Two Birds, One Stone

by

Janet Yeager

Men and Women of Valor

Two Birds, One Stone

Cover Art by *Tina Lynn Stout*

The Wild Rose Press, Inc.
PO Box 708
Adams Basin, NY 14410-0708
Visit us at www.thewildrosepress.com

Publishing History
First Edition, 2025
Trade Paperback Print ISBN 978-1-5092-6370-7
Digital ISBN 978-1-5092-6371-4

Men and Women of Valor
Published in the United States of America

Dedication

A book begins as a dream and then a possibility. Add encouragement and advice, and the story starts to take shape. Thanks to Ally Robertson for her editing skills and the continued support I receive at The Wild Rose Press. As always, thank you to my children and grandchildren, Scott, Kathleen, Chloe, John, Eric, Janet, and Ginger. I love you all. Most of all, a "green felt tip pen" debt of thanks to my wonderful husband, Greg, who offered sage advice on how to give this story the wings it needed to fly. I love you.

Acknowledgement

Though the character of Jess is not based on anyone in particular, their inspriration comes from Jonna Mendez, the Central Intelligence Agency's first female Chief of Disguise. In articles and interviews, Ms. Mendez states that in the course of her career, she used props and disguises to appear to be both male and female in her assignments. Thus, the character of Jess was born.

Chapter One

When you commit to the life of an encryption officer, there will always be a niche with companies or governments hiring you for your services.

The participants of the "Encryption in the Modern Age" Conference held in the London Financial District's swanky Windsor Star Hotel are not here to collect Continuing Learning Education credits, drink and consume the contents of the sponsor's buffets, or make contacts to add to their online profiles. They want to know, or say they know, how to be a spy.

Here's my reality.

The rock in my shoe hurts like hell as I hobble out on the stage to give my presentation on Encryption 101—Security in the Modern World. The crowd is primarily middle-aged and bored. I unscrew the lid of a water bottle provided and launch into my talk.

"Hello, my name is Iris Blackrail, and I'm an encryption officer working for Bolton's Valor Security Forces, based in Winding Creek, Colorado. Encryption breaches cause disruptions to banking institutions and cryptocurrency exchanges and can cause companies to pay ransom demands due to weaknesses in their security systems." I change the slide to show the image, taken from a popular film, of an actor hanging precariously from a large British Pound sign. "Once the subject of popular media presentations, and contrary to popular thought, the weaknesses don't always come from the dark forces believed to work in the universe. Sometimes,

1

they are closer to home."

I change the slide on the screen to a screenshot from the Times Report. "Here's a recent article regarding a data breach caused by a trusted employee who figured out how to hack into the encrypted data and steal millions from their company."

The audience straightens and leans in.

I have them, and we all know it.

"Hiring encryption officers or getting or continuing the training in being one is no longer a luxury." I change the screen and continue my talk, pleased that people are scribbling or typing notes. My talk continues for several more minutes, and I announce that I'll take questions.

As expected, the questions are of the "what-if" variety and are, in fact, similar situations. I answer by giving a tailored spin so that the person in crypto thinks they got a different answer from banking, or the random, unfocused question is treated as thought-provoking.

I lift my right foot in an effort to ease the throbbing, shooting pain and reach for the bottled water, silently cursing that I left my pain reliever at my hotel.

A voice interrupts me in mid-swallow. "Miss Blackrail? I checked your profile, but the information about you seems to be protected behind your employer's firewalls. What makes your experiences valuable to us? You're an expert in encryption. Why would a bank that caters to ski towns hire a high-powered individual like you for encryption work?"

A sneer is a sneer in any accent. In this case, it's neither English nor American. Based on the way the person pronounced encryption as *awn-creep-shawn*, my guess is French, but I can't be sure.

I limp from behind the podium to the side of the

stage, a plastered smile on my face, to where I can see the questioner, a pale, thin person with close-cropped hair.

They don't smile. Instead, they scan me from the top of my wig, continuing over the too-tight business suit and coming to rest their gaze on my knock-off sensible shoes. "What information can you give us about your background and why you are especially suited to be the one to give us this talk?"

Heads swivel, and several people turn back to me with benevolent smiles.

The person pronounced information as *in-for-mush-on*. I run through a number of accents but come up short.

"Great question," I reply, my eyes scanning the room to see who might be in league with the questioner, and glad to see only genuine interest. "I was surprised when Winding Creek Bank contacted Bolton's Valor Security Forces about using me in the position of encryption officer, as I worked in a number of capacities for various companies but none in a financial institution. My background in Southwest Asian Studies with minors in Russian and Farsi isn't exactly what you'd expect. I've worked in areas that deal with 'enemies, both foreign and domestic,' for a while, and that's what led me to law school."

There are twenty-three people enrolled in my seminar. Twenty-two lean in, but the questioner isn't one of them.

I continue. "Winding Creek is a beautiful area located near Denver, in Colorado, and caters to the needs of ski towns and their clients. People have discovered the charms of ski towns across the American West and are moving to Winding Creek, Aspen, and other places. It's my job, as contracted by Bolton's Valor, to keep their transactions secure. Does that answer your question?"

The person nods but raises an eyebrow. "That's great information." Again pronouncing the word *in-for-mush-on*. Again, I can't place the accent. "Thank you for sharing it with us."

I step back, tempted to take another drink from the water bottle, but I suspect there are people in the room who would view this as a tell. While Bolton's Valor Security Forces does employ me, and I am an encryption officer overseeing the security of Winding Creek Bank's transactions, every other detail, down to the speaking of Farsi and the work with enemies, both foreign and domestic, is a complete lie.

****

Pam Clayton's capped-heel hand-tooled cowboy boots announce her presence ten seconds before she appears. Breezing past the Snowshoe Montana Winding Creek Bank mineral department receptionist's protests, she takes dead aim for me. Her beaded suede purse sails onto my desk, sending my pen holder and the cherished picture of my father and me onto the floor. Dropping like an exhausted pack horse into the chair opposite me, she flicks a stray auburn strand from her face.

I remind myself to breathe and not blink. Pam does this every month.

"Miss Clayton, how can I assist you?" I ask, raising my eyebrows with an expression that questions why she has brightened my existence with her presence. Though we have known each other since high school, she insists on being addressed in a way befitting her current station as the executive assistant to my largest client.

Owing to my workplace status or title, Pam feels it

necessary to remind me of her elevated status every month.

I remind myself to breathe and not blink about that, too.

"Oh Jeannie, can you help poor little old me? I don't know what to do. Mineral leases for Linda's properties in Texas were sent to her home address. You're supposed to prevent that from happening. To make my life more difficult, they're offering a ridiculously abysmal amount of money. What do we pay you and the bank for?" Her whine tells me she would have been the terror of the cereal aisle when she was an overtired two-year-old. She certainly threw a similar fit when she wasn't chosen as Homecoming Queen decades before.

"Did you bring the offer letter with you?" I ask, losing the battle of mentally shaking the images of her in a diaper with a rhinestone tiara dangling from her head. "I'd like to look at it, and as part of our agency agreement with your employer, Linda, we will negotiate the terms for her."

Pam heaves a sigh, causing her heavy turquoise necklace and chandelier earrings to sway, and then fishes a manila envelope from her purse. "It's important that you get things processed, and all I see as Linda's executive assistant are mistake after mistake. She isn't happy with you, and I'm not either." She dabs at her nose, and as she pulls her finger away, drops of blood run down her lip.

"Pam! Are you all right?" I gasp, my hand opening a desk drawer, taking a tissue out, and then handing it to her. "Do you need me to call Linda? Tilt your head back, and I'll get you a glass of water." Without waiting for an answer, I leap from my chair and run to the bank's breakroom. Opening the safety kit, I get a bandage and a styptic pencil, then take a glass from the sink and fill it with cold water. Turning out of the kitchen, I nearly collide with Dan Werner, our bank's president. "Pam Clayton has a nosebleed," I say, rushing past him.

Pam sits in my office, tilting her head back. As I enter the office with the styptic pencil, Band-Aid, and water, she turns to look at me with a weak smile. "I'm sorry, Joanne, about the mess. I have been under a lot of pressure lately and should be taking the medicines my doctor prescribed for me." She takes the pencil from me and then dabs it against her nose, wincing at the sting. "I forgot there is a check that I received, er…Linda received, that needs to be reviewed. It's in my purse."

I reach into her bag, extracting an envelope from Alamogordo Oil from the morass of makeup and medically sized tubes. Dan appears at Pam's side, kneeling on the floor and taking her hand. "I didn't see you, Dan," I say as I walk around my desk, placing the envelope and the relationship before me under consideration.

Pam drops Dan's hand as she rises from the chair and, without a word to me, walks out of my office and into his office.

****

Michael Laysan's sense of humor doesn't lend much of itself to laughter, so the exchange in my office must have appeared highly comical. "Her money? Your office is a shambles, by the way."

In the twenty years I have known of my British pen pal from when I was in high school, we never spoke by phone, only communicating through mailed letters. His letters detailing Arthurian myths and the flora and fauna of the land surrounding his village in the Cotswolds were often exhausting to read. But then there were the stabs at sweet poetry he'd send that kept me writing back to him. In my letters to him years before, I'd wondered what his hands felt like. I'd wondered about a lot more than that. Over time, our correspondence dwindled, but I often wondered what became of him.

He showed up on my doorstep unannounced six weeks ago at the height of Snowshoe's busy tourist season. Michael said his new job with the Forest Service was starting in a few weeks, but the promised temporary housing had fallen through. The amount he was willing to pay to cover his portion of my rent was generous. I could understand the crunch, so with equal measures of reluctance and curiosity, I'd said 'yes' to allowing a relative stranger to stay with me.

"Thanks for noticing about my office." My smile registers somewhere between Get Out and What Now. "Pam's purse knocked over a few things. Did you hear from Bolton's Valor about the rental? Will you find another place to stay?"

"Her money?" Michael repeats, his lower teeth biting his upper lip in contemplation. "Is there a way that you can assign this account to someone else? Why does Linda Taylor keep her? She's awful. And to not know your name?"

"Michael, please close the door if you are going to ask questions like that," I say, sitting on the floor to pick up the pens. Turning over the framed picture of my father and me in Alpine National Park, taken a few weeks before he died, I frown at the glass spiders in the corner of the frame.

"Why do you keep an odd number of pens in your

pen holder?" The door clicks closed as Michael asks the question. "Moreover, you should complain to that superior of yours about your workload. I see you. Every night, after hours, face in your computer screen, looking like you are ready to cry. And do you ask for help?"

Who pays attention to the number of pens I have? Who cares? I pretend to look for another pen but only find a dust-covered wrapped mini candy bar. I don't have answers for Michael, and even if I did, he would only pepper me with another string of questions.

His proffered hand is warm as I stand. "I was depositing a check and heard that woman prancing down the hallway toward your office. What an atrocious sight. You need a break." His brown eyes search mine. "You grew up in the Columbia Valley. Do you know about Willow Creek Meadows Lake? We could take my Rover and have a picnic tomorrow morning. I have some research to conduct, and I want to get a feel for the area."

I pull my hand from his. "Is your work in the Forest Service as interesting as it was in England? Snowshoe has to be a big transition from London. Why didn't you go to Colorado and work on your grizzly project?"

Michael sniffs. "Joanne, Colorado's last wild grizzly was killed in 1979. Other than private reserves, which already have forensic biologists, there'd be no work for me there. But *Ursus arctos horribilis* has a significant presence in and around Snowshoe, even though it is actually a Great Plains animal. It was classified in 1815…"

I raise my hand. "I have work to do, and I have plans."

"Well, you know where to find me," he says, squaring his six-foot frame and giving me a hopeful smile. "I could use your help. The others in the office aren't from here, so I could use more of a local perspective. Please consider it."

I'm startled as Dan raps on the doorframe and peers in through the window. Reaching for the doorknob, I nod to him, and as I open the door, Michael turns to me. "Please consider it. You'd be doing me a favor." He then nods to Dan, who nods back.

"Your childhood pen pal is settling in, is he?" asks Dan as Michael disappears down the stairs leading to the parking lot of the bank.

"I was getting a report on the history of grizzly bears in Colorado, so you saved me," I say in a flat tone. "How is Pam? That nosebleed probably needs to be looked at. Did you sign the agency agreements from Georgina Hinerman? I can't wait to get started on managing her piece of business."

"Pam says she forgot to take some medicine. Are you familiar with the You Who Foundation?" Dan hands me the signed agency agreements that I shared with Georgina two months ago when I was in London. "I'd like to bring you in on a conference with Wally Harmon and Alan Greene. As you know, both are on the bank's board of directors and are involved with the Foundation. They'll be here in a few minutes."

"Wally and I attend the same church. Did the You Who Foundation receive some oil and gas interests? Pam brought a lease offer and checks that need looking into…" I swallow hard, hoping that Dan suggests taking the meeting himself.

"True, it's timber and ranch acreage, and we'll bring in those departments when things get more formalized, but if you could pop in and say hello, I'd appreciate it."

He raises an eyebrow. "I'll leave you to dig into Linda's project and will message you when Wally and Alan are here."

I nod and give Dan my best optimistic smile. "Great. I look forward to seeing how I can contribute."

As soon as Dan goes into his office, I slip out of my office and walk to the bathroom. After locking the door, I sit on the toilet and take the deep breaths my therapist recommended when I feel a panic attack coming on. I visualize a meadow and push away the thoughts of Alan's hands sliding all over me so many years ago.

****

A few minutes later, I return to my office, where a pulsing message from Dan appears on my computer's screen. "You Who meeting's rescheduled. Can you prepare a bullet point report? Environmentalists versus Timber? Don't want to anger people."

I glance out of my office. Dan's office is dark, and I silently curse yet another time that I've worried over nothing.

I have three projects that I need to work on and one that clamors at my curiosity. Leaning back in my office chair and picking up Georgina Hinerman's signed agency agreement, I admire the sweeping, cursive 'G' and 'H' of her signature and wonder if she took a page from the world-class artists whose Western paintings and sculptures grace her London mansion.

Georgina had taken two months but had agreed to become one of Winding Creek's newest clients.

The encryption conference where I gave a talk as Iris Blackrail on "Encryption in the Modern Age" was over.

I'd returned to the bed-sit off of Ebury Street, blocks from Victoria Station, spending the evening as my alter ego, putting details to a report to be sent to my bosses at Bolton's Valor. The following day, I was happy to return to my true identity, Joanne Corvus, a tourist visiting London.

The cab called earlier waited for me, and when I gave Georgina's address to the cabbie, she raised her eyebrows. I had assured her that I was an expected visitor.

The cab rounded Buckingham Palace, where crowds gathered for the Changing of the Guard and Trooping of the Colors, before stopping at a narrow side street. Exiting the cab, I discovered the road wasn't narrow at all. What I thought was a gate was actually a bow-shaped entrance with a guardhouse on the left side. I walked up to the building and gave my name to the guard.

London's famous rain hadn't started, but dark clouds gathered above my head. The guard said, "The driver will be here in a minute. Please wait over here." He pointed to a small door surrounded by brick and ivy. Opening the wooden door, I sat on a bench, then gasped as the view revealed an expanse of manicured lawn complete with a number of marble sculptures.

A Rolls Royce comes down the lane and stops in front of me, and a young woman alights from the car. I am gaping at a marble cowboy statue when I realize the woman is asking if I'm Joanne Corvus.

"Yes, I'm Joanne. Sorry, I was admiring the statues," I say as the chauffeur opened the back door of the opulent automobile. The car moved slowly past a statue of a cowboy and a steer. The cowboy, complete with hat, chaps, and a handlebar mustache, held his hand high in the air, riding a bucking stallion. Tethered to a corded rope held in his hand was a calf, its eyes bulging with distress at the rope lassoed over his head.

"A gift from the Remington Family. They were neighbors to the Hinermans in the West, I believe. The house's interior was decorated to celebrate the family's time in Wyoming and Colorado," said the driver in a rote way.

As we rounded another corner, the Hinerman mansion came into sight. We passed a fountain and entered a courtyard with a grand staircase leading to a handsome building. The driver stopped, then ran to my car door and opened it as a young man came down the stairs, calling my name.

"Hello, Miss Corvus, I'm Daniel, an assistant to Georgina Hinerman. She's expecting you. Do come in."

I followed him up the staircase, through enormous doors, into a foyer filled with Thomas Moran's, Charlie Russell's, and what appeared to be another Remington. In the center of the foyer was a small bust of a young man wearing a cowboy hat. Above the staircase to my right was a large painting of the same man, sucking on a grass straw, his cowboy hat pitched back on his head. A kerchief was tied around his neck, and tiny beads of perspiration dotted the man's brow.

"Edvard Hinerman. Returned here after the war, the Great War. He's buried here, but he wanted to remember his life in Wyoming and Colorado anytime he strode through the home. Madame is expecting you in the drawing room."

He opened the doors to a cozy drawing room filled with antiques. A tall woman, her hair pulled back simply at the base of her neck, stood next to a stack of books. Behind her, sitting on a table bathed in golden light, were balls of yarn and knitting projects. She waved me over and gestured to sit down.

"My knitting. It's how I work out problems. I'm Georgina Hinerman, but please call me Georgie. Everyone does," she said as she settled into the chair. Her fingers reached for the yarn, and she separated the strands between two long, elegant fingers. "You don't mind, do you?" she asked, pulling the knitting toward her and dropping her head to begin. "I don't want to seem rude, but it distresses me to look people in the eye, so knitting is a great way to alleviate things."

"I knit, too," I said, leaning forward as Georgie's fingers danced across the strands. "I use a bowl to keep my stranding separated."

At this, Georgie looked up at me with a shy smile. "I've read your proposal and talked to my cousin Linda. She speaks highly of you. My question is how I would receive the money. Would the method of receiving funds be difficult?"

"I know what you mean," I replied, trying to keep my thoughts on her question and not on how she knitted so fast. "Twenty years ago, a requirement to have safeguards in place to prevent money laundering was enacted. A money-laundering prevention officer is in each bank. Another protective measure is to have funds go through an intermediary. The funds we process at Winding Creek Bank for foreign clients are transferred to a larger bank that scrutinizes the funds and ensures that the funds are coming from a known source."

"And you are the bank's money-laundering prevention officer?" she asked. As she talked, her hair fell over her shoulder, but she paid it no mind.

"One of them, that's correct. I've gotten the certifications and work with law enforcement should any need arise," I said with a smile.

"The papers are signed. You requested two copies."

"Yes, our bank president, Dan Werner, will sign both copies and return one original for your records. I can have those overnighted to you when I get back to Montana," I said, happy that my reputation had been a good one.

"Do you work with Linda, or do you work mostly with her assistant Pam?" Georgie's head remained bent, and for a second, her fingers slowed as she mentioned Pam. She stopped, then unpicked a stitch.

"Linda definitely keeps an active hand in her investments. I talk to her from time to time at the bank. Pam's previously worked with charitable foundations, and I think that's how she met Linda and got hired by her. Linda is helping Pam learn more about her business ventures," I said.

Georgie's fingers hadn't picked up her knitting. I sensed that she didn't like Pam for some reason. "I admire loyalty—Linda's one to learn more about her investments. Two summers ago, I visited the ranch, and she showed me the planes and drones that she uses for her timber holdings. I'm pleased that your bank has experienced people in timber and ranch management. Linda asked me to invest in some upcoming projects, so I suspect that you and I will be working together in an expanded capacity." Georgie tipped her knitting needle into the dropped stitch to correct it, then looked up at me with a smile. "I have an appointment in the center of London, and I can have my driver drop you off."

I rose, and Georgie did the same, setting her project into a handsome brocade knitting bag. "It's been a pleasure, but your driver doesn't need to drop me. I have some errands of my own. Look for the signed originals to be sent to you in an overnight mailer when I return."

Georgie walked with me into the foyer, and I stopped to look at the cowboy painting. I noted that Edvard, Georgie, and Linda share the same deep-set eyes and half smile. I also noticed the faint outline of Long's Peak in the painting's background.

"Long's Peak is near our headquarters. I'm happy to see that it figures into the painting of your ancestor."

Georgie glanced over her shoulder and nodded at me. "It's been a pleasure meeting you, Joanne. I look forward to working with you." She walked with me to the door, then shook my hand again and gave a wave to the driver who waited outside.

I descended the house's stairs past the western sculptures, which I realized had a perfect place on the grounds as they represented a big part of the family fortunes.

****

Weeks later, after putting the Hinerman agency agreements into a folder, I rubbed a minor ache in my calf before deciding to stretch my legs and become Iris Blackrail.

Snowshoe, Montana's neon-clad restaurants teem with late summer tourists eager to swim in Snowshoe Lake or take gondola rides on Snowshoe Mountain—the Friendliest Ski Area!—which overlooks Alpine National Park's peaks. My favorite restaurant is an easy three-minute walk from Winding Creek Bank's offices. The Hare, or more properly, The Snowshoe Hare, is my home away from home now that Michael is staying with me.

Emelie, the bartender, calls out to someone in the back as I walk in. "Make sure the Snug is open. Have the usual?" A transplant from Aspen and Jackson Hole, Emelie supplements her river-guiding income with bartending at the Hare. Nearly everyone here has two jobs in order to make ends meet.

That includes me. Michael's help with the rent and cooking is helping my budget. Still, I would have opted that he not live with me, but that's how it's currently working out.

I walk to the back of the restaurant to the Snug, where a panel with only a small latch announcing its presence stands open. I slide into the small alcove and close the door, take out my Bolton's Valor Security Forces-issued laptop, and rap on a sliding panel on the wall above my head. It slides open, and Justine peers in. "Your usual is coming. The Moose Drool will be here in a sec, and you'll have the Steakhouse Burger with sweet potato chips?"

I nod, and the panel slides shut, leaving me in splendid solitude.

The encryption project data is registered to Iris Blackrail. Bolton's Valor contacted me nearly a year ago to investigate a potential breach within Winding Creek Bank's protocols.

My work within Winding Creek Bank as Joanne Corvus is legitimate. So is my work as Iris Blackrail, working for Bolton's Valor Security Forces. As part of my work at the bank, I am required to take two weeks off each year. Moreover, I surrender my work laptop and telephone for review of potential conflicts of interest.

Bolton's Valor set up the speaking engagement in London. Knowing that Georgie Hinerman lived there and had expressed an interest in having the bank's Oil and Gas Department manage her assets, I did my work as Joanne, then sent my phone and laptop to Winding Creeks's corporate offices outside Denver and went to the encryption conference in London as Iris Blackrail.

I open the laptop and then reach into my bag, sliding on a thin, flesh-toned latex glove. The index fingertip of the glove contains tiny ribbed impressions that mimic a fingerprint. Taking out a VPN token, I place my index finger on the security feature, log in under Iris's name, and enter a ten-letter and number password. The food arrives, and only after that, I pull out the UFED—the Universal Forensic Extraction Device. Justine and Emelie know that I will knock on the sliding door if I need anything. Otherwise, I'm to be left alone.

As an encryption officer, my job is to notify clients of software updates and potential security breaches. As my fingers tap the keyboard, I think about the lengths to which I had to cover my tracks while I was in London.

Now, in the Snug, munching on a burger and drinking from a stein of my favorite beer, I look for anomalies in the data I'm reviewing. The transaction glows red, and I begin a trace of the source. The last time this happened was while I was in London. The route came from Colombia to Miami and then to Snowshoe, and then it disappeared.

"Software doesn't launder money. Bankers do," I say under my breath. The funds in Snowshoe haven't varied, and neither have the loans, fees, nor any other sources of income.

However, the computer says there is an encryption problem, and it's my job to find out who is behind it.

And I don't have a clue.

Hours pass, and I decide it's time to go home. The sun is low in the afternoon sky, and the neon of

Snowshoe's restaurants, emboldened by the dimming light, illuminate the path leading to the maple and pine tree-lined boulevard where my rental home sits.

Michael's Rover isn't in the driveway. Stepping into the kitchen, I'm greeted with the heavenly smell of cooked chicken and rosemary. A pasta pot sits on the side of the sink, and I let out a groan as guilt settles in.

Setting down my bag on the kitchen table, I walk to the dining room. Sitting on the Mission-style table is a candle, which, based on the wax puddling at the candle's base, has been lit for several hours. A filled wineglass and a plate of fettuccine alfredo—my favorite Italian dish—sit next to a note.

'Thought you could use this after the day you had—Michael.'

I rub my mouth as waves of 'I'm a total idiot' wash over me. I don't have a clue. I really don't.

Chapter Two

Michael's Rover didn't show up in my, er, our driveway for two days. In his absence, my phone calls to his cell phone and his office went unanswered. I drove west of Snowshoe, past the golf course, to look at the parking lot of the Wildlife Services office, hoping that I'd see the Rover.

On day three, upon spotting the olive-drab English car he'd had shipped here, I ran up the bungalow stairs to find him in the kitchen, fileting two Dolly Varden trout. He moves to the oven, extracting toasted almonds from a cooking sheet, and then sets them on the countertop. Then, and only then, he turns to me.

"Fancy a sauvignon blanc to go with the trout, or would you like a Portuguese Vinho Verde?" he asks, taking off an apron. As he lays it over a kitchen chair, I grin, the only smile I've had in two days. The apron is made up of tea towels from the Cotswolds. He lowers the heat on a small pot and then reaches again into the oven to remove spiced carrots. "I made up a fresh batch of garam marsala when I got home and thought it would pair well with the trout almondine and limed rice."

"Where—" I begin, but his shoulder blades tighten through his shirt as if he's been punched. He straightens and, without turning to look at me, takes plates from the painted cupboards, setting the trout, the rice, which he mounds with lime zest, and the carrots on plates.

"Michael, I had work to do," I say. "I should have

19

told you, but an issue with the bank came up, and I needed to look at it."

His eyes don't quite meet mine. "Let's eat," he says. "We can see if the trip to Willow Creek Meadows can work into your plans. I'd like your input." He takes the plates into the dining room, then squats in front of the wine refrigerator, removing a narrow green bottle. He takes down two glasses and a corkscrew from the sideboard above the wine refrigerator and places them on the table. He turns on the overhead light and then dims it, but not to the level of the solitary candle.

Taking the cutlery from a kitchen drawer, I join him in the dining room. "What do you need to know about Willow Creek Meadows?" I ask, figuring that question is as low-level as I dare. I want to ask where he has been for two days, what the solitary candle was about, and if maybe he should call the rental agencies in town.

"Let's sit. I don't want the trout to get cold." He waves to the chairs.

I take my seat, and he uncorks the wine with a professional ease.

"Where'd you learn to uncork wine like that? Did you work in a restaurant?" I ask, looking for another way to ease the tension between us. He pours wine into the glasses and brings one of them to me.

He sits, takes a sip from the glass, and then begins to eat the food.

"You were asking about Willow Creek Meadows?" I ask, taking a bite of the almond-coated trout. "The fish is delicious. What do you want to know?"

A mound of rice, carrots, and trout balances precariously on his fork. "Do you remember a snowmobiling accident near Willow Creek Meadows

Lake several years ago?" he asks as he swallows the mixture. "This is good if I do say so myself. Two people died due to an avalanche."

"Yes," I say, welcoming the easier path but puzzled by the trajectory of the conversation. "Willow Creek Meadows Lake is a remote location with terrible cell-phone reception. They weren't locals who would have known to bring a satellite phone, which would have helped with the recovery. As I recall, two men tried to outdo the other and were caught in the slide." I take a bite of the trout and recall another detail.

"The force of the avalanche caused the ice to overturn, and the fish in the lake were sent flying. Some of them were skewered by the bare willow branches. In the spring, after the grizzlies came out of hibernation, they had quite a sushi feast."

"Those grizzlies are part of my study. And they don't hibernate. Hibernation is a state of--"

I drop my fork down on the plate with a clatter. "Michael, I don't need to know what hibernation is. I grew up here. You asked for my help, and I was busy. Then you disappear—not that it's any of my business where you went—but you disappeared. No phone calls. Nothing. You want my help. Tell me what you need my help with." I pick up my fork, which looks like a fulcrum. If the balance goes one way, I'm going to press him to move out. If it goes the other way, I get some answers.

Michael takes a sip of his wine. "It's the fact that you are a local that makes you useful to me. When we corresponded, I could always count on getting fascinating stories in your letters. And you always encouraged my interests. You're sensible. I have a lead that I'm following that I dare not talk about just yet. It doesn't make sense. That's why I had to leave. Too many questions to answer on things I don't have an answer for. I promise that your coming with me to Willow Creek Meadows Lake will help me clarify things. Can you spare a day for me?"

My phone buzzes. I raise my finger, holding my answer. "I turned off my personal cell but forgot to do so on my work phone. Sorry. Let me check what is going on." I walked through the kitchen and dig into my purse. Dan's message is to the point.

--You Who meeting 9 am tomorrow. Have you worked on the presentation?--

Pursing my lips, I typed my reply.

Yes, I'm ready. See you tomorrow.

With that answer, my stomach churns, and then I race to the bathroom.

"Joanne, is it the trout?" Michael holds a towel in his hand. He kneels beside me.

"No, it's work. It's a presentation for some people I'd rather not see. I wanted another person to do the presentation, but Dan didn't listen." I raise my head, take Michael's towel, and then wipe my mouth. "He doesn't know, and I need to be professional. It was years ago."

"What was years ago?" Michael asks, but I shake my head hard and shiver as I recall Alan Greene's hands on me.

"Oh, no. You have to tell Dan," he says, resting his hand on my back.

Again, I shake my head. "I can't do that. Please don't ask any more questions. Please." Tears run down my cheeks. "You made a wonderful dinner, and I've ruined everything. I'm so sorry."

Michael stands up. "I'm making you a cup of ginger

tea."

As I rinse my mouth, the clatter of dishes on the kitchen countertop reminds me of a responsibility I've shirked. "Michael, let me help clear the dishes," I call over my shoulder. Walking from the bathroom to the kitchen with its painted table for two, I see Michael's apron still hanging over a chair. "Tell me about the Cotswold tea towels and who made the apron for you."

"I made an apron as a gift for my mum as part of a Boy Guides project. I badly overestimated the number of tea towels, and I ended up making two. As for the tea towels, they show the routes I would go on during my great trods. I think I wrote about them to you." Michael scrapes the food into a waste bin and then slides the plates into the sink filled with soapy water. A teakettle whistles, and he takes it from the stove before retrieving a saucer and teacup from a cupboard, then sets it in front of me. He returns to the cupboard and rummages for a second, bringing out a tin. "They're digestive biscuits. They, and the tea, should help you set things right."

Pouring the amber liquid into the cup, he sets it, along with the biscuit, in front of me, then pulls out his chair and sits across from me. Waving his hand, he says, "Drink it. You'll feel better."

The tea is hot, and I pull back.

Michael jumps up and goes to the refrigerator, taking out a carton of milk. "Do you want this in a pitcher?"

I laugh and shake my head as he pours the milk into my cup. "No, what you have done is better than anything that I could have asked for." I sip the tea and close my eyes. "I have taken great pains to push a part of my life away. I did a bad thing years ago, and it's coming back to haunt me."

"Stuff and nonsense. You haven't done anyone or anything wrong," Michael says, his chair scraping the linoleum floor as he sits down. "I don't believe that."

"It's true, I'm afraid. I exchanged my silence for a new car." I open my eyes, looking briefly into my roommate's brown eyes, then closing my eyelids as tears fall. I wipe the moisture away with my sleeve and bow my head. Shaking my head, I recall the panic I felt as the old family car wouldn't start on that bitterly cold evening, Alan running down the steps of his office, wiping his sleeve on the iced-up window, and asking that I come inside to warm up. I did as I was asked, my boots squeaking on the snowy steps, the warmth of the dental office flushing my cheeks. Inhaling sharply, I shake my head at the memory of what happened next.

"And now you must face this person." Michael's voice is clipped as if holding back a rage. "You have to tell Dan."

"I can't. I kept silent. I took the gift. I used the car. My parents..." I say, seeing their faces and the shame in their eyes. "I can't."

His hand creeps across the table for two. I sit with my hands in my lap, and then, as my tears fall, my fingers move to rest on top of his. As I look up, I see tears falling from his cheeks, too.

****

Fluttering burgundy maple leaves dance in an early morning breeze. I'd had a fitful night, worrying about the meeting with Alan at ten o'clock at the bank, worrying about Michael's whereabouts and his feelings toward me, worrying about whether I should bring up that I can't find a breach in the encryption data, though the blinking red light on Iris Blackrail's computer clearly shows one.

Stepping from the house, I look at the skyline and the maple leaves, which mimic the shapes of the mountains behind them. Did an early settler notice the similarity in the shapes and decide to plant maple trees? I smile at the thought as I walk down the wide sidewalk toward the business district.

Sipping the last of my coffee and glancing at the empty driveway, I decide to tell Dan before the meeting about my reservations about working with Alan and suggest that he bring in another analyst.

"Good morning, Songbird. We've missed you at choir practice." Wally Harmon gives me a friendly wave as he stands in front of the church we attend. He holds a coffee mug bearing the Norwegian flag. "I dropped off our choir schedule to Pastor Jen. Our choir isn't the same without that voice of yours."

"It's nice to see you," I say with a smile. Wally stands behind me in choir practice. I can always count on him to be an enthusiastic, if slightly off-pitch, tenor. "I've been meaning to come back. You'll be at our meeting at the bank?"

"Wouldn't miss it for the world. The You Who Foundation does good work in the community. This social media exposure is reaching new opportunities to help and bring in new donors." He tosses the remains of his creamed coffee on the lawn by the sidewalk.

We reach the business district and walk toward Winding Creek's three-story glass and brick offices. Wally bumps my shoulder and says with a smile, "I understand you will be giving the presentation. Not to worry. Pretend we are all cabbage heads. Do you remember when you said that in choir? It helped my daughter Marilyn with her solo. She's never forgotten it."

We step inside the airy atrium, and Wally peels off toward the commercial lending section. "I have a meeting with your lending team about an expansion I'm mulling over. I'll see you at ten. Break a leg!"

Forty-five minutes later, after responding to e-mails and signing off on oil and gas ownership verifications called division orders, I visualize the presentation's setting with Dan and Wally listening. As I think of Alan, a lurch hits my stomach. I start again. I visualize Michael's face as he held out his arm last night, and I vow to see his face instead of Alan's at the meeting.

Dan raps on the door. "Ready?"

The conference room is on the third floor and overlooks a portion of Snowshoe Mountain and, if you know where to look, a hint of Snowshoe Lake. The lake lies beyond a low hill where a glacier pushed sediment in front of it, creating a moraine. My back will be facing that view.

I take a deep breath and walk into the room where Wally sits with an older man I don't recognize. Wally and the man rise, and the stranger offers me a soft hand with manicured nails.

"Paul Allegretti, this is Joanne Corvus, our senior mineral manager. Paul is a new addition to the You Who Foundation's Board, and I wanted to introduce the two of you," says Dan with a broad smile. "Alan Greene couldn't make it today but looks forward to meeting you, Joanne."

Dan's words about Alan sucker punch me. I blink my eyes rapidly at this news and give a thin smile to the three men. Drawing in a long, ragged breath, I try to focus on the bullet that I had dodged and how happy I should be that Alan isn't here. Alan's fingertips had been cold as he pushed me against the metal cabinet. As cold as the imagined air going down my back right this second.

I blink again.

Wally raises his cup with the Norwegian flag on it as a salute, and I begin my presentation, growing more comfortable with every sentence, drawing on my experience and that of the bank's departments. I deliver what we do and how we can help the You Foundation to Wally's benevolent face, knowing I will be safe.

In return, Wally tosses softball questions, which I readily answer, with Dan chiming in. Paul remains quiet.

Wally is all smiles as we exit the conference room. "You were great. We'll be in touch soon. And I'll tell the choir to expect your lovely voice among them shortly," he says, squeezing my shoulder.

Still chuckling over Wally's choir remark, I walk back to my office, recalling my getting sick last night, my tears, and all of my worry. I had worried for nothing. Again.

Michael picks up on the first ring.

"Do you want to go on a picnic this afternoon?" I ask, inventing the excuse I will use with Dan if he questions me about taking the time off.

"Yes, I can manage that. Let's meet at the house around one. From the tone of your voice, it sounds like the meeting went better than expected. You need to trust yourself. You're better than you know."

I laugh for the second time and send Dan my out-of-office request. I call into the Hare, order sandwiches and sides to go, and then walk home.

The maples flutter in the breeze, mimicking the sharp-edged mountains of the Kennedy Range. I am going on an adventure with a good friend. Life is good.

****

I'm pulling on my hiking boots as Michael leaps up the front steps. He shifts his weight back and forth on the landing. "We'll pack a picnic and drive the 47.3 miles to Willow Creek Meadows Lake to check out the strange story I heard. Apparently, it's so weird that we need to see it to believe it."

Standing up, I take my backpack from the closet and sling it over my shoulder. "I've called into the Hare. We can pick it up on our way."

"I'll get the trekking poles and meet you in a minute." He angles past me as our bodies graze in the doorway. As I walk down the steps, he calls out, "I told you to believe in yourself."

The Rover's doors are locked, so while I wait, I pluck a leaf from one of the silver maples. The burgundy top hides the silver underside.

The doors unlock, and I slide in as Michael opens the back, putting his backpack, bottles of water, trekking poles, camera, and another bag behind us.

"The Hare will be our next stop. I hope you like Reuben sandwiches," I say, putting my backpack behind me.

"Right you are." Michael flashes a big grin and starts the car. "I'm sorry that you put yourself through all that torture, but I'm delighted you called and are able to take the afternoon off. I'd like to treat you to a proper dinner tonight if you don't mind. I made reservations at seven thirty at the Hennessey House."

We arrive at the Snowshoe Hare a minute later, and

I go inside, picking up the sandwiches from Emelie. I pay, then walk back out into the bright, sunny day.

After a few minutes, we pass the turnoff to Snowshoe Mountain Ski Area. "You know this country like the back of your hand, Joanne." Michael's voice turns serious. "What do you remember about the Willow Creek Meadows Lake accident?"

I shake my head. "Just rumors. A couple of out-of-towners, maybe from Florida, with not much experience. One of our choir members said that one of the victims was the son of someone famous, maybe a client of ours at the bank, but I didn't recognize the name. The newspaper ran an article about the accident but didn't list the names because they hadn't contacted the next of kin. The whole thing was dropped." I pinch my mouth and raise my hand to indicate the story's finality.

Michael's Rover bumps as it leaves the pavement and goes onto the dirt road between Snowshoe Lake and the low hills below the ski area. We pass into a treed area, and Michael slows the car. He cocks his head toward mine, his eyes never leaving the road. "I saw the report that last winter, a couple of people on snowmobiles came up here. One of the snowcatters decided to challenge the other to take a run up the side of the mountain just above the lake. Up and down—a small game meant to show how strong and brave they were. Two guys showing off."

Michael drops into a lower gear as the Rover climbs up a hill. His voice rises as he continues. "On the fourth pass, a chute of snow unfurled. According to the witness' report, he didn't glance behind him, and even if he had, it would not have much mattered. In less than ten seconds, he and his snowmobile were part of the rocks, trees, and snow tumbling and churning down the narrow chute leading into the lake."

I nod. "That much I knew. The snowslide hit the lake with such a force that nearly all of the ice and fish were thrown, then impaled onto willow branches."

Michael's mouth did a quick line of consternation. I am keeping him from the story.

The afternoon sun's rays cast deepening shadows around us. As we begin to climb higher, pine, ponderosa, and tamarack trees give way to lodgepole pines.

A brown and gold sign points to Upper Snowshoe Lake Road one way and Thayer Lookout the other way. "We want Upper Snowshoe Lake Road," I say, pointing to the left as a truck with a rowboat passes us.

"Is the fishing up here any good?"

"Graylings mostly, I think. Maybe some trout. My dad, Thew, took me here for ice fishing." Recalling a cold ride in the back seat of a Willy Jeep beside a metal bucket and bamboo poles. "That's Upper Snowshoe Lake. We walked over to that large boulder over there." Pointing to a fifty-foot-high rock jutting out of the south end of the lake. "He told me that it was a pothole lake formed by a remnant of a glacier gouging and pushing a large boulder."

I point to a small sign on the left. "There's the campground. The host was murdered here a few years back, and no one found the guy for nearly a week."

Michael nods. "Our office manager said that it was a drug deal that went bad. Have you been to the lookout? Our office handles registrations at cabins and lookouts, but I don't think Thayer is on the list."

What looks to be a Newfoundland dog scampers across the road ahead of us, but the gait is off.

"That's a good-sized black bear," I say. "How's

your grizzly project coming along? Can you talk about it?" I ask, but Michael doesn't answer, his focus on the series of switchbacks on the mountain before us.

"There are five switchbacks, as I recall," I say as I crank down the Rover's window, letting the scent of pine into the car. "Mmmm. So nice and fresh up here. Amazing."

Willows and red sarvis berry plants dot the hills. "Water," I murmur. Michael reaches back, but I shake my head. "Where there are willows, there is a water source." I tap my head with a laugh. "Scout or Guide training, ya know."

We gasp at the landscape. A fresh scar is on the side of the mountain. Uprooted trees lay like matchsticks, and their branches tipped akilter. The dirt looked freshly overturned.

Michael turns into a wide spot in the road and shuts off the car.

We get out and walk to the boulder pile lining the road. Most of the rocks are half the size of the car. I scramble up the ones closest to the mountain and reach for Michael's outstretched hand. He joins me, hands on his hips, his head turning every which way.

"The service had a crew up here." Michael points at the damage path. "This reminds me of a wound that hasn't bound up properly. It started up there"—pointing to a small chute—"then gained speed, until" his hand traces the trajectory into the pool of placid water before us—"so the fish went…"

"Michael?" I turn as he jumps down and lopes around the rocks. As I scramble to catch up, I catch a glimpse of his plaid shirt disappearing into the willows. Following his general direction, I push aside the greenish gold branches, faint with red streaks.

A tangled branch snaps free, swatting my cheek. "Oww! What the…" Just to my right, a small, dull eye peers at me. I step back. A willow leaf protrudes from its mouth. A tiny spine dangles from the limb. "Michael, come here."

He appears and then laughs like a kid getting a longed-for treat. "Oh, it's true, look at this place." As if we need illumination, the sun appears from behind a cloud to reveal the whitened bones of fish hanging like tinsel. Hundreds of tiny spines litter on rocks and tree limbs.

That's when we hear a woof.

Two sets of puffing breath rustles and crashes through the sarvis berry plants, not ten feet from where we stand, followed by another woof. A guttural inhale of breath comes from behind us.

Michael and I freeze.

I crane my head in every direction, then point to a path on our right.

If Michael is afraid, he's not letting on. "Make noise. Whistle. It should want to run away," he says.

Another woof and another long sniff come with a breaking of brush and a flash of grayish-brown fir.

"Let's hope it's not a sow with cubs." I'm wracking my brain, trying to think of words or actions that will make the bears run away from us.

"God save our gracious King! Long Live our noble King, God save the King! Send him victorious, happy, and glorious, long to reign over us, God save the King!" Michael clasps my hand, his voice the best and only baritone that I'd heard since we got here. Together, we begin slowly walking backward toward the road.

He begins "God Save the King" again, and I join in warbling the only version I know. *My country 'tis of thee, sweet land of liberty, of thee I sing...*" I shrug as Michael gives me a stern look.

The bears crash and sniff where we had just been a minute before.

"Sweet land of liberty..." I bellow as Michel joins in on my version. The boulders appeared beside us, and they never looked so welcoming. Slowly, we turn toward the Rover.

The sow stands on her haunches, its brown eyes looking at where we are. "As long as we are not between her and her cubs, we should be free and fine," says Michael.

The bear drops onto all fours as a small ball of fur flies past us.

"Oh shit. We are now between the cub or cubs and her. May I suggest another chorus while we walk toward the Rover?" Michael's voice is straining for options.

Then, the bear looks away.

And so do we.

A whirring sound and a blue light buzzes up the road, about one hundred feet above our heads. "A huge dragonfly?" I think as my mouth gapes. I flush at the stupidity of my thought. The device's four wings stand stock still, and a portion of it appears to swivel to where we stand. Forgetting the danger behind us, we run over to the top of the hill as the blinking light heads south. Dangling from it is a small black container.

As we turn back, the hump of the grizzly is visible at the end of the Rover. Her two cubs scramble up the scree and into the woods.

The sow pauses and, in what appears to be a look of

disbelief on her part, shakes her head.
  I shake my head back. "Me neither."
  What had we just seen?

Chapter Three

The best sounds of the day are the Rover's doors unlocking, my pulling on the handle, and the closure of the car's door. Sliding down a little into the seat, I look to where Michael should be.

The hinges of the hatchback creak, and a rush of cold air chills my head and shoulders. Twisting in my seat, I shield my eyes against the bright sunlight that shadows Michael's face. He lifts a rectangular bag and unzips it before setting it back. His hand hovers above the bag as if selecting a particular piece of fruit. He finds what he wants and then zips the bag shut. Closing the hatch, he walks up to the driver's door and slides in, starting the car before taking a cord with a little box attached from his pocket and plugging it into the Rover's console. He holds a walkie-talkie in his hand.

"What is that?" I ask as he twists a dial. The device gives a loud squawk before silencing. A green light, like a cat's eye, blinks slowly, and a little screen has computer numbers on it.

"Roger, Roger, this is MTS341 calling FS341, over?" He presses his thumb on the transmitter. "MTS341, calling…"

A woman's voice crackles over the phone. "FS341 to MTS341, over. What is your location? Over?"

Michael turns to look at me. "What are the longitude and latitude of Willow Creek Meadows Lake?"

"What?" I ask, my mouth opening in astonishment.

"Seriously? Why would I know that?"

He holds up his hand to silence me like he's stopping the class idiot from embarrassing herself further. "MTS341 to FS341, we are at Willow Creek Meadows Lake. Please keep the office open so that I can address concerns with the warden. Over?" He lowers his hand and asks, "It shouldn't take more than an hour before we return to Snowshoe, right?"

"Oh, now you need my help," I mutter, shaking my head before turning to look out the window.

"Our local person, though a local, doesn't know our exact location, so I will guess that after dropping her off, I can be there in ninety minutes. Over and out." He drops the walkie-talkie next to the console.

Putting the car into gear, we drive for a few miles before I break the silence. "Can I ask what that was about? What is a drone doing near Willow Creek Meadows Lake? Do you think kids were navigating it?"

At the last question, Michael actually rolls his eyes, opens and shuts his mouth, and takes a long sigh. So, I'm back to "I'm an idiot mode." Great.

"Fine. Okay. Well, not okay. I don't appreciate your assumption that I would somehow automatically know GPS coordinates, and when I didn't, you treated me like I was an idiot," I say, crossing my arms and turning to look out the window. I sit like this for about ten seconds, and anger takes over. "I'm not an idiot. We both saw the drone and the bears. Can you speculate on any of this? Why do you need to talk to the game warden?"

Michael runs his tongue along his gums as he approaches the mountain with the five switchbacks. "I have to drive, and I need to concentrate. Do you mind?"

"Unbelievable. Do you hear yourself? Yes, I do

mind. A lot, in fact," I say, yanking my seat belt around me tighter and turning back to the window.

Five switchbacks. I bet he skids out, and it'll be me that has to bail his sorry ass off this middle of nowhere. But, as I count, to my increasing anger, he navigates the switchbacks with perfect ease. Soon, we are off the mountain and driving toward Upper Snowshoe Lake. More moments pass as we drive by the campground where the host was murdered. A pickup truck is silhouetted against the sun, and I want to tell Michael to let me out. I will hitchhike or whatever to get away from him. Stealing a glance in his direction reveals a man impassively staring ahead, not at me, not at the phone, just at the road.

I count in my head, hoping to reach three hundred, plotting how I can walk back up the campground and see about bumming a ride to town. The silence, what we saw and nearly experienced, weighs on my mind.

"FS341 to MTS341, over?"

"MTS341 here, over."

"FS341 Warden will see you. Once you get cell-phone reception, you can call with an ETA, over."

"Copy that, over and out. I will take you to the house, Joanne, and then I need to go to the office."

"I gather that," I say, hoping the sarcasm lands. "I'll call the restaurant and cancel the reservations."

"Fine. Good. Thanks," he says, his eyes never leaving the road.

More minutes pass, and my stomach growls. "I forgot I brought lunch. I'm unbuckling for a second to crawl into the back to get the sandwiches out."

"No, you're not. I will pull over," Michael says as he slams on the brakes.

I get out of the Rover and walk back to the hatch. Opening it, I retrieve the bag with the food in it and take out two bottles of water from the bag. Closing the latch, I walk back and stop before getting into the car. The temperature has dropped, and I estimate that we are twenty miles from Snowshoe.

The Rover starts, and Michael's eyes bore into mine through the glass.

"Fine," I say, opening the door and sliding back in. I put both water bottles on the console, and he takes one, placing it between his legs as he puts the car into gear. Rummaging in the sack of sandwiches, I take out one, unpeel the wrapper, and take a bite of the salty Reuben sandwich.

"I'll take one of those."

"You speak!" I say, pulling out the other sandwich and handing it to him.

He slows the car as he pulls the wrapper off, bouncing through a pothole as he does so.

I take it back from him and unwrap the sandwich.

"Thanks. I have a lot on my mind. I don't think I can tell you things, so let's understand that," he says, his eyes never moving from the road.

We stare straight ahead, munching on our sandwiches until the lights of Snowshoe illuminate the hill by the lake.

Minutes later, we arrive at the house. I get out of the Rover, and Michael U-turns it toward the west side of Snowshoe. As he pulls away, I see him speaking.

I walk up the cottage steps, go inside, and take the encrypted laptop for Iris Blackrail from the hall closet. Another message shows another attempted encryption breach. The coding comes from another sector, so I send an email to my counterpart at Cheyenne Mountain, Colorado, stating that if she needs any help, she should let me know.

Looking outside to the Maple District, where the residents of a Craftsman cottage hold secrets with potential consequences, I'm not sure I have an appetite, but I crave normal.

****

"Michael can't go to Hennessey's, and I don't want to waste the reservation. You want to join me at seven?" I ask Belle Conure.

"What's he done now?" my sounding board, knower of dirt, and all-around creative genius friend replies dryly.

I open up my mouth, then close it fast, not wanting one of Belle's patented blunt talks. "Michael plans things, then dumps them for some all-secretive missions, which is probably an excuse to go on a hike that resembles his precious Cotswolds. I promise not to talk about him. I want to know about you."

"If I had a penny—"

"See you then?" I ask, imagining her performing the perfect Pilates roll-up from the purple upholstered fainting couch she'd gotten for a song. She's damn near perfect, except she can't sing. Not that that detail stops her at karaoke night and church choir.

Belle is loyal, intelligent, and tells the truth. That can be a two-edged sword, especially in matters of the heart. When I separated from The Hole, she didn't refrain from a more than occasional 'I told you so,' but she was first in line to clear the paths to my eventual recovery.

I look at the candle on the dining room table and

decide that maybe Michael's communication skills aren't the only ones that need improvement. Picking up the phone that goes to my roommate's voicemail, I leave a message. "I didn't know when you would be back, but Belle and I will be at Hennessey's. Join us if you can."

Grabbing my purse, I pull out a pen, scribble a note, and leave it on the dining room table, resting against a candlestick.

Bounding down the stairs, I walk through the Maple District, then go south to the site of Snowshoe's first hospital, converted years ago to a steakhouse. Belle's red and white 1964 VW Bug hugs the curb, and I stroke the hood of the car, which is one of the many rituals passed between two good friends.

Jazz piano favorites play over the speakers as Belle waves me over to the table overlooking the side garden, where late summer Denver daisies peek over the windowsill. I sit down, and a French 75 and a purple concoction, Belle's favorite, a huckleberry martini, are placed before us.

"I left a message for Michael. He might join us," I say. "We went up to Willow Creek Meadows Lake this afternoon and ran into a grizzly sow and her cubs." I hold off on relating the details about the drone.

"Mm-hmm," Belle says, opening the menu and cocking an eyebrow at me. "Refresh my memory. Do you like your potatoes and stories half-baked?"

I sidestep the heaping side of sarcasm. "My presentation went well. It looks like we may get another piece of business. Wally from the choir was there, and so was a man named Paul Allegretti. Do you know of him?"

"Nice tap dance around the obvious. No, I haven't heard of that guy you mentioned. I did hear from Pam, though," she says.

I read somewhere that the drink French 75 is named for a cannon. As I reach for the drink to steady the explosion of poise inside me, the lemon curl and half the drink flies out of the glass, rendering the starched, white tablecloth and my friendship sticky battlefields. "I'm sure you didn't," I say, glaring at her. "We can cut the dinner short if you're going to be that way." I lean down to pick up my purse, then rise from the chair.

"No, she paid you a compliment. Really, it's a good story." Belle's words fly like buckshot and miss their target. "I'm sorry. Truly, I am. Please sit."

"No, this was a bad idea." I fish two twenties from my purse and place them on the table. No one looks up from their banter as I walk out of the restaurant. Dodging two cars as I jaywalk across the main street, I slow my pace as soon as I'm out of the line of sight of the restaurant. Only then do I allow my tears to fall.

"Joanne, please wait up, please!" calls Belle. Her beaded key fob jangles against the metal purse strap. As she reaches me, she takes the back of my arm. "I'm sorry. Pam came to me about catering a luncheon for a foundation. She heard from some of the directors that you will be managing the minerals and how impressed they were with your professionalism."

I wipe my tears from my eyes, but my anger, actually the taunting tone Belle had used, hasn't gone away. "Belle, you know how I feel about Pam. She gossiped about me in high school and then crowed about my separation and the divorce and how The Hole deserved better. She makes my life a living hell every single week—stupid questions and entitlement. And I have to endure it with a smile on my face. And I was expecting Alan Greene to be at the meeting this morning. I've been sick for days."

"Oh, no. Alan was supposed to be at the meeting? Pam said she has always been impressed by how smart you are. She relies on you. She does." Belle is practically shadow-boxing away from her stupid remark.

"You should know better," I spit, causing Belle's brown eyes to widen at my anger. "I canceled my afternoon because I couldn't wait to get the hell away from that place. If there is any way, any way at all, to get away from Pam and the foundation, I will do it in a heartbeat. You," I say, practically putting my finger into her chest, "you, of all people, should know not to bring her up. I wish she were dead."

"You don't mean that," Belle whispers.

I raise my head, my eyes staring hard into hers. "Don't I? I wish I could disappear using a different identity. Assume a different life."

Sidling beside me, she puts her arm around me. "Let's walk this off. C'mon, it was a stupid remark on my part, and I'm sorry for that. But disappearing? Unthinkable. Let's walk over to Maple District Park. We can get this sorted." She pulls on my shoulder, and we walk together, eventually slipping arm in arm.

No one is in the park as we sit down on a wooden bench dedicated to one of the park's donors.

"Now, how can we get all of this sorted out?" Belle asks me. She nudges me. "C'mon, tell me."

I open my mouth to answer, but my attention is drawn to a whirring sound above my head. I crane my head to see a small drone circle slowly above us before landing in the grass about fifty feet away. A teenage girl runs past us and picks it up, then calls out, "Sorry, I didn't see you there. They can be loud."

"Excuse me, but can you answer a few questions?" I call. The girl stiffens, but I smile at her. "Oh, you're not in trouble. I was wondering about the range of drones. How far do they travel?"

She walks over, and I recognize her as one of St. Olav Church's members. "I'm sorry, I got it as a birthday present and am learning. I don't know very much. It doesn't have much of a range. I'd have to trade up to be able to do that. My dad's in real estate, and the agents use them for aerial photos of properties they are selling. He got a used one for me so that I can look at the landscape and houses."

A sedan pulls into the parking lot behind us, and the driver honks the horn.

"That's my mom. I have to go," says the girl, running back to where the drone sits. She waves as she runs past us before getting into the car. "Bye," she calls as they leave.

"Let's plan a do-over on dinner. I'm sorry that I snapped at you, Belle. Let's walk back to your car, maybe get a nightcap before you go home," I say, but I know I will be terrible company, as I secretly hope that Belle will decline my offer.

"I appreciate the offer, and yes, let's plan another dinner. I'm sorry that I upset you." Belle holds out her pinky finger. "Friends to the end?"

I take her pinky finger in mine, an old Guide tradition from our summer camp days, then shake it twice.

"You don't have to walk me back to the car. Besides, your house is less than two blocks away," says Belle, rising from the bench.

I stand, and she hugs me. I watch her walk away until she rounds the corner toward Hennessey's. The silver maple trees shiver in the evening breeze. As I reach the Craftsman cottage, Michael's Rover is nowhere in sight. Stepping inside, I see my note on the kitchen table.

I pull out the Bolton's Valor laptop and, using my special glove, log in as Iris and then send a message.

Hi-

Who is our resident expert on drones? I have some questions.

Iris

As Michael's Rover turns into the driveway, I close up the laptop and, tucking it and the glove away, turn back into Joanne Corvus.

****

"The meeting went longer than I had expected. Have you eaten?" asks Michael.

Actually, I hadn't. "I meant to. Ignore the message about Belle and me going to Hennessey's. We ended up not going," I say, glancing at the clock. "Do you want to go to the Hare? I think they are open." I walk back over to the closet I'd closed only minutes before.

"Yes, that sounds good. What a day, huh?" says Michael, walking to the front door and holding it for me. As he closes the door, I hear the ping of a phone message.

"Do you need to get that?" he asks as we stand under the porch light.

I am sure that I turned off the Iris Blackrail computer, but I blanch at the thought that I might not have turned off the Bolton's Valor-issued telephone. "No, it's probably Belle wanting to talk. You know her and her personal life," I say with a smile. "I'm craving a

44

steakhouse burger." But I stop as I realize that I want to sort my day's problems out.

Descending the steps, I stop. "Actually, it's probably too late for orders, so let's see if we can rustle up something from our refrigerator. Do you mind? Maybe we can make fettuccine alfredo and crack open a bottle of that sauvignon blanc?"

Michael nods, the porch light highlighting the frown on his face. "Yes, I guess that would be okay. A Washington State Pinot Noir would be the perfect wine, but I don't think we have any of that. The terroir around the Willamette Valley and the high volcanic content of the soil exposed by the Glacial Lake Missoula Flood or floods provide the perfect soil. Some suggest that there were multiple floods, exposing mafic—"

"That sounds fascinating," I say. While the last thing I want to hear is about Glacial Lake Missoula, I learned through Michael's letters that I can lead him to what I do want to talk about. Tonight, it's the drone we saw. I need to lay out a path. "Didn't you tell me a great flood formed the English Channel?" I ask.

He turns toward the front door, again holding it for me and swiping at a moth fluttering against the porch light. "I'll start the pasta, and you can look for a suitable bottle of wine."

I walk over to the wine refrigerator and kneel on the polished fir floor. "I found a pinot," I say, rummaging through the dozen bottles of wine. "We're in luck. Let me open it, and I can set the table."

Michael leans back, glances at the bottle, and takes it from me. "I'll take it. I can use some of it in the sauce," he says, setting the bottle on the counter. He then turns back to the stove, pouring a quarter cup of pasta water into sauteed tomatoes, chopped basil, and cream cheese. Roasted, cut-up chicken sits on a cutting board.

A ping comes from the closet, and I inwardly groan, but with a laugh in my voice, I say, "There goes that phone of mine. Let me see if there is a crisis or if I can turn it off. Belle and her clients. I should write a book about that."

As I walk toward the closet to shut off my other life, and I hear the sizzle of the meat hitting the pan, Michael's voice registers as sharp and clear as the maple leaves against the mountain range outside. "Are you answering Iris Blackrail's phone or the one where you are Joanne Corvus?"

My hand shakes as another message pings on Iris Blackrail's phone. Opening the closet door, I take out the phone from the satchel and look at the message. *I have information regarding your request. Please update us on the encryption project. – JM*

I shut off the phone and put it back into the satchel. Drawing a deep breath, I walk into the kitchen where Michael is plating the fettuccine. He slides a look and slices of chicken on top of the pasta to me.

"It's work-related. All I can say is that I have a project where I'm Iris Blackrail. I won't tell you why because I'd be breaking my client's trust. That's all." I hold my chin level and think I've done a good job of selling the story. I can't tell him about the encryption project.

"I saw the satchel last week and thought that it belonged to your family. I won't pry," he says, but his clipped voice sounds like he has been stung.

Drawing another deep breath, I again keep my voice at a monotone. "The food smells delicious. Shall we?"

In the moments that I looked at the phone message and debated what to say, Michael uncorked and poured the wine, gotten the cutlery, and plated the food. He brought out two glasses, handed me a glass and a plate, and motioned for me to sit at the dining room table. He then turned on the sound system as one of my favorite soundtracks played.

I raise my glass to him in a toast. "Here's to complicated people," I say with a smile. "Cheers."

Michael touches on his absence by simply saying that he was reviewing data on the grizzly bears. They are being seen in new areas where two conservancy groups and logging companies have questions.

Twirling the last of the pasta against his spoon, he smiles at me. "They want answers on what these new movement patterns mean. I have a conference in Billings soon and will visit Bozeman and Yellowstone National Park."

I nod and wave the nearly empty bottle of wine in his direction. He shakes his head. "Maybe we can have some port instead. It's still a nice evening, and we can sit outside for a while."

Clearing the plates, I take them to the kitchen. Michael digs around in the Mission-style sideboard and takes out a liquid-filled handblown bottle and two matching glasses. "A gift from my grandparents," he says, "I can't leave them in storage." He pours the tawny liquid into the glasses and walks to the back door. I step outside and breathe in the pine-scented night air before walking to two cushioned chairs next to the outdoor fireplace.

Brushing off maple leaves from the cushions, I sit down. "It's been only a few hours since we saw those bears and the drone," I say, taking a sip of the sweet, rich wine and closing my eyes in pleasure. "What do you think about what we saw?" I open my eyes and look over at him. I can't see his eyes, only his profile, so I have to rely on his voice and his body language.

His elbows rest on his knees and remind me of a philosopher working out an age-old problem. He twirls the glass between his hands, then brings it to his lips. Michael takes a sip of the port and stares at the mountain range. "I don't know what to think. It's curious, isn't it?"

After a few moments of silence, he rises, then yawns. I nod as he goes into the cottage, left with the sense that he knows more than he's saying, and he can't talk about it. Bears are showing up where they shouldn't be. That's the only clue I'm going to get.

Chapter Four

"Good presentation yesterday morning," says Dan with a smile, his hand resting on my office's doorjamb. "Wally and Paul were pleased with what you talked about. However, Alan, after talking to Wally and Paul, has a few questions. He's waiting in the conference room." He pushes off of the frame, then stands in the doorway as if trying to right himself.

"Do you need the number of the massage therapist that I recommended?" I ask, not unkindly.

"I'll have to take you up on that. Old football injury that's come back to haunt me," he says, his sense of balance restored as he slowly walks toward the conference room.

My nemesis faces the lofty windows, taking in the view of Snowshoe Ski Area's broad alpine runs. He unwinds, catlike, extending a hand to Dan and then turns to me. "You must be Joanne. I'm sorry I wasn't able to make it yesterday. I had an emergency surgery to perform."

Dan shifts his body, searching for a bearable equilibrium, before motioning to the seats, and Alan walks around the table to face us. He looks at Dan as we sit.

"Buddy, that old golf injury acting up?" Alan throws a conspiratorial wink in my direction. "Don't believe the old football injury story. The story involved a golf cart." His gaze shifts from us to a large aerial photograph of the

Columbia Valley. "The valley has certainly changed since that photograph was taken. Snowshoe was a tiny lumber town. My dental practice in Tamarack was building. And look at the valley now. It's hard to believe all the changes that have occurred."

I'm weighing his banter and his mannerisms, looking for a clue that he knows who I am. I freeze, barely breathing, hoping Dan will pick up the conversation thread.

"Yes, lots of changes, both good and bad," says Dan, shifting his right leg and grimacing. "Alan, here, challenged us to a putting contest, but he neglected to put the brake on the cart. It rolled…"

"Oh, buddy, it wasn't my cart, and it was a level path." Alan gives me another wink and a smile that doesn't extend to his eyes. "Don't believe him, Joanne."

"I remember Dan's rehab took months," I say, recalling Dan's transition from a walker to a cane and triumphant removal of his handicapped sticker from the Audi. "That was right after I started working here. Dr. Greene, I understand you might have questions regarding the bank's services?" I ask, my voice rising. Does he remember my voice or my appearance?

"No. Yesterday, I got caught by an old-timer who lives near the border. He's a great old guy, but he cracked a molar and didn't want to drive down that rutted Outer Park Road to see me. He tried to give me mule deer venison as payment, but I waved him off," says Alan, again winking at me.

This is the part where I'm supposed to remember his charity or remark upon it. I give him a thin smile. "That's nice of you, Dr. Greene."

"Wally and I go way back," Alan says, changing the

conversation. "We met Paul at a conference about a year ago. He lives here for part of the year. He heard about the You Who Foundation and the scholarships provided to needy kids and families and wants to be a part of that. He worked with some conservation groups to have an easement on his property where we are proposing a summer camp be built."

"That sounds interesting," says Dan. "Where is Paul's property?"

"He has several tracts of land around the Columbia Valley. The parcel he's thinking of donating is north of here," Alan says. Rising from the table, he strolls over to the photograph, studying it for a minute, before pointing to the upper left corner. "It's probably forty miles from here." He gestures to a peak in the distance.

"When he deeds the land to the conservation group, we would like to know, as the foundation will need to put that on its books. We'll research how these transfers are handled and will work with the conservation group if they need us," I say as a knot forms in my stomach. Hadn't Michael mentioned a conservation group that he was working with? Could they be the same?

Dan rises from the table, again resting his hands on its edge to balance himself. "We appreciate your stopping by, Alan. Let us know if you have any questions," he says, extracting a business card from his billfold. I pull out a card, handing it to Dan to give to Alan.

Alan takes the cards from Dan and then slaps his arm. "We have to do another golf game or maybe go for a hike one of these days before the snow flies." He nods to me and walks ahead of us down the hallway.

Dan and I stand in the lobby, watching as Alan

bounds down the bank's outside steps. As we turn to return to our offices, Dan rests his arm on my shoulder, bringing his leg to be square under his body.

I know better than to ask. For far different reasons, Dan hates Alan as much as I do.

****

Abbie, our oil and gas mineral department's receptionist, calls out to me as I walk back to my office. "I signed for boxes from England. I've put them in your office. Let me know if you need me to help with filing or scanning the documents. Oh, and I put some treats in the breakroom."

"Thanks," I say with a smile as I step into my office. "I will be happy to accept your help."

Along the bottom third of a wall are ten bankers' boxes stacked into three groups. "The Hinerman Legacy" appears on four of the boxes, while "Wyoming Purchases" is on three. The remaining three boxes are labeled "Colorado Legacy Lands."

Abbie walks up beside me in the doorway. "I've never heard of a legacy in regard to oil and gas interests. You get such interesting things to do," she says, the ache for additional knowledge palpable.

"It's time, isn't it?" I say with a grin. "I would like your help with opening this account. We are lucky to have a template that we can follow. Can you create a folder for Georgie, Georgina Hinerman, and then copy Linda Taylor's Colorado and Wyoming interests into them?"

I walk over to the boxes and take off the lid on the first Wyoming box. Inside are file folders neatly labeled with the state, county, range, township, and section. I nod with satisfaction. Motioning to Abbie, I pull the box off the stack and put it on my desk. "Look. A landman created these files. Do you see how the files are labeled? That's what we are supposed to do. But," I say, pleased that she is holding a pen and a notebook, "we usually talk about S-T-R's—Sections, Townships, and Ranges— when we talk to clients. It's a funny thing, but it's information to keep in mind."

I pull out a folder that holds division orders. "Abbie, look how they have organized the division orders. Tabs indicate the operator." I flip pages looking for another teachable moment. "Ah, here are the calculations confirming the ownership interest. Write this down."

Abbie sidles next to me, her pen poised above the paper.

"The Hinermans homesteaded first in Weld and Adams Counties in Colorado. Edvard Hinerman and his brother Joseph came to raise cattle but soon found that returning to their old business of being grocers was much more profitable. When people could not pay their bills, the Hinermans would ask the land owners to deed over their minerals as a form of payment for the food they sold."

Abbie frowns. "That's predatory."

I nod. "Yes, I suppose you could say it was, but if you've been to Colorado, you don't think of it as being rich in oil and gas. Access to water was far more important to ranchers, so by giving up their minerals, the ranchers also knew that they had a way for their crops to flourish. Call it an extra incentive."

Penciled calculations line the margins of the division order. "The calculation comes from how much space the oil company needs to drill the oil well and how many acres you own." I point at the number in the form of a decimal. "That is the royalty rate based on the negotiations between the landman, or owners, and the oil company. Multiply this formula, and you should come back to the ownership percentage here."

Abbie walks behind me, pulls out a folder, and opens it. "The deed shows that it went from a person named Johnson to Edvard Hinerman," she says, like a student puzzling out a complex math problem.

"Flip farther back. Five bucks say there will be a homestead deed coming from the US Government to Mr. Johnson," I say with a smile.

Abbie thumbs through some pages and then holds the folder up for me to see. "Sure enough! Look at that!"

Her desk phone rings, and she scampers past me to answer it.

I take the folders, put them back in the box, and return them to the stack. Returning to my desk, I pull up the Columbia County tax assessor's website and type in "Conservancy." One hundred fifty results pop up, and I grimace at the thought of looking at all of them. "Allegretti," I type, and I sigh as the computer informs me there are no records under that name.

An evil thought creeps into my head. "Greene, Alan." My lips pucker in dissatisfaction as one address comes up, which, based on its location in Tamarack's business district, registers as his office. I type in the name of the You Who Foundation and get a postal box in Snowshoe.

I pull out an envelope where I've written down the code for the passwords I use for the websites I've used with other clients. Foundations are required to file information tax returns, which list their revenues, expenses, the names and addresses of their board members, the names of any employees, and their salaries.

****

Dan knocks on my door and motions for Abbie to come over. He holds up his car keys. "Let's go to lunch at the golf course. It's Par For The Course day, and I think Par-k Burgers and Par-Boiled Ribs would taste great. You two have been working hard, and it's my treat."

Abbie and I look at each other and grin. I grab my purse, and Abbie goes to her desk to retrieve her bag. The three of us walk out the back door of the bank to where Dan's red Audi sedan sits.

We get in, and I admire the luxurious interior of the car. Dan sits, then grabs his leg and pulls himself in.

I open my mouth, thinking that I will tease him about the massage therapist, but stop myself as I see a look of pain cross his face.

Seeing my frown, Dan smiles in a jolly way and says, "I'm starving, aren't you? I thought it would be a good idea to start having these team meetings every few months. I see all of your hard work and want to know how I can help or if you know of ways to build our business."

He starts the car, smoothly guiding the car out of the parking lot before turning west toward the Golf Club.

Abbie, the newest employee, appears nervous, but Dan, ever the good manager, talks about gardening and a movie that is coming out.

"I like to garden, but with my apartment and my roommates, I don't find much time. We don't have the space anyway," says Abbie.

"Are you allowed to garden at your place, Joanne?"

Dan asks.

"I don't have much of a green thumb, actually. I never really learned how. My roommate Michael will probably start gardening. A few nights ago, he was walking around the backyard, looking at the yard, and then he went into his computer and began making notes," I say.

Dan slows the car and turns into the pine tree-lined parking lot. "I called ahead, so I think we can get my favorite spot near the fireplace."

We get out of the car and walk inside the log cabin structure overlooking the eighteenth hole. Golfers stroll toward the pro shop and wave to Dan as we walk by.

"I can't wait to get my knee straightened out so that I can play again. I played all the time, but recently, I haven't been able to do so. Abbie, didn't you win some state awards?" asks Dan as we walk in and are seated in front of the restaurant's massive stone fireplace.

I face the hearth and smile at recalled dinners with my parents, sitting in the same chair.

Abbie beams and gestures to the golf course. "This course is one of the more difficult in the state. I played here a few times when I was on our college team and liked their Par Three course. I go here after work several times per week."

Fingers slide down my back, stopping just above my bra. I inhale sharply.

"Buddy, taking your ladies to lunch? Aren't you the best boss ever," says Alan, who hasn't removed his hand. His index finger makes a small circle just below my shoulder blade and then presses the finger into my skin.

My cheeks flame, and Abbie's eyes widen. No, I think, not here. Not now.

Pushing my chair back, I hit Alan's thigh and he steps to the side. I stand, then turn to face him, completely unsure as to what to say. As I face him, his cheeks flush, and I recognize that he hasn't planned for this.

"Alan," I say, taking a small step in his direction. It's not in his face, but it's enough for him to take another step backward. I then turn my back so that it faces toward Abbie while still keeping Alan in plain view. "Abbie? Alan traced a spot on my shirt that I must have on my back. Can you come with me so that you can point it out to me?"

I scoot past Alan, and Abbie follows me into the bathroom. Abbie rests her back against the bathroom door. "I'm confused," she says. I twirl in the mirror on the chance that there really was a spot.

"You don't have a spot on your shirt. And he touched you? Why—" But then clasps her hand to her mouth. "Oh, he's one of those," she says, her body seeming to shrink into herself. "He's a creep." She walks over to me and puts her hand on my shoulder. "Are you okay? I liked how you handled it, but you weren't blunt enough."

"He's part of a foundation that promises to bring in a lot of money to our department," I say, brushing off imaginary lint from my shirt.

"He's a dinosaur. He's a hashtag away from losing his business," she says, already working out a media blitz that has ended others' bad behavior. "I'll know to watch out for him. I was going to switch dentists, but not now and certainly not to him."

I pat her on the shoulder, and she opens the door to the din of a restaurant where Dan sits alone, nursing his iced tea. Alan is long gone.

****

"Are we friends again?" my friend with the off-key voice and boundless enthusiasm asks as we put away our hymnals and prayer songs of our church choir.

I close my cubicle, locking it securely, before turning toward Belle. "I don't get why anyone would want to steal the hymnals. That's ridiculous. Yet, two of them have gone missing in the last three months. Is there a black market for them?" I say this with a laugh. "If you're talking about the other night, it's been forgotten. Besides, I faced down my would-be predator at lunch earlier today at the golf course, so I'm feeling a little feisty."

Belle rubs her eyes, her lips thinning.

I sigh. "Are we continuing the conversation from the other night? Is that it?"

"You're going to get upset, but I'm your friend, and friends tell the truth," she says, her voice lowering. "Can we talk in a place with terrible acoustics? I can't tell you this here."

Shirley and June, two sopranos who have been part of the church choir since I was little, are whispering about the brown shoes Pastor Jen wore at the Lutheran Home. I look at the tiled choral room, then raise my eyes to where the chapel is. "Okay. St. Olav Church's acoustics are excellent, and we don't want eavesdroppers," I say, nodding toward the two women who are now talking about the length of one of the tenor's hair. "But this better be good."

We walk out of the choral room and up the stairs, saying goodbye to the two women who are now discussing who makes the best hot dish. They don't look up.

"The Hare should be noisy this time of night," I say as we step outside the church building. A whiff of tobacco is in the air. As I round the corner to the alley, I see Wally Harmon leaning against the church wall. He holds the cigarette in his hand but hasn't taken it to his lips.

"Sometimes, I like the smell of it. I quit years ago, but I light one up from time to time to smell the tobacco," says Wally, with a guilty expression on his face. "Promise you won't tell Beth. She'll wring my neck."

"Aww, your secret is safe with us," says Belle with a grin. "You sounded good on that solo. It'll be good on Sunday."

"Thanks," he said, drawing the cigarette under his nose and inhaling. He then drops the cigarette onto the gravel and extinguishes it with his boot. He straightens, giving us a wave with his hand, and walks down the alley toward the church's side parking lot.

Emelie is on duty as Belle and I walk into the Hare. "Is the Snug open?" I ask, and she nods. Taking two menus, she walks us back to the secluded booth. As Belle and I slide onto the benches, she closes the door, leaving us alone.

"Let's order, and then we can talk," Belle suggests, and I give her a nod.

Belle traces the menu with her index finger, and I look at it as if I don't have it memorized. "Lots of good choices. I'll have the Southside Salad. Have you had that?" she asks.

I haven't, but it sounds good, so I shake my head. "That sounds good. I'm buying."

True to form, Belle raises her head in protest, but I

smile at her. "My treat." I then knock on the wall, and it slides open. "Two Southside Salads, water for me, and—"

Belle says, "The same."

Two glasses of water are handed through the sliding door, and then the door closes, leaving us alone.

"Well?" I ask, "What am I not going to be happy about now?"

"It was yesterday afternoon. My customer was having highlights done on her hair. I'd walked over to the burger shack across the street to get food for her and me, and when I came back, Pam was sitting in Courtney, the other stylist's chair, talking in that obnoxious way she has."

Belle leans forward, her purple-lidded eyes widening. "My customer was under the dryer, so I sat at my booth, pretending to eat my burger, but Pam's conversation was awful. I debated telling you, but after you blew up at me, I took the only steps I knew to have you believe me. I reached into my purse, pretending to scroll my messages, and then I recorded her conversation." She pulls out her phone and earbuds and shoves them across the table. "You need to listen to this."

"You—" I say, as a knock on the door announces that our salads are ready. Opening the door, I take them and place them in front of us, smile to the server, and then close it, saying, "That will be all," as if my life is humming along perfectly.

"You did what?" I repeat, looking at Belle, who rocks and pushes the phone and earbuds to me.

I put the earbuds in and hit play. Pam's voice comes in loud and clear.

'I met him at a charity event. Our eyes locked, we

smiled, we both just knew—such a cliche. I had been sitting at a banquet table, grumbling about the terrible food. His hand rested on my shoulder, and then they just slowly drew back down my back to my shoulder blade. I must admit I shivered! Alan's not exactly handsome, but he has a nice smile. That was my first impression.' I press pause. "How long is this recording? Is it about a catering job? I'm not listening to this—"

Belle takes a bite of her salad, raises her eyebrows, then leans over and presses 'Play.'

'Alan was different. He seemed to care about making me feel special. Like I am a young woman, not a woman skidding toward middle age. He said, 'I'm actually getting an award, so stick around. It might be worth your while. Such a flirt!'

I shake my head at this nonsense. In response, Belle presses 'Play.'

'A few days later, he called me. He had been thinking of having a gathering. I suggested that lunch might be convenient for discussing what to serve and how many guests would be attending. Now, a year into this, we have done things that I would have never done before.'

"An affair? Pam's having an affair with Alan—" I say, "Oh my word. I thought she and Dan, but Alan?"

"Shh! You can be heard!" Belle shakes her head. "There's more. There's a lot more. But you can't say anything. I was hoping the Hare would be crowded, but you can't say anything. People will hear you." She lowers her head and crooks her finger at me to lean in. "You haven't gotten to the part about you."

I turn the recording back on. Pam's voice has dropped to a conspiratorial tone.

'Like cocaine, for instance. Oh, don't get huffy, it was legal until the 1930s! Really! Now, that had surprised me. Alan said that he had a friend who was a distributor—his choice of words is so amusing—like a home party plan with extra gifts for the hostess? He said it felt great. There were no real long-term side effects from the stuff that he had, and if I liked it, he knew where they could get more. And he's in the medical field, so he would know! The white crystals stung my nose. Hunched over a small table in his office with a drug pamphlet rolled up tight, I inhaled. The effect was way better than I had hoped for. Intense, sweet, and so much desire. I felt warm, and I craved the chance to curl into this feeling and make it last. Alan's touch is more than a caress. It is like being slathered with buttercream frosting, and he is the only person who is going to lick it off—buttercream frosting. Light, sweet, and I wanted Alan in a way I didn't think possible. Like a romance novel!'

Belle stopped eating, and I had no appetite. A bell rang in the beauty shop, and Belle talked to her client about getting rinsed out. Belle and the client's shoes click on the floor as they walk to the sink.

I'm left with Pam's obnoxiousness.

'I curled into Alan on the floor, my legs at an angle to him, my head just below his heart. We sat on the floor of his office for a long time, not saying anything. The stubble on Alan's chin was sure to chafe my skin. I drew my fingers back slowly, tracing an abstract design on his throat, and then got up and left.

Of course, I was back the next afternoon and the one after that, and I started craving my time with Alan and the little "upper" that I get. I feel fearless, unstoppable, and on top of my game. I finish projects.

Well, here's what I was getting ready to tell you. One afternoon, after a line of coke had gone up my nose, Alan whispered something to me. We were in his office, and he had told his receptionist that he would be out of town, so the office was closed. He pointed over to the supply cabinet.

'You know Joanne over at Winding Creek Bank? I had her right there.' His fingers did a slow circle in the direction of the supply cabinet. 'And she liked it. She begged me for more. She did everything for me. I gave her a car, and she gave me…' and he pointed downward and grinned at the memory. 'Yeah, she was fine.'

I pick up the salad bowl and fling it at the wall. Croutons, eggs, and chicken smear the wall. The bowl cracks in half. By then, Belle's grip on my shoulder is like a vise. I start, the tears stinging my eyes. Belle pushes me down into the chair and vehemently shakes her head. She mouths "Bitch" and "No!"

Emelie opens the door, a questioning look on her face.

Belle's voice is soft. "A little accident, she thought the chicken tasted off, and as she tried to return it, her hand slipped. We'll pay for it. You might want to check the chicken." The door clicks shut.

Meanwhile, I listen to Pam's feigned innocence. *'I was incredulous. 'Joanne—the woman that handles the investments? My boss Linda has an account with her. When did this happen?'*

Alan didn't answer at first. He wiped the blood from his nose on his sleeve, waggled his fingers downward, and said, 'Oh yeah, she's a fine piece.'

Pam swallowed some water, gargling her words. *'Enough of that hag. What makes our new meeting place so great is the abundance of huckleberry bushes, but I will never tell where they are.'* The beautician laughed at that. No one ever reveals their huckleberry sources.

I listen to Pam talk about loving this new hike and doing it every evening around seven p.m. Had she mentioned that it was an out-of-the-way place? Hard to get to? Great huckleberries? Belle sticks her fingers in her mouth and pretends to vomit. I crook my finger at her. "I've heard enough. Let's go."

Belle twists her hands in a choking fashion, but I shake my head. I don't have a plan. If Pam knew what had really happened, surely she'd understand and not blab to Dan or Linda. But is Pam a reasonable woman?

I'm not sure whose life will be destroyed, but someone's life is going to be drastically altered.

Chapter Five

The streetlight across the street exaggerates objects within its sphere of light. The shapes I stare at from my bedroom window are long and narrow, like the bow of a boat. The summer breeze makes the shadow appear to go up and down, and I recall a time when I saw a boat coming across Snowshoe Lake toward my father and me.

My father held up his fishing bucket and slapped my shoulder as we waved to the man in the boat. The motor had slowed, and the boat sliced the water as it approached us.

"Hi Thew! And is this Joanne? You've gotten so tall." Wally Harmon pushed his sandy-blond hair from his forehead. The boat hit the gravel on the beach with a decided crunch. My father put down his bucket, and we caught the rope Wally had thrown at us.

Wally nimbly jumped from the ski boat, his boat shoes looking like brown canoes under the water. He came up behind me, but as I tugged, both he and Thew lessened their pulling, leaving me to pull mightily on the rope.

"Thew, she's a strong one. She's pulling the boat in by herself," laughed Wally. He reached down and tousled my hair, and then the three of us pulled the boat onto the shore. "I have to put Beauty up for the season. Do you want to ride with me up to the blockhouse and put the boat away, Joanne?"

Thew nodded, and I watched Wally run up the hill,

start the pickup, and back the truck and the boat trailer straight down the boat ramp. After a few moments of work by my father and Wally, the boat was loaded onto the trailer. Wally leaned over and opened the truck door for me, and I climbed in, pulling the door shut behind me.

Wally drove the truck up the hill and began backing into the driveway to the blockhouse. I watched the boat trailer turn in the opposite direction, almost perfectly in line with the garage door of the blockhouse. Wally set the brake, got out of the pickup, and walked toward the wooden garage door. Instead of reaching into his pocket to pull out the keys like my dad Thew did to open the door to his bar in Tamarack, Wally removed a pocketknife and slid it along the trim of a window. There was a flash of metal, then he cupped his hands and caught the key in mid-air. He inserted the key into the deadbolt lock and pushed the garage door open.

Getting back into the truck, Wally put it in reverse, and the boat went into the garage.

I climbed out of Wally's truck and walked over to where my father waited in our car.

Wally walked over to the car and said, "There's better fishing out on the lake than from the dock. Anytime you want to borrow the boat, Thew, just let me know." He slapped the hood, then lowered his head again. "Are you going back to town?"

Thew grinned, pointing to the coffee cans in the back seat of our car. "Huckleberry picking spot is nearby."

Wally clasped his ears as if not wanting to hear the location of the secret spot, and I said, "We're not supposed to tell, Mr. Harmon! Everyone knows that!"

We laughed, and Wally walked back to his truck, waving goodbye.

A mile down the road was our favorite huckleberry-picking spot. It lay in the prime location—between 3,500 feet and 4,500 feet in elevation, on a north-facing slope. When we got out of our car, I groaned as we had company. A girl of my age sat on a log with purple coloring around her lips. A pile of berries lay at her feet. She looked bored and afraid.

"I spilled the berries, and my parents are going to be so mad," she said, staring at the purple, plump berries puddled between her feet.

"There's plenty more. You only have to go up the hill, and you'll find some good spots," I said, but the girl shook her head, continuing to pout. "I don't want to be here. It's so boring."

I nodded, deciding that I didn't want to be friendly with her even though Pam Clayton was my age. I walked past her.

It can't be a coincidence that her trysts with Alan are where she had picked berries all those years ago.

I wasn't sure if Wally still had a boat. Getting out of bed and padding to my phone, I give myself a mental shake, recalling his mention of its sale a few years back over coffee in St. Olav's narthex. But did he still own the blockhouse? I open the tax assessor's website and type in Wally's name, then smile at the results. I reach for my clothes and get dressed.

I would need to hide my car. Tiptoeing across the backyard, I open the small garage that backs onto the alley behind the cottage. Glancing around, all I see are darkened windows, though a faint rosy glow highlights the mountains to the east of me.

Backing my car from the garage, I drive down the alley and then toward the huckleberry patch. In another hour or less, joggers and bicyclists will be exercising along the road. I want to be back at the house long before that.

The blockhouse has some moss on it, but otherwise, it looks the same as when I was last in it years ago. I get out of my car and listen for any sound of movement. In the distance, I think I hear an owl, but otherwise, I appear to be entirely alone. I take the flashlight out of my backpack and peer inside the garage door windows. Boxes lie on the floor, but otherwise, the garage is empty. Squatting down, I point my flashlight along the sill of the window, hoping for a glint of metal. Again, I smile but hear a racket as squirrels chatter angrily in the treetops above me, and I freeze.

I don't know if the squirrels are upset by me or if they sense other dangers. I'm not taking any chances.

Running toward the car, I start it, then turn around and head back up the hill and to town, where my neighbors' windows are still darkened. I drive down the alley, put the car back into the garage, and as I walk back to the house, I see a creature scurrying by the woodpile left next to the house for building toasty fires.

A pungent aroma stings my nostrils. Do I want to bother the rental agency with getting rid of a packrat, or do I watch for signs of them wanting to burrow under the cottage? As I walk up the steps and enter the warm kitchen, I decide not to do anything about the pack rats.

As for Alan and Pam, well, that's another story.

****

"You're up early," says Michael, coming out of our shared bathroom, wearing the green twill pants and olive-brown shirt of his uniform. "I'm making madeleines. Fancy a cup of tea?"

The question hit me as being not a question.

He takes a few steps down the stairs, and I turn and go back to the first floor to wait for him. "You seemed fitful last night. I could hear you tossing and turning," he says as he steps off the bottom stairs and walks toward me. He puts his hand on my shoulder, then moves it to cup my chin. I pull back but then stop as I fight back tears.

"It's that asshole, isn't it? Dan needs to reassign you, or you may need to leave that job if he doesn't make a change soon." Michael leans toward me, then takes his finger and dabs under my eye. "There's no need to cry. We will get this sorted out."

"I might not have a job for much longer," I say, following him to the kitchen, where he opens a kitchen drawer and pulls out that ridiculous apron. Although he is pulling out ingredients from the cabinets, his head is cocked to where I stand.

"Belle recorded Pam's conversation." As Michael opens his mouth, I hold up my hand. "No, please, I need to say all of this out loud to another human being to see if I'm crazy. Pam is having an affair with Alan. They have a rendezvous point near a huckleberry patch, and I think I know where it is. I planned to hide my car in an old garage that I know about and go spy on them since their tryst would either be in one of their cars or outside."

"And blackmail your blackmailers?" asks Michael, setting down the bowl full of batter on the counter. "What if they don't care?"

My mouth opens in horror as Michael continues. "You accepted a gift from a man. And that makes you what exactly? How far are they into the Stone Age? You were barely eighteen?" He turns toward the cupboards, returning the ingredients to the cupboards next to the stove. "Belle has recorded proof that Alan is a predator and Pam has a cocaine problem," he says over his shoulder.

"How do you know about the cocaine?" I ask as he turns on the stove.

"Seriously? You've lived this long and don't recognize the signs of cocaine use?" Michael's tone is more incredulous than sarcastic. "Well, I have always thought you had a sheltered life. Living over a pub, fishing with your dad, it's all so placid, now isn't it?"

That was delivered with the reasons I don't want him living here.

"That's it!" I say, pounding my fist on the wall. "I confide in you and want your perspective, but all you give me is blathering on about arcane subjects that nobody cares about. Pam and Alan are going to paint me as the town whore. Maybe you don't get how small this area is, but I do. I'm living with you. I'm sure people think we are more than roommates."

"You want a pat on the head and to be told you're still the good girl. And to prove that others aren't as good as they portray themselves to be." He stands still as if my words are in the air and he can read them. "I thought my being here would be of help to you. I won't blather on and continue to annoy you if you think that's all my friendship with you means."

I hold my hands in a prayer position as I see how much I've hurt him. "Michael. Oh, I'm so sorry. Please forgive me." I step toward him, but he puts his arms out, palms forward.

"No. You need time to yourself. Our sharing of the house wasn't a great idea. I'll ask the rental agency to find other accommodations for me." With that, he strides out of the kitchen, through the living room, opens the closet door, retrieves his jacket, and walks out the front door.

I run after him, but he's already in the Rover, already has it in gear, and is already driving out onto the street. I'm left to watch him turn west toward his office.

Behind me, the oven beeps, ready to bake the madeleines. I walk back inside and turn off the oven. Engulfed in silence except for the increasing din of cars passing by, I find myself longing for the sound of gravel on the driveway. The knot in my stomach only grows as I recall the pain in his face and the rush of air as he walked out the door. Mostly, though, I put my hand on my chin and think of his warmth and the kindness in his gestures.

What have I done?

****

Of course, my phone calls go to his voicemail. Of course, before I get to the office, when I drive past the Forest Service office, the Rover isn't there. Of course, I've messed things up.

Of course.

In tears, I drive to the office. Drying my eyes, I park the car and then walk into the bank. My office carries a vague scent of onion skin and musty, foxed pages, and right now, it's the most comforting smell in the world. I pull open the box labeled "Hinerman Legacy." Within minutes, I'm looking at range maps and homestead deeds conveying interests to Edvard and Josef Hinerman.

I recall meeting Georgie in London and admiring the

man in the painting, and I remember how his eyes and the smile tucked under his mustache showed amusement.

Opening another folder, I come across Josef Hinerman's death certificate. I look at the bottom of the page to where the coroner has listed his death as being from a fall from a horse. Then, curiously, tucked in the notes are notes for the sculpture I had seen in London. I gasp as I look harder at the design. Josef died in 1889, and the commission notes are from 1891.

"A tribute to Josef," I say out loud.

Abbie, who came in while I was knee-deep in reading, called out. "Do you need anything? There are huckleberry muffins in the breakroom."

"No, I'm reviewing documents and came across the design for a sculpture. I saw the actual sculpture while I was in London visiting Linda's cousin, Georgina," I say, determined not to show my bewilderment at how my morning started.

"Did you go for a walk by the lake this morning? I thought I saw your car," says Abbie. She bites into a muffin and continues to look at her computer screen.

"I went out to scope out the bicycle path, actually. Where'd you see me?" I ask as nonchalantly as I can.

"I was coming down Ski Hill Road, and I thought I saw your car. I was finishing up a run," she says, her words muffled by the morsels of huckleberries and streusel.

Another reason not to spy on Alan and Pam, then. Witnesses. I'm not as good at spying as I think. Unless…a workaround comes to me.

As I contemplate buying workout gear two sizes larger than my frame and painting my bicycle, the phone rings. "Joanne Corvus, Winding Creek Bank, how can I help you?"

"Joanne, it's Linda. Linda Taylor. Do you have time this morning for me to stop by?" Her voice is calm, even happy.

"Sure, I'd be happy to talk to you. We received Georgina's files and are processing them," I say. "Coffee with two sugars, right?"

"Yes, good memory. Great, I'll see you in about an hour," says Linda, then hangs up.

I return to the files, then pull up Linda's asset listings on the computer and compare them to Georgina's asset holdings. Opening a second screen, I access the Weld County deed clerk and recorders website and compare the recorded ownerships to Georgina's records.

Abbie stands in my doorway. "Ms. Taylor is here to see you. She's in the conference room. I overheard how she takes her coffee and am getting that for her. Do you want coffee, too?"

I nod as I look at my watch, realizing that an hour has gone by. Taking a notepad from my desk drawer, I walk down the hallway.

Linda faces the window, looking at the ski area. She turns as I come in, gesturing to the view. "It doesn't get old, does it?" She walks to me and then takes my hands in hers. "I'm glad you got to see Georgie. She's my favorite."

We move to the conference table, clasping hands where we sit like old friends.

"The design for the sculpture in her garden is in the boxes she sent over. The rider with the steer?" I say, hoping Linda can fill in the blanks on whether it was done as a tribute to Josef.

"Josef befriended the Remingtons. My grandfather

Edvard ran things. Still, Josef must have been an interesting man to be around," she says, "though he didn't die in an exciting fashion. His foot caught in the stirrup of a horse, and he fell, hitting his head on a post. One of his friends had the sculpture commissioned, but Georgie's mother saw it and had it shipped to England rather than keep it on the Colorado ranch."

Linda ends this story with a flat tone, and I get a sense that there is much she isn't saying.

"So, how can I help you today?" I ask.

"I need an inventory of my assets. I have Winding Creek and my other brokerage working on my stock portfolio, but I need to know if you could work with me on the ranch and timber properties. I came across some information that seems odd, and I'm not ready to share it with the ranching team and forestry team at Winding Creek."

My eyes widen. "I didn't realize you were unhappy with their services. I can get Dan—"

"It's probably nothing, just lights in the sky or ATV marks and clearings that look odd. I was hiking and saw the ATV tracks, which led to a timber cut that I didn't know about. I don't know if you know of anyone with drone experience, but I need some reassurance."

"You mentioned lights in the sky?" I ask, thinking of what I had seen at Willow Creek Meadows Lake and the Maple District Park. "Are you thinking there are drones? Are people using the drones that you have without permission?" I reach for my notebook, but she takes my arm.

"I use the drones in my farming acreages and have expanded their use to my timber sales. No notes. Just for now, no notes. Two friends talking. That's what it will have to be." Her voice lowers, and I lean in to hear her. "Pam can't know about it. I can't put my finger on it, but she's been acting differently lately. I know she and Dan have been seeing each other for a while, but—" She sighs, releasing my forearm. "—call it foolishness if you like." I nod, and she smiles. "Come by the house tonight for dinner. Around six?" She stands and leans in to hug me. "Thank you, Joanne."

****

Linda Taylor's house would have been considered large when it was built. Set off the road leading to the ski area, the Mid-Century Modern house tucks itself into a copse of aspen trees atop a bluff overlooking the large meadow, clawed out by the lobe of the Cordilleran Ice Sheet that formed the landforms in this area.

Unlike her cousin in London, there are no gates, no security, no grand parkways, and certainly no statues of ancestors to drive by, but Linda shares a great many of her cousin's sensibilities. For one, she takes her surroundings with grains of respect and salt.

Her dog, Dane, an enormous wolfhound, greets me at the door with a sloppy lick of my hand while Linda shoos him aside. "He's huge but harmless. Just a big lug," she says, scratching his ears. "Go on, you!" The dog scampers across the wooden floor and heaves himself into a sofa the exact shade of his fur. "I figured that it would be easier to give him his sofa to lounge on, and while I was at it, I found a fabric that matched his fur. Win, win!"

She motions to me to follow her to the kitchen. I lean down to take my shoes off, and she points to a heaping bag of colorful slippers. I giggle as I pull out a pair of curly-toed court jester ones and hold them up to her.

"Always good to tell when someone has imbibed too much, don't you think?" she says with a laugh.

I settle on a pair of felted wool ones and slip them on.

"Good eye. Georgie made those. She and I went to Lerwick, Scotland, two years ago, and she let me pick out the yarn."

I pad into the kitchen, where Linda tends a pan of lamb chops and sliced potatoes. "I picked rosemary from my greenhouse. That'll go on top. I hope you like Tuscan reds. That's what we will have with the lamb." She nods to the opened bottle and the two wineglasses and turns down the heat on the stove. "This should sit for a few minutes."

I pour the wine and hand her a glass. "This is lovely."

"My ex, Marshall, thought Montana was too cold, and he spent part of his childhood in Connecticut." She shook her head at the silliness of that thought. "My grandfather Edvard had many skills. He ran a grocery store in Germany, but he also was a woodworker. He didn't much care for the plains of Colorado and wanted Josef to go to the mining camps, but my great-uncle insisted the future lay in the sugar beet and wheat fields outside of Fort Collins. It turns out Josef was right about that, but he knew how much Edvard missed the forests of home, so as their business grew, Edvard bought timbered land."

Linda walks to the dining table and sets the plates next to the stove. Taking a spatula from a tray, she lays a lamb chop on each plate before putting the sliced potatoes beside them. "Come, let's sit."

We sit at the table, and she raises her glass. "Salut!"

she says with a smile.

I cut into the lamb, and the tender morsel, hinting with rosemary and coarse pepper, is delectable. "Mmm…" I say.

She takes a bite, then takes a drink of her wine. "Edvard took me on long walks in the woods when I was little. He's looked at a tree and told you what it could be used for. Quite often, he brought small logs back with him, and I would watch him strip the bark, plane the wood, and create toys for me and gifts for the family." She takes another bite of the delicious meal and then sets down her fork and knife.

"I sell a portion of my timber each year. Before the sale occurs, I like to walk the woods where the timber will be cut and talk to the loggers about what they will be doing. I have great respect for their work. But—" She breaks off, rises from the table, and goes to a sideboard behind me. "Roads and trails are being put in the middle of the forest that the lumber company swears they didn't create. We have set up cameras to see who goes in, but all we see are things dropping from the sky and people coming in on ATVs, picking up packages and leaving."

"Ms. Taylor," I say, but she shoots me a look telling me that we are way past the formalities. "Linda," I begin again, "I'm an oil and gas manager, and I don't know anything about drones," raising my hands to limit her scope of inquiry.

"True," she says, "but you find things. I noticed that when we had our meeting two years ago. There was a problem with what I was told was a minor issue, but you picked up on that and dug in. Do you remember what you found?"

I blush at the memory, and Linda gives me a

Cheshire Cat grin. "Yes, but the money sent to the state would have been found by your portfolio managers. I'm sure of that."

"Perhaps. But you want to run a tight ship. I like that. Your diligence is noticed." She holds up the bottle of wine. I nod, and she pours another glass for each of us.

"Have the buyers changed from year to year?" I ask, probing for an anomaly. "There has to be a reason for these small clear-cuts and the ATVs. Can you pinpoint where the clear-cuts are and when you noticed them?"

Linda stands up. "Would you like to see the planes and drones I have? They are down in the barn area. I have cameras on the barn because we have bears and coyotes around, and they spook the horses. Four days ago, Dane went wild, barking at the door, and when I let him out, he raced for the barn area. I ran after him, but when I reached it, nothing was amiss. I checked the cameras and couldn't find anything."

At hearing his name, Dane jumped off the sofa, placing his massive head under Linda's hand. She opens the back door, and we pass a greenhouse on our right. A stone path leads to a paved sidewalk. As we walk down the trail, motion sensor lights come on.

The 'barn area' is a polite way of saying, "This is how the other half lives." A large hangar hugs the bluff, shielding it from the eyes of anyone with a home across the pasture. But there are no lights across from the barn because I'm confident that Linda owns that land, too.

A riding arena is to our left and connects to a large red barn. Linda walks past both of these and the hangar to a smaller barn, which is connected by a breezeway to the barn. She punches a code into the lock, and we step inside, where three larger versions of what I saw earlier this week lay on the floor. Laptops sit on three tables, as do six large monitors.

"The code to these buildings changes every two weeks, and so do the codes to the laptops," says Linda, her voice carrying a tinge of pride. "I like to feel secure." She walks to one of the tables and opens one of the laptops. "Let me pull up the footage, and I can e-mail it to you, or at least the stills of what I found. I'll include the GPS coordinates."

"Are these connected to you by Bluetooth or cable?" I ask.

"Bluetooth," she says, opening a file and motioning me over to look. "Here's the security footage from earlier this week." I look at the date stamp and see the foothills below the ski area. I lean in, wondering if my hunch is correct.

The drone Michael and I had seen at Willow Creek Meadows Lake had taken about thirty minutes, but the size and the package it carried were unmistakable. The drone flew about one hundred feet above the pasture, like a giant mosquito, never stopping, just blinking as it continued down the pasture before disappearing.

Linda opened two other files and printed those images out. "Here's the timber footage. I included the ATV tracks, too, though I'm not sure those will be of much help." She cranes her head as if looking for additional information but then looks at me with a broad grin. "Let's go back to the house. Maybe over some brandy and apple pie, we can talk about the drones."

As we walk back up the pathway, Dane stops and, with hackles raised, lets out a low, ominous growl. Linda reaches toward him, but he turns back, his eyes blazing. Baring his teeth, he suddenly leaps forward, diving into the trees, barking and growling.

"Dane! Dane! Come here!" Linda shouts. "I don't want to go in there, but he hasn't acted like that before. I thought he would bite me!"

We stand still, illuminated only by the pathway lights. A short distance away, Dane let out another aggressive bark, but the cracking of branches increases, and he lopes onto the path about twenty feet away. His long tail thumps the pavement at the sight of Linda, and he pants happily, pleased that his mistress is out of danger.

I open my hand to let Dane sniff it before reaching to pat his head. "Good Dane. Good dog," I say as calmly as I can. The wolfhound, Linda, and my head turn to where an ATV revs its engine.

Chapter Six

This time, I catch on.

Moments later, after leaving Linda's house, I walk past the woodpile in the dark, where, fortunately, I don't smell the packrat. Michael's Rover is still gone. Unlocking the back door, I walk into the kitchen, where the madeleine batter sits in the mixing bowl, a thin skin clinging to the sides like the first ice on a pond. Walking to the sink to dump the contents, I catch sight of a recipe card lying on the counter, and a pang of guilt hits me.

The handwriting isn't Michael's. With lesser pressure and more generous swirls and loops, this was written by a woman. What had Michael told me when we first began corresponding when I was sixteen? His father had been Polish and had escaped with his parents just before the Second World War broke out. His mother is English, but Michael mentioned going to Bretagne and other coastal parts of France during the summer holidays to visit family.

The temperatures are in Celsius, as are the measurements, but I take a look at the oven dials and am pleased that Michael has written the Celsius numbers on the dials in pencil. "Okay, you win. I'll bake the madeleines." Setting the temperature, I re-butter and flour the madeleine forms, drop the batter in, and then reach into the cupboard above the oven, retrieving a cooling rack.

Putting my purse in the closet, I reach down and pull

out the Iris Blackrail bag. Opening the phone messages, I see that Jacy has left a message. *Another attempt to beat the encryption in your sector. Please review.—JM.*

The message was written minutes ago. Walking back to the kitchen, I set the Iris Blackrail laptop out and log in using my special glove. Three VPNs, with addresses in Somalia, Nigeria, and Belarus, are those I recognize as known hackers, and I send that information on to our senior cyber security team's office outside of Cheyenne Mountain, Colorado. The fourth is the one that has Jacy concerned. For a millisecond, the hackers had tested our branches' protocols, breaking several levels before stopping.

The oven beeps, and I get up, put the madeleine batter into the oven, and then set the timer. "This has to be a coincidence, right?" I say to the universe. I watched or heard something in the woods with Dane and Linda, and at that exact moment, a hack occurred on our branch and, more specifically, our department. "Why would anyone want to hack into our revenue department and look at our data? It's oil and gas revenue. Nothing more."

As I study the VPN and recall Linda's video, I pull open the e-mail from Jacy from three days ago. I go to the closet and then return to the kitchen table and open my personal laptop. Opening the video file from Linda, I look at the drone as it passes by her pasture and then disappears. Moments later, a VPN shows four attempts to hack into Winding Creek's security. Again, the first three came from Somalia, Nigeria, and Belarus. The computers were different, but the origins were the same. The fourth, also a millisecond long, had been local.

The oven beeps, and I pull open the oven, pulling out a dozen puffed, golden madeleines. I set them on a cooling rack and then return to the computer. There's no coincidence. The hacks come from Tamarack, which I know all too well.

Michael romanticized the idea of my childhood living above a pub. Thew's bar, The Tamarack Springs Bar, sat on the main street of the town. After my mother died, Thew and I lived above it, in rooms converted from a brothel. The VPN for the hack comes from within ten meters of my father's bar—more specifically, from my old home.

****

Closing up my computers and returning them to the hall closet, I walk back outside and get my car from the garage. I need to think about what I expect to find, so rather than take the highway, I take the back road.

As a kid, I'd used this section line road that parallels the railroad line to go to Snowshoe Lake. Now, the section line houses the site of Heritage Farms—pioneer homes and gardens converted into a group of trendy shops selling organic produce. Although the owners eschewed the idea of having too many modern conveniences when they opened, they insisted on having three miles of gravel and dirt roads paved.

Several minutes later, I drive into the town of Tamarack and turn onto its Main Street. Tamarack's heyday had been years before I was born, but that wasn't a deterrent to Thewford Strong, known in local and collegiate circles as Thew.

My father had baseball skills and had even been recruited by some franchises, but when he tore out his knee, his career as a baseball player ended.

His co-captain on the team was from Tamarack and had family connections. He knew of two opportunities—

a dress shop where a woman was retiring and a bar where the owner hadn't paid taxes. Thew opted for the bar.

Half of the businesses on Tamarack's Main Street are shuttered and dark, but one is still open. The Tamarack Springs Bar, its green and gold trees lit up, appears on my left. I park across the street and walk over to the building.

The framed photos of local sports teams are long gone, replaced with generic posters of local attractions. Gone, too, are the yeasty, beer-soaked carpet and heavy wooden tables. Two bartenders, both college-aged, stand behind the bar, ignoring the lone patron in the place.

I take a seat at the opposite end of the bar, and one of the bartenders takes my order. "Moose Drool," I say. She points at the draft options, and I nod, although typically, it wouldn't be my first choice. Although I grew up in this bar and seem to be in the company of strangers, I ask where the bathroom is, and the bartender nods to the back.

The new owners haven't replaced the swinging doors, which I remember hanging from when I was young. I slip into the women's bathroom and close the door. I curse the new owners who changed the sink's configuration, replacing the cabinet with a simple basin. Putting the VPN tracker into the ceiling might be difficult. Maybe I'll have better luck with the men's bathroom. After a minute, I step back into the corridor. Smoothing my hair, I look in the corners and inwardly groan as I spot a lock on the door leading upstairs and a camera in the corner capturing my every move.

Returning to the bar stool, I appear to be the lone patron. "Quiet night," I say, and the bartenders nod before going back to wash the counters and bring glasses back to the kitchen. It occurs to me that the bar will close earlier than I think and they want me to leave. I nurse my beer for a few minutes, and the bartender slides me a tab. "Okay," I say, fishing money from my purse. "Thanks." Standing and walking toward the door.

I'll return on Tuesday, which will be another slow night, and go back to the bathroom again. Unless the new owners put in another apartment above the bar, which I doubt, the living room is over the corridor. If I lift one of the tiles above the men's toilet, I can put in a tracking device to see where the VPN transmits information. I'll put in a request with Bolton's Valor Security Forces and have the order expedited so I can get information on the people who live above the bar.

****

I already know the answer, but I drive past the Forest Service building anyway. The parking lot is empty. Returning to the cottage, I'm saddened to see that Michael hasn't returned. I put my car away and walk back into the kitchen, take two madeleines, and sit down by the kitchen table. I look up at the clock on the wall, knowing that I might be waking him. In a way, I hope I do.

Hi – I made up the batch of madeleines. I'm sorry about this morning. I could use your input on a problem, but you will have to keep what I tell you a secret. – JC

Three dots appear on my screen, then disappear. They begin again, then disappear. A minute passes. I hold my breath.

I had no right to say the things I did to you, and I am sorry. I would like to apologize to you in person. Let me know if that is possible. — JC

Can we talk over lunch tomorrow? I'll be back by

then. ML

My fingers dance across the phone in answer. *That sounds good. Can you tell me where you are?* I stop, then erase the last sentence, dead sure he's somewhere he can't talk about. *Text me when you are ready tomorrow. Thanks! —JC*

Okay. Good night. ML

Using my Iris Blackrail laptop, I send an e-mail to Jacy requesting the VPN tracker and asking if local authorities need to know about the device.

****

Climbing into bed and reviewing my day, I'm not sure I'm much of a sleuth. Even though it's been years since I'd had childhood and young adulthood celebrations within those four beer-soaked walls, I should have been identified by, if not the barkeep, at least one or two customers. But I wasn't.

It might be better to have a stranger put the devices in at the Tamarack Springs Bar since the possibility of running into a local who might remember me is pretty high. As for spying on Pam and Alan, what would I say if discovered? That I just so happened to be out for a hike. And would I be in disguise? Again, they'd recognize my voice.

I wake up to the idea of asking someone to place the tracker for me or figure out another way to see who is living there. Madeleines are a great way to start the day. I take two for myself and then put the rest on a plate to take into work.

Abbie is in the breakroom. I set the madeleines on the counter, and she beelines for them. "If you haven't checked your e-mails yet, we got the go-ahead from the You Who Foundation and they provided information on their assets," she says between bites.

"Great!" I say, "I need to contact their contacts over at the conservancy and get an idea of where the new camp is going to be. I want to find out if they are leasing the land for the camp or how that ownership will be structured."

Abbie's eyes widen. "I have a lot to learn."

"When I start those conversations, how about you join me, and I carbon copy you on the correspondence?" I walk to the cabinet where the coffee cups are, then pour myself a cup of coffee. "I like to 'get the lay of the land,' " I say, my fingers using air quotes, "and see if anything is different."

I take my coffee and sit down in my office. After opening my work e-mail and answering a few questions, I'm happy to see the e-mail forwarded by Abbie from Wally Harmon labeled You Who Foundation. Wally has used an automatic signature, and I forwarded the document to Dan, who will need to sign it as well.

Another e-mail from Wally, this time sent to Dan and me, gives the contact information on the conservancy and attaches a map showing the properties' locations. I purse my lips because the description isn't a description—it's an aerial photo with a red mark around it. The highway is in the background, and it makes a jog as if hugging a mountain range. What had Alan said? It's a property north of town that Paul owns. Mentally, I pull up images of the highway, recalling a bend in the road as the road veers from northwest to almost due north.

Frustrated with the lack of information, I give up. My voice dripping in charm, I call the Conservancy Group, hoping for a sympathetic ear. "Hi, this is Joanne Corvus at Winding Creek Bank in Snowshoe. We are working with the You Who Foundation. Paul Allegretti is donating land to the conservancy and will have a camp on the property. Do you have the legal documents for its location? And, it's an ask, and I'm happy to send you the agency agreement, but do you have recorded copies of the deeds that make this conveyance?"

The receptionist takes down the information and promises that I will get an answer shortly.

I open a website of the deeds recorded in Columbia County to confirm my thoughts. I type the name Paul Allegretti into the search engine and get zero matches.

That's odd, I thought to myself, rolling my head from one side of my shoulders to another to stretch my neck. Okay, let's try The Conservancy, and I get a hit on a recorded deed conveying a surface interest from the conservancy to the You Who Foundation. I make a note of the sections, townships, and ranges, as I can narrow my search to transactions regarding that area.

Putting the legal information in reveals a transference from Allegro Enterprises to the conservancy. I print out those deeds and then save them in the You Who Foundation legacy folder that I've now created.

I am not one to miss an opportunity. I type in Allegro Enterprises and get pages of conveyances. Habit tells me to start at the beginning, and I pull up the earliest documents that show a sale of a commercial property in Tamarack. The physical location is listed along with the legal description, and my blood runs cold.

Listed below it is the transference of a liquor license from Thewford Strong, also known as Thew Strong, to Allegro Enterprises. I lean back hard in my chair, recalling the conversation that led to the selling of my father's business.

"Jo-Jo," my father had said, inhaling deeply from his oxygen mask, "it's a guy out of Florida wanting to make a change. He doesn't like the weather, and he wants to be close to the park. He's paying cash." He coughs and then wipes what is, based on other coughs this hard, blood from his lips. His appointment with the oncologist was the following week. Not that I could persuade him to try for an earlier appointment.

Three months later, he was gone—the cash from the sale paying the medical bills and the remainder of my student loan. I'd mucked around for a few more years, marrying a man who I knew was a bad fit from the start, and then divorced him two years later.

In truth, I don't know if I should be grateful to Paul Allegretti for buying my dad's bar when he did. I pull up the section township and range, and there is a conveyance to another company in Chelan, located in Washington State.

I might as well go down that rabbit hole. I type in the name of the LLC and see paired conveyances. Allegretti Resources, LLC to Bon Ami, LLC.

"Have you heard from Dan?" asks Abbie, pulling me from my train of thought.

I shake my head, then look away from the computer to her.

"You've been quiet. What are you working on?"

I don't know what I'm seeing, and the disruption has made me angry. Which, by Abbie's expression, I must have told her nonverbally when I looked up. "Oh, sorry. I was in a rabbit hole," I say, smiling sheepishly.

"I'm getting messages from a deed retrieval website. Are you charging this to a particular client?" Abbie asks me, but I catch a whiff of sanctimony in her question.

"I'm getting a feel for a landholder's assets. They may be a potential client for the bank. I am curious as to how this pans out. I do that from time to time." I say this last sentence as casually as I can, knowing that what I need to do now is do my research on my home computer and keep the bank out of things until I track down my suspicions.

"I called Dan about another matter, and it went to voicemail. It's odd for him to be out of the office. He would tell us, right?" Abbie glances over her shoulder at Dan's darkened office.

I smile, knowing what my weekend project will be, and nod as if I had paid attention. "I'm sure it will be fine."

"What will be fine? What is it?" Abbie says with a frown.

"Oh, sorry. I meant that Dan will be fine."

And as if by magic, through my office window, I see Dan's red Audi, caked with dust, pull into our parking lot.

Dan pushes against the car as he gets out. From his rumpled appearance, I would swear he's wearing the clothes he wore yesterday. He disappears, clomps heavily on the stairs, walks past Abbie and me, closes his office door, and then pulls down the interior window shades in his office.

Abbie and I huff in surprise. We stare at each other, then glance at Dan's office, and then our eyes slide back to each other.

"Don't check on him. I think he wants to be alone," I say. "He'll come out when he's ready." Abbie nods.

"Do you think it's Pam?" she asks in a conspiratorial

whisper.

"I don't know. I don't know anything about their relationship. If they are seeing each other, it's news to me," I say, thinking back to Pam's bragging about her relations with Alan. "It's probably none of our business." Looking up at her with a slightly, but only so slightly, less sanctimonious look.

Abbie blushes and then returns to her desk.

I pull out the Hinerman Legacy files and begin to read through them, knowing that Abbie can't track my whereabouts and what I'm working on. A recollection from a training class pops into my head. "Know Your Owners," said the instructor at the banking conference. "Remember, machines don't launder money. People do."

I'd kept Thew's bank statements as I was his executor. The bank accidentally posted revenue into our account after the sale, and I returned the funds. I would need to find the statements and look at them tonight because I would swear I sent the overage to an address in Chelan, Washington.

Chapter Seven

The text is to the point. *Lunch at the Hare? Noon?—ML*

Yup. I reply.

Dan's instant messaging stays off, and his office blinds and door remain closed.

Minutes before lunch, I walk past Abbie, and she shakes her head, looking over her shoulder at Dan's office. In turn, I shrug. "I'm meeting Michael at the Hare. I'll be back in an hour or so."

Though the temperature is warm, clouds form in the western skies. Crossing the street, I'm relieved to see Michael turn the corner across from the Hare and park. He alights from the car, walks around to feed the meter, and then sees me.

Though I am a hundred feet away from where he stands, his smile is unmistakable. I smile back, and he waves. We meet at the corner in front of the Hare. He reaches out and squeezes my shoulder.

I am hoping for a hug. Oh, why not? I slip under his arm and wrap my arms around his chest. His hands fall onto my back, and for a second, he pats me like I'm a pet. Drawing back, I smile a thinner smile. He steps back and then opens the door of the Hare.

"I asked for a quiet spot, and they recommended a place in the back called the Snug. Are you familiar with it?" he asks as we step inside. Emelie sees me and gives me a wave, then pulls two menus from under the hostess table and walks us back.

We step inside the Snug, and I look to where I threw my salad earlier this week, relieved there are no traces of egg, chicken, or dressing anywhere.

"Your favorite place. I can see why." He slides closer to me so that we sit adjacent rather than across from each other. "You need my input. That's nice to hear." He scans the menu before setting it down.

"Michael, I said things I didn't mean," I say. "I'm sorry." His brown eyes reveal no emotion. "I need to talk to you about the drone we saw on Monday. And—" I'm interrupted by the opening of the sliding door behind Michael's head. "I think we're ready to order. I'll have the steakhouse burger, but I want iced tea instead of my usual drink."

Michael scans the menu again, then leans over to me so that he can see Emelie. "That sounds good. Let's make it two." He then sits up and closes the sliding door.

"I need to tell you a secret," I say, leaning forward. "I work on the bank's encryption and monitoring security breaches. It appears the drones pass by Linda Taylor's house with the VPNs coming through four places, the last of which appears to be my father's old bar in Tamarack. Paul Allegretti, a guy from Florida, bought my dad's bar, which he sold to another LLC in Chelan, Washington. The drones seem to be having a connection with attempted hacks on the bank."

Michael looks at his hands and says nothing. He then draws a breath. "Is there more?"

"Yes, Linda has timber interests. During the last few timber sales, clear-cuts in the forest and ATV tracks have been discovered, though the lumber company doesn't know anything about it. She wants me to investigate," I say, noting Michael raises his eyebrows at that, "and I thought you might be able to let me know if the Forest Service is aware of it."

"You mean like your boss waiting in strange places and at strange times? This morning, I saw him driving out on a Forest Service Road miles from anywhere."

"Where? How did you see him?" I ask, wishing the chatter in the kitchen behind us would quiet down so I can catch every word.

"I've seen him when I'm in the lookout. Dan's flashy Audi tends to attract attention. We pulled surveillance of the roads, and Dan had been driving near Willow Creek Meadows Lake, waiting for a while and then driving to another spot. At that point, he disappeared from my view, but he's done this at least twice in the last few weeks." He pauses, then slides over and whispers in my ear. "He was only a few miles from us when we went to Willow Creek Meadows on Monday. Had we gone back toward the highway, we probably would have seen him."

He then slides his arm around me and pulls me toward him. He leans into me, our noses practically touching before he holds the back of my head and whispers, "You aren't the only one with secrets." There's a rap on the door, and Michael says, "Oh, come in." Then he kisses me with our eyes open, and with the slightest shake of his head, he indicates for me to say nothing.

****

I raise my eyebrows, then bat my eyes at the man I had dreamt of kissing for decades, and then turn to look at Emelie, who flushes at the intimacy.

"Sorry, I can come back…" she says. I shake my head and point to the table. "No, that's fine," I say, pulling back and wagging my finger at Michael as if he is a mischievous puppy. "He said he was hungry. I thought it was for a burger. I'm rather clueless!"

The three of us laugh, and Emelie grins. "So if you need anything, he's got it covered. Okay!" she says, pointing at Michael before giving us a wink and closing the door.

"It was the only thing I could think to do," says Michael. "You didn't mind it, I hope." He slides away from me as if distancing himself from an unfavorable response.

"You're full of surprises," I say, with a smile, "and good at thinking on your feet."

We stare at the huge burgers, and I unwrap a straw and put it in my iced tea. I bring the burger up to my mouth but can't find an appetite. The kiss was, at best, okay. It was not a peck. It was not passionate. It was not familial and certainly not one a friend would give. It was, as I looked at him with new eyes, inexperienced.

I smile at that thought, thinking of the English boy who wrote of Arthurian legends and mudlarking in the Thames and Deen Rivers. That boy sent me poetry, and in those letters, he wrote of hope. Some of those hopeful ideas seemed to be directed at me. That gave me hope, too. For all of his other experiences in the world, there are portions of him that might not be so experienced after all.

I nudge his elbow, and he nudges me back as we take bites of our burgers.

He speaks softly, so softly that it requires me to lean in. In doing so, I smell the clean, soapy smell of his skin. My mind flashes to actions I probably shouldn't contemplate. His voice lowers, and I realize he's telling me important information, and I've not heard a word.

I couldn't say what I was thinking, so I asked him to repeat the last sentence.

"The grizzly bear project is only part of what I am working on. I've been at the Hornet Lookout and others in the area," he says.

"How did you see Dan? He's a mess, by the way. He came in this morning looking like he hadn't been home, and then he went into his office, closed the door and the blinds to his office. Neither Abbie nor I dared to knock on his office door to check up on him. Can I ask what you are looking for when you go up the lookout? I'm not sure grizzlies would go up near a lookout unless they had to."

"I hiked from Thayer to the mountain above Willow Creek Meadows Lake because I suspect a drone caused the avalanche two years ago. No one would have noticed above the noise of the snowmobiles." He takes a sip of his tea and dabs the sweet potato fries on his plate into the blue cheese dressing and then the ketchup. "You Americans. Why not dip these in the proper British brown sauce."

He leans toward me, his wrist brushing mine. "I found the remnants of a drone. It's unregistered, so I am tracking who might have access to a device of that size. It must have crashed because it came in contact with a rock or tree or maybe the weather. But it dropped its cargo, which someone hiked up to retrieve. We know that because there are scratches, and a portion of the wrapper was wedged under a rock. It's probably too deteriorated, but we are hoping that it will reveal evidence of its purpose."

"Drugs?" I ask, barely able to breathe.

"Yes, probably cocaine." He takes a bite of his burger and then licks his fingers. "My mother would slap me for licking, but this burger is delicious. You can't repeat any of this to anyone, do you understand?"

"It would appear, then, that we are working together. If it is cocaine trafficking, how would we be able to figure out who is sending the drugs and from where?" I ask, taking another sip of my tea, then glancing at my watch, I groan. "I have to get back. Dinner tonight, or do you have to go to the lookout?"

"I'll be at Thayer Lookout," he says. "I have to go back and look at some grizzly data. Ken and I will be spotting tonight, but I could meet you tomorrow morning. It's a drive, but would you consider coming up to Lodgepole Ferry and meeting me at the Merc? We could drive into Alpine National Park and go to MacFarland Lake."

I nod, slide out, and stand.

Michael does the same, and we face each other. In my shoes, I come to the top of his eyebrows. To lean in or not to lean in? That is the question.

Instead, I reach up, cup his chin, and look into his eyes, looking for a change. "Tomorrow morning, then. See you, Michael." As I open the door, I imagine what a sashay might look like and do not look back. Why break the spell?

As I step back outside, the sun shines brightly, as if granting a wish, before disappearing into the reality of a cloud.

****

Abbie isn't at her desk, and Dan's office door is open. I walk into my office, pushing aside thoughts of what I contemplated. I look out at the parking lot and see that Dan's car is gone. Probably at lunch or making a delivery, I think, though a wave of guilt washes over me. *Dan's not like that. Something is wrong. But am I the one to ask about it?*

"Good lunch?" Abbie calls, setting down a lunch bag. She sits down in her chair and starts typing.

"Yes, I ran some errands, then grabbed a burger. When did Dan leave?" I answer.

"After I did. He never came out of his office, and he didn't make any office calls. I hope he's all right," she says, but her tone changes with her question as if I will chastise her for her nosiness.

"His car is gone. He might have an appointment," I say as blandly as I can, standing up and walking out of my office.

Abbie says nothing, her eyes fixed on the computer monitor in front of her.

I walk to the breakroom to retrieve the mail in my inbox, but other than two division orders, it's empty. Dan's inbox bulges, and I peruse the contents. I pull out two letters that appear to be lease offers and two requests for approval for work on wells. A postcard-sized card flutters down on the ground, similar to those advertising upcoming seminars. Absently, I pick it up and return the card to Dan's inbox.

For the rest of the afternoon, I research and log lease offers and approve the budgeted expenditures for work to be done on two wells in Colorado. As I work, I reflect on the kiss and Michael's embarrassment or tepid response. My stomach churns with anxiety as if I have, yet again, misread a situation. Maybe it was a response to keep me quiet. I sigh. Perhaps we are both inexperienced.

A vacuum cleaner whines to life in the building. Abbie's desk sits empty, but Dan's office light is on, so I walk over, turn it off, and close the door, being sure to lock it.

Gathering my things, I shut my office, then step outside, where the sun continues to play peek-a-boo with the clouds hovering above Snowshoe Ski Area. A breeze has lowered the temperature by at least ten degrees. I walk down the street toward Sain Olav's Lutheran Church. As I pass by, faint music comes from inside. Opening the church door, I slip into the back of the sanctuary as Shirley, the church organist, plays the final stanza of the hymn "Lord of All, we sing your praise," and I join in.

Shirley stops, cupping her hand to her eyes to see who is singing.

Clearly, I've startled her, and I call out, even though the church is not large. "Sorry, I heard the music and thought I'd come in."

"Hi Joanne. I was glad to see you at choir practice. It will be nice to have you back."

I walk toward her, my feet bouncing slightly on the thick carpet leading to where the organ sits on the left side of the church. As I approach, I smell flowers. "I was walking home and heard the music. It's a comforting hymn, isn't it?"

Shirley's fingers hang in mid-air over the keyboard. She hunches forward, staring intently at the sheet music.

Well, that's a dismissal. "I'll see you Sunday," I say, blanching at my intrusion. I skulk through the sanctuary and into the narthex to check my inbox. Empty again. I glance to where Shirley sits at the organ. Her shoulders rock gently, and she dabs at her eyes.

Walking into the late summer evening's light, I think about Shirley and what I know of her. She's been a fixture in the church for as long as I have been around. With her ramrod-straight posture, hurricane-proof hair, and steel-rimmed reading glasses, she presents disgust without a word when we come in a beat too late. Come to think of it, I've never heard her laugh or seen her smile.

I pull out my phone and call Belle. We never greet each other, preferring to dive into the questions or comments we may have. She picks up on the second ring.

"Didn't Shirley Thorpe date someone after her husband's death?" I ask, crossing the street to where the cottage sits.

"Odd question."

"I'm an odd person," I say with a laugh. "Husband died, a period of mourning, and then, there was someone, but I don't remember who."

"You must. It was the talk of the town. Old Steelback Shirley met a man who lived in the South and began flying there to see him. He never came here. Shop gossip said she found out he was married, and then she never dated again. Well, no, that's not true," says Belle, "his wife died, and she's rekindling the flame."

"This stays here. She appeared upset when I saw her at the church. Dabbing her eyes," I say with a firm voice.

"Hmm…" says Belle. "Shirley doesn't come into our shop, but one of the other caterers on our team did a catering job for her a few months back. I could ask her."

"No! Don't do that," I say, looking around to see if anyone is out on their porch enjoying the evening and likely to hear our conversation. Two doors down from where I'm walking, the red-orange glow of embers rises to someone's mouth. Several seconds later, it drops again. "I'm being gossipy. Forget I mentioned it."

Avoiding the eyes of whoever is smoking that cigarette, I jaywalk toward the cottage. I go inside onto the porch and sit down on the settee, removing my shoes. The smoker also sits on the covered porch. I don't know him or who lives there, and I shiver as full-blown paranoia sets in. *Get a grip. You have no evidence of him eavesdropping. Will he connect you to Shirley? And for what?*

Opening the door to the cottage, I take a last look at the smoker's house. I'm jarred by the sight of the embers, jarred by Dan's absence, and jarred by Belle's willingness to snoop and, more likely, blab about my questions. A bubble of anger rises, and then another and another—Shirley's coldness, Belle's gossipy nature, and my stupidity about Michael.

****

Scrounging in the refrigerator, I pull out the half-opened bottles of wine and the remnants of attempted meals, place the food on a plate, and pour myself a glass of the Vino Verde. As the food heats up in the microwave, I contemplate how much evening light I have left and how long it would take to bicycle out to the huckleberry patch. I don't even know if they are having a tryst. Michael is right. I shouldn't go out there to spy.

The microwave beeps. I take the plate over to the kitchen table and sit down, weighing my options. I should do what? If I bicycle, I might come home in the dark. They might not be there. What if they see me? What if I walk above the road somehow? Would I cross the properties out there with houses on them? I could play stupid. The berries would not be ripe yet, but maybe they would be getting near. I could accidentally see them. They're being in the wide open like that if Belle was right.

Gulping the rest of my wine, I take my keys and go outside to the garage. I get my car from the garage and then drive through the Maple District to the road that parallels the railroad tracks. Crossing the bridge, I drive north, past Linda Taylor's house, past Abbie's running spot, past the entrance to the ski area, and on toward the blockhouse. I pause at the bottom of the hill and contemplate whether I should hide the car and walk the rest of the way. A glimmer of headlights comes toward me, and I look for an exit. A road that leads to the beach is on my left, and I drive down it. Halfway down the hill, I see a red Audi pass by. At the base of the hill, the road makes a sharp left turn, but the wide space at the base continues to be used as a parking space.

I park with the nose of the car pointed to the lake but then decide to turn it around so that I can see who drives down the road above me. The lake is like a mirror. In the distance, the sun hangs low over the Thayer Range, which Michael and I passed days ago. A bird flies above the lake, but as I watch it, I don't see a flapping of its wings. Getting out of my car, I race toward the boat ramp and see it fly toward Snowshoe, heading southeast.

The echo of a car's engine reverberating against the hillside is behind me, and as I walk up to the top of the boat ramp, a blue crossover car drives slowly past. It continues on the road, switching gears as it goes up the hill toward the highway.

As I walk back to my car, get in, and drive back toward Snowshoe, I don't see taillights ahead of me on the highway. Thinking about drones and vehicles, I believe that home is an excellent place to be. Crossing the bridge back into Snowshoe, my thoughts center on one idea. There's a lot of traffic on the road used for huckleberries and trysts.

Chapter Eight

Minutes after arriving back at the cottage, I connect my Iris Blackrail computer. No encryption breaches have been reported.

The blue crossover had nothing to distinguish it from the hundreds of vehicles like it in the Columbia Valley. Still, it can't be a coincidence that Dan's Audi was on a lonely stretch of Heaven's Rest Road, and a few minutes later, it was followed by a blue crossover.

Before going upstairs to bed, I check the weather forecast and groan as there is a sixty percent chance of rain tomorrow. As I undress and get ready for bed, I reflect on the day, knowing I'm missing a clue. But my eyes close, and before I know it, my alarm goes off.

I prepare a thermos of coffee, grumbling that I don't have any madeleines. Then again, the Lodgepole Ferry Merc is known for its huckleberry bear claws and enormous cinnamon rolls. Maybe Michael and I can have lunch or dinner at the Aurora Borealis Saloon. I put a waterproof jacket and pants in the back of my car along with trekking poles as Michael had talked of a hike near MacFarland Lake.

I drive from Snowshoe to Tamarack and again drive north on its Main Street past Thew's Tamarack Springs Bar. The lights are dim. Nevertheless, I drive around the block to see who parks behind the bar and if I recognize their car or cars.

A logging truck rumbles down the main street, bits

of sawdust and bark flying off the back of its truck bed. As it passes by, I catch the name of the owner, "Elizabeth Logging Company." I'm not familiar with that company, but a number of businesses have sprung up as log homes are being built.

The parking lot behind the bar is empty. Disappointed, I turn right at the next block and take a left, following the narrowing road until the river appears on my right. Across the river are the western flanks of the peaks that make up Alpine National Park.

As I drive the increasingly potholed dirt and gravel road, lodgepole pine trees stand like sentinels above the river. I reflect on how Thew and I made this trek on a sunny spring morning. A song had come on the radio, a familiar song to us both, but with a twist in the genre. We sang along, belting out the lyrics of the country song, now done to a jazzy beat. "You need to find out who is singing that. They are good," said Thew.

That was my introduction to The Modern Retellings. I dig into the car's console, extract a compact disc from its jacket, and slide it into the player. I sing along, thinking of my father's baritone and our laughter about the band's inventive twists on popular songs.

Soon, I see the sign for the entrance to Lodgepole Ferry. Enormous logs frame the road to the Lodgepole Ferry Merc, with another log on top and a moose antler rack in the middle. The red building with its massive painted sign saying MERC in bright white letters is about a quarter of a mile down the road.

A familiar figure nurses coffee in front of his Rover, and I break into a grin. I honk, and he looks up, using his silver thermos cup as a wave. I pull into the parking lot, cut the engine, and hop out into a fine mist.

Michael steps under the porch and waves me in, holding the door for me. "Any trouble on the way up?" he asks. "I was going to buy some rolls, but they had choke cherry, huckleberry, and normal cinnamon rolls. It seems to be an important decision, so I thought I'd leave it to you."

"Good call. I do love the smell of freshly baked treats," I say, breathing in the sweet scent of berries. "I'm partial to cinnamon rolls, but their huckleberry bear claws are legendary." The clerk hands two of them to me and gives Michael an expectant look. "I'm not sharing these," I say with a grin.

"Better get some more of those, then." He fishes out a twenty and hands it to the clerk. "I thought we'd come back here for lunch, but we have special plans for dinner."

The clerk winks at me, and I blush. "Okay…" I say in a joking fashion. "It'll be interesting, I'm sure."

Michael opens the Rover's passenger door. I run over to the back of my car and retrieve my rain jacket, pants, and trekking poles, then place them on the back seat of the Rover. Closing the door, I look over at Michael. "We have lots to talk about."

"Let's close up shop first. 'MS341 to FS341. Over. Off duty today and until tomorrow at sixteen hundred hours.' "

"FS341, Roger that. Enjoy your days off. Over."

Michael points to the lodgepole pines that look like blackened matchsticks. "Part of a forest fire several years ago. The cones only open when there is enough heat. Usually, it is a forest fire, and the first flowers to come up after a fire are fireweed, which is known for its fuchsia flowers."

We check in at the park ranger station and then drive the seven miles of dusty, twisting, rutted road. Michael gears up the Rover, and I jump in with what I want to talk about.

"I saw another drone last night. I was out at a boat ramp on Snowshoe Lake, and it flew by," I say.

"You went out to spy on them?" Michael doesn't look at me but issues a sigh that is enough to let me know his thoughts on what I was doing.

"Dan drove by in his Audi, and then a blue crossover drove by. I didn't go to the huckleberry patch." As I say this, I recall being in the principal's office, which is not far off from how I'm feeling now.

"Well, that is strange. Who owns the blue crossover?"

I shook my head, thinking I might have gotten a hall pass. "I don't think the car belongs to Pam. But I'm left to wonder if the drone, Dan, and that other car are connected."

He lets out a sigh before slowing to avoid a giant pothole in the middle of the road. "Of course they are. But you don't know if Dan sent the drone or if it is anything other than a toy. It's not helpful and could be considered gossip."

"Okay," I say, completely deflated. "What is your news?"

"Drones are a hot topic. There's talk of replacing the fire lookouts with drones and studies to determine if they are more cost-effective than keeping a building, sometimes built over one hundred years ago, manned by people in a remote location and paying them a living wage to stare for days on end at nothing. Or once in a while, a whole lot of something when a fire erupts."

Michael veers sharply to miss a pothole in the road but can't avoid the one just after it. We bounce sharply upward and land hard on the Rover's unforgiving seats. "Plus, the octocopter drones can carry payloads of over two hundred kilos—nearly five hundred pounds—which can help with construction projects. Drones are expensive, but you can leave them for hours and days and months on end, and they will never complain about loneliness or needing time off to vacation with their friends or go back to school. However, they are subject to costly mechanical issues. And—" He breathes what sounds like a sign of relief as we turn into MacFarland Lake's parking lot. "—they lack the human touch."

We get out of the Rover and walk toward the lake's shoreline.

I gasp. "This is stunning," I remark, taking in the long, narrow lake flanked in the distance by two steep mountains. A headwall of a third mountain is at the end of the lake. "Is it me, or does this look like a smaller version of Lake MacDonald?"

"It definitely does resemble Lake MacDonald. Of course, it's part of the Lewis Range and part of the Belt Super Group, so the Precambrian mountains, or the Old Rockies, have overthrusted over the New Rockies." Michael rattles this off, not with the intent to impress, but as if stating the weather in the most general of terms.

"So, if that theory is correct, there's a possibility of finding fossils along that headwall in the background," I answer, thankful my geology courses and field trips as a high school student are paying off at last.

"You remembered those facts from the letters I wrote you all those years ago. I'm impressed," says Michael.

I open my mouth to correct him, as I definitely don't recall any letters on any such topic, but I'll let him have this point. Walking along the shoreline, I spy a trail marker and walk toward it. "Do you want to hike for a little bit on this trail?"

Michael shakes his head. "I have other places to show you. We have several stops and will need to go back to Lodgepole Ferry to cross the river. We can talk in my car, but I don't think it will be safe to talk about drones or any of our mutual work concerns while we are here."

"That sounds ominous," I say, nudging his elbow. "Are you sure the Rover is safe?" He nods but puts a finger to his lips, then crooks his finger at me. "I need to hug you and tell you what we have discovered. You can't act surprised."

"Oh, Michael," I say, falling into his open arms with a heaping dose of overacting. "You are so wonderful."

His fingers stroke my hair, and he leans in to whisper in my ear. "Your car is bugged. There is a tracking device, and we know where you've been in the last few weeks. You didn't need to drive by the Forest Service office to look for me, by the way."

I pull back, my mouth falls open, and I raise my eyebrows in shock. "You have been tracking me?" I can't walk back to Snowshoe from MacFarland. I'm stuck with Michael.

"Keep your voice down and get in the car. My car has been scanned thoroughly, and it's clean, but yours is not. Now, let's smile like we love each other and get back in the car, okay?"

I do as I am told.

Michael starts the car, and in a few minutes, after

getting to a non-bumpy part of the road, he speaks. "It's a shock, I know. But you can't do anything different— except not go back out to the huckleberry patch. I'm on a project to track grizzly bears and why their migration patterns are sporadic. We think there is a connection with the drones passing too close to them. I'm going to ask you to do something when we get to the Canadian border. It will not be normal, but please go along with it. We are going to drive on a forest service road that we think isn't monitored. I'm going to inflate a doll, and you are going to drive to the border. The doll will be in the passenger seat, and I'm going to hide in the back. You are going near the border to take pictures. I'm going to honk the car horn like I'm angry, and you will accidentally drop a pack on the ground. The pack has special equipment in it."

"Sounds like a spy novel," I say in wonder. "We are hoping to get whoever is sending the drones on camera?"

"More like a task force partnership with Canada. It has to look unplanned," he answers.

"But people know what I look like." I counter, not seeing how this could work.

"Yes, as Joanne Corvus. But you're not always Joanne. The limp, the padded clothing, and the wig in London made you look like a different person. When we reach the border, can you be Iris Blackrail?"

I gasp. "How do you know what I look like? How long have you known?" I ask, but Michael smiles and shakes his head. I'm not getting any information from him about my supposed disguise. "Won't the surveillance cameras pick up on the Rover? It's distinctive. And my wig?"

"That has been sorted out. Just become Iris Blackrail

after we drive up the Forest Service Road and definitely be her when we get to the border."

"People will notice that a blonde left Lodgepole Ferry. Where is my wig?"

Michael points to a large paper bag in the back seat. "You have less than a mile to create your persona."

I reach back and pull out a wig that is similar to what I use, lean forward, and adjust my hair into the wig. "I'm going to need a ball cap unless you have one in the car."

Michael gives a small whistle. "Hello, Iris. That was fast. I think Ken might have left a cap in the glove compartment."

I look at Michael. He's wearing a tee shirt under a flannel shirt and a puffy vest.

"Pull off your puffy vest."

Michael slows the car and removes his hands from the wheel. He pulls the vest over his head and hands it to me. It smells of soap and is warm to the touch. "Just keep driving," I say, and he laughs as I shuck my top, put the puffy vest on, then the shirt, and reach back to get my rain jacket. Opening the glove compartment, I take out a well-worn Forest Service cap and place it on my head. I look for the final bit of disguise. I settle on a small screw lying on the console, bring up my right foot, and take off my boot and sock. I put the screw in the bottom of my sock and put the sock and boot back on.

"There. Say hello to Iris."

****

As we drive past the parking lot of the Mercantile, I ask Michael to stop. "I need to use the restroom."

Michael shakes his head. "We can use other facilities up the road. Sorry, but I have to be careful about this, Iris," he says, pausing to look at me. "That's amazing."

"How do you know the car is secure? They, whoever they are, could have hidden a mic anywhere in the car, or my purse, or who knows? This whole charade might be for nothing."

Michael slows the vehicle as a lumber truck rumbles past and overtakes us. It's going faster than I think it should, but with its girth, the driver seems to think that might must equal right.

"Odd that a logging truck would be here," says Michael, as if he could read my thoughts. He stops the car. "Actually, Iris, why don't you drive, and I sit in the back?" Michael slides out of the car and motions for me to slide over onto the driver's seat. He opens the back driver's door and removes a vinyl square from a bag. Walking around the car, he opens the front passenger door, places the vinyl square on the front passenger seat, and then touches a button.

I don't know if I should be horrified or laughing. I chose to laugh at the vinyl man with a surprised expression. Michael takes off his flannel shirt and puts it over the doll's shoulders. He then slumps down in the back seat and says, "Okay, see if you can follow the truck."

Fortunately, the road straightens out, and I'm able to spot the logging truck less than a mile ahead of us. "Do I get to ask who put in the purchase order for our new friend? And how was the invoice done? One sex doll for use in diversion, oh, that's a bad word," I say, as Michael breaks into a grin.

"Entertainment—"

"Education," I say, trying not to look in the back seat and see Michael's expression.

"They have uses—"

"Oh, cut that out. I'm trying to drive. How far behind the truck should I be? I'm trying to be serious here, and you have a, well, we probably should name him if he's going to keep us company. How about Dick? Though we don't know much about that."

"Oh, Henry?" answers Michael. "I didn't know the mouth would be so, so—"

"Inviting? If you are into that, I suppose," I say. "How far are we from the border?"

A minute later, the dust trail is gone, and we are back in a sunny meadow. A brown sign announces Trail Creek Road and that the border crossing is ten miles ahead. Reaching down behind the doll's surprisingly realistic and hairy leg, I take the bag of treats from the Mercantile, retrieving a huckleberry bear claw. Biting into the roll, I savor the tart yet sweet filling, wiping the sugar coating from my mouth.

Suddenly, a bear, unmistakable in its color with its silver tips and tawny brown coat, runs in front of the car. I slow down, taking in its huge, shaggy frame. "Michael, Michael? There's a grizzly twenty feet from us."

"Oh, it has a collar. I'll be able to track who it is when I get back to the office."

Two yearling grizzlies barrel past us, crossing not ten feet in front of the car. Oblivious to us, they run pell-mell up a low hill before disappearing down the bluff above the river.

Michael points his finger and tries to roll down the window but can't because of the child's lock. "Curses! Where is that bloody drone? Where are you? Slow down so that I can look!"

I bring the vehicle to a crawl as we scan the sky for

anything that resembles a drone.

"Stop the car! I need to get in the front seat!"

Dutifully, I slow down and put the Rover in Park.

The doll appears to question my driving skills with its awful open mouth too close to my face. Michael opens the back door and runs around to the passenger side. With a terrific yank, he jerks the doll out of the car and then tosses it on the side of the road. "I think I see it! Turn around, turn around, now! Let's go!"

I do a J-turn with Michael cursing at me under his breath. "It's getting away. You need to speed up. I'll keep a lookout on it and see where it goes."

Anger seeps to the surface. "Stop yelling at me! I'm doing the best that I can. Are we going to the border? What are we doing?" I yell. "Change this. Change that. Do this. Do that."

I look in the rearview mirror to see if any of my messages are getting through, but Micheal's focus is on the sky.

"I still see it. It's going south and headed that way," he says, his eyes fixed on the binocular lenses, and he points with his index finger. "I have it in my sights. Let's follow it. It's not going that fast, and it is carrying a package," his voice has changed to a gentler tone. Message received. "I'd like not to lose it, but if it goes onto places that don't have roads, we might be out of luck. Do the best you can."

We pass Trail Creek Road, and I slow, but Michael shakes his head. "It's veering across the valley. I wonder, oh, it's following the river. That's clever. It can drop its package into the water. Maybe that's how it's picked up. That makes what you saw last night reasonable. It drops the package in the water, and then someone takes a boat or kayak out to pick it up. Still, let's see where it goes and if it turns around after it drops the package."

The drone goes above the tops of the pine trees and disappears from view.

Oncoming cars distract me from looking, but Michael keeps his binoculars trained on the river. "I don't think this is going to work. The road goes away from the river, and we can't see it. The only way to know is to see if it comes back up the river. Turn around, we are going across the bridge and going down the road inside the park."

"What? No."

"Turn around," Michael says, but his tone has changed from collaborative to a growl. "You need to do what I say, or we won't get this solved. Understood?"

"Yes, sir!" I say, irritated to be ordered around like I'm an idiot. No, that's not good enough. "Michael, what about our going to the border? And what about the doll that is lying on the side of the road with your shirt? We're supposed to drop your original plan to go inside Alpine National Park—"

"The park will make exceptions—" says Michael, his head swiveling.

"No, they won't," I say, waving my index finger at the mountains and then pointing it at him. "This is a wild goose chase. I get wanting to see where the drone is going, but you told me that I was needed, me specifically, to help you with a drop at the border. What happened to that plan, huh?" My mouth opens in a sneer.

Michael scans the river and the surrounding area, then sighs in frustration. "Let's drive for twenty more minutes, and then we will turn around and get back to our original plan. Wait! Is that what I think it is?" He points to a large object. The object flaps its wings. "Being led around in circles. I don't know what to do." Michael's frustration erupts as he pounds his fist on the dashboard.

"I doubt anyone would be on the river, Michael. It's too early in the season. It will be a miracle if we see the drone."

"We have to try. We have to follow up on this hunch, Joanne."

He continues to look to where the river meanders out of sight.

"The Rover is getting low on gasoline, and we will need to fill up soon," I say. "Is it too late to drive back to the Canadian border? Maybe count off one success in your plan?"

Michael grimaces but says nothing.

I take a road that heads toward Four Lakes and the train trestle. Dropping down to the secluded area, we have a commanding view of the slowing river.

Michael takes his binoculars and scans the river in both directions. "Nothing. Nothing at all. It could be anywhere on either side of the river. We don't know." He sets down the binoculars and then brings his knees up to his chest, a man confounded by so many close calls and no answers.

****

Nestled in the charred remnants of a crown fire, the raven huddles against the rain, watching the human dig a hole, placing meat and a shiny object into the dirt.

After a few moments, the human walks away.

The bird flies down to the lumped site, its tallow eyes peering around for fellow foragers before pecking and tugging voraciously at the meat and shiny object.

Wresting a twig-like object free, the raven flaps its wings, brushing off the duff, and begins its flight to the large aerie in the crook of a sturdy pine tree a mile away. Gaining height, it soars on the air masses coming off Snowshoe's ski area and lake. Nearing a garbage heap, the bird spies a fish head lying on the ground. Swooping down to get the fish head, it drops the shiny object, which tumbles before coming to rest in the branches of an Oregon grape plant. The raven sets its talons into the fish's head and flies away.

That evening, a pack rat, attracted by the shiny object, takes it back to its midden tucked into an old woodpile behind the rented Craftsman home.

Chapter Nine

Dan's red Audi sits in the cottage's driveway, and its owner slumps on the steps, impervious to the drizzling rain. My boss looks up as I slow the Rover, parking it on the street. As I cut the engine, Dan raises a tear-streaked and blotchy face. Michael and I get out of the car. As I take a closer look at my boss, I shiver.

"Dan, let's go inside and get you a cupper. I've never known a situation that couldn't be solved with that," says Michael, who clasps Dan on the shoulder.

Dan stands up but visibly shakes as he turns on the step. I press my hands against the back of his soaked shirt to steady him, and Michael leads him onto the porch and inside the house. Without a word, Michael points Dan to his favorite chair, and he sits. Michael strides into the kitchen, and I hear him call, "Putting the kettle on."

Michael walks back out and squats beside Dan, who holds his hands in front of his face. "Joanne," he says, raising his eyes toward my head, "can you get some tissues from the bathroom for Dan, please?"

Shit. I'm wearing a wig, a puffy vest, and a ball cap. Maybe Dan didn't notice?

I scurry into the bathroom, toss the wig in the cabinet under the sink, take off my rain slicker, toss the vest and ball cap under the cabinet, and then remove my boots and shoes. Tossing my hair, I look like Joanne again. I walk out and remember I forgot the tissues, then go back inside and retrieve them.

The kettle whistles loudly, and Michael goes to the kitchen to fetch Dan a cup. As I pass by Michael, I cough, and he looks me over and gives me a thumbs-up.

Dan's huddling and staring at his hands reminds me of a wounded animal, so I squat beside him and speak softly. "Dan? How are you?"

Michael walks around the two of us, setting a plate of bear claws and a cup of tea beside Dan, and then motions with his hand for Dan to eat.

"Dr. Greene has been in the valley for fifteen years or more. He's regarded as an old-school dentist, happy to go to the outer stretches of the area to help patients who cannot come to him. Over the years, some old-timers who lived in the northern reaches of the county would come to rely on him to check on their general health," says Dan, taking a long sip of the tea.

He sets the cup down and goes back to regarding his hands. "Dr. Greene told me he often came home with a package of deer meat or smoked fish as payment," he says, his voice adopting a robotic quality. "More than once, fur skins were his payment, and he took those to a taxidermist to resell them and receive the cash he needed. Now the old-timers are dying off, and the deer and fish payments are a rare occurrence."

Dan leans forward, placing his forehead in his hands. "I haven't seen Pam lately. Part of that is my trips to Missoula, which are longer than usual, and my always being on the phone with my current or prospective clients."

I rise and walk over to the chair opposite Michael, widening my eyes in a motion that I hope conveys my incredulity.

"I worked for Dr. Greene when I was a teenager. He

talked about the old trappers," I say. "I didn't know he had expanded his business."

Dan continues to stare at his hands. I motion to the plate of bear claws, but he raises his eyes and then drops them as if the sweets are objects he doesn't understand. I take one of them for myself.

"Pam heard me speak once, very slowly, to a man whose English is not that strong, and she got suspicious. The man talked about getting people into a new investment, and he just knew this was the next big thing." Dan twists his fingers in his hands. "I proposed it to our board members, and they passed. I created a loan to invest in it for myself, but the paperwork hasn't been approved. I mentioned to Pam that I was thinking of telling Linda about it and her cousin Georgina, and she flat out blew up at me."

"More tea?" asks Michael, and Dan nods, though he has barely touched the cup he has. Michael rises and then stops as Dan continues his story. "Dr. Greene, er, Alan, told me the investment involves the sale of diamonds held in a bank in Washington. They can't find the heirs, though they tried diligently. The diamonds are old and large. That's what Alan says. They belonged to the wife of one of Alan's old fur trapper clients, and the old guy died, leaving nothing but his bank account here at the bank. We are the Successor Trustee of the trapper's bank account, so it's up to us to dispose of his assets, and the members of the bank's board think that should include the wife's diamonds. Alan thinks it's a great idea to get the diamonds from the bank in Washington, hold on to them, and then turn around and sell them at a profit."

"Dan," I say, "has a judge signed off on this? Don't the probate courts have to approve the bank getting custody of the account? If the diamonds belonged to the trapper's wife, is there a legal trail that shows that the trapper would get them upon the wife's death? Aren't there notifications that need to go out? I can always help with that, or we can have one of the other wealth management offices handle it."

Dan's mouth tightens, and, as he wipes his hand across his cheeks, I notice that his tears have dried. "It's a good investment," he repeats.

"Aren't you and the board too close to be impartial about this?" asks Michael. "I'm sure you have appraisals already done and provided to the board so that they know what they are buying, correct? It's not like they would be buying cubic zirconias?"

Dan jumps up. "I knew it was a bad idea to come over here. Michael, you don't understand how banking works in the United States, so butt out," he says, narrowing his eyes. "Joanne, I came here to tell you that Pam has complained and wants you off Linda's account. You'll need to apologize to Pam for the way you treat her. If you don't, I'll have to talk to human resources about it. I value your work, Joanne, but you have a prejudice against Pam that goes back years. And now I'm noticing it with Alan. This behavior is affecting your judgment. I've arranged for you, Linda, and Pam to meet in the conference room on Monday so that you can formally apologize to them. We'll have to look at whether it would be a conflict of interest for you to work on Georgina's account."

My mouth drops open, my tongue touching a molar as I look hard at my boss and, until a few seconds ago, someone I considered to be a friend. "Dan," I say softly, "Dan, this isn't like you. I don't understand. Not even a little about any of this. You want board members to invest in assets technically owned by another bank. But the diamonds aren't here. They are in a bank vault in Washington. Is it one of our branches?" I pause, not rising from my chair, watching Dan's stance change.

"Dan," I continue, my voice going for a lullaby and failing, as Dan squares his shoulders and then grimaces as pain shoots through his face. "Dan, walk me through all of this and how it happened. Pam complained to you, her friend, about me. She involved her boss, Linda Taylor." I pause as neither Dan nor Michael have moved. In fact, Dan doesn't seem to be blinking.

"You are taking out a loan so that you can invest in this diamond scheme, which our loan department declined. Have the other board members—Alan, Wally, and Paul—approved? Are they overriding the bank's standard practices? Are the senior corporate banking officers aware of this? I would think they would have to be notified, don't you? Otherwise, it would be a conflict of interest. Help me understand because I don't."

My boss, who I thought was my friend, shakes his head and walks to the door. "See you Monday."

"Dan?" I call after him, still not rising from my chair, still believing that he will see the idiocy of this. "Dan? Help me—"

He slams the house door and the porch door, and I rise from my chair, walking to the living room window. Against the streetlamp's glow streaking the rain-spattered street, I watch him get into the Audi, back onto the street, and into the darkened streets of the Maple District.

I see the glow of a cigarette on a neighbor's porch. The figure stands, twists their arm to put out their cigarette, and then walks inside the house.

****

Michael picks up the teacup and the bear claws and takes them into the kitchen. I follow him and slump into a kitchen chair.

"He's a nutter. Stressed-out nutter," he says, putting the cup in the dishwasher, then pulling it out and examining its rim.

"Do you think he's on drugs? We can't call the cops because we don't have evidence of any wrongdoing," I say.

"Who has seen the diamonds? Only Alan, right? Or did Dan say that?" asks Michael. "Dan has taken out a loan through the bank, but the bank will want collateral. His house, no doubt. Dan's the one person I know in this town that doesn't have two jobs. Does he come from money?"

"Not that I know of." Recalling what my boss might have said in meetings with clients. "Like a lot of people, he came out here for a summer job. He worked as a rafting guide on a river. He was in the corporate offices and met people who had mineral interests. He'd also worked as an oil and gas operator for a summer, so he developed our oil and gas management department."

I sit back in the chair, thinking about Dan's pain. Then, a sobering thought hits me. "Michael, you might need another roommate unless you've already gotten a new place to stay." I say this while working on what I would or might have to say to Pam on Monday. "I might get fired. In fact, I will likely get fired."

"Oh, stuff and nonsense. Dan probably will apologize to you on Monday and say that he was taking medicine that hindered his judgment and that he's sorry for the intrusion."

"If I'm working at Winding Creek, come Monday, I probably should check on something Dan said about the trapper that died. He said the man had his wife's diamonds in a safe deposit box in Washington, but Dr. Greene treated him at his cabin. That likely would be north of Tamarack."

I stand, walk over to the hall closet, and retrieve my laptop. Setting it on the coffee table in the living room, I log on and then access a newspaper database. I type in "Tamarack," "died," and "trapper," narrowing the date range to the past three years.

Seconds later, I have a list of four names. Michael crouches beside me.

"Didn't Dan say that they had posted Probate or Heir Finder notices in the newspaper? In England, and I'm sure they do that here, they would post it in the last known residences or where they had a business. Are there any from Washington?"

I scroll through the obituary notices, looking for a link to Washington State or a wife who might have died in Washington. I come up empty.

"It doesn't make sense, does it?" asks Michael. "It's like the grizzly bear project. While bears can and do wander, they have territories or areas they stay in. Over the past two years, we've seen the animals show up in places that are closer to humans, though they are not attacking ranch animals. In fact, they are becoming a group that lives along the margins between the outermost parts of their normal breeding habitat and where humans live."

I open a newspaper article associated with the first trapper and a screen with the Columbia County Tax

Assessor's Office website.

"What are you doing?" asks Michael. "I don't see the connection."

I gasp as I see the owner of the trapper's cabin. "It's an LLC, a Limited Liability Corporation," I say. "Michael, I can't prove it right now, but I'll bet dollars to donuts that every one of these trappers sold their properties to Allegro Enterprises, who then sold it to an LLC based in Washington State. Why would they do that?"

Michael squats beside me and opens a laptop. "Dollars to donuts? You Americans obsess about food. Keep the assessor website open."

"How did you...where did you get your laptop? I didn't see you leave?" I ask. "You're like a ninja."

Michael glances from his computer to mine and drops a tag on a location. "Hmm..." Taking his finger and pointing. "This is Thayer Lookout. The drainages in this area"—pointing to the locations of the cabins—"aren't easily visible, but look how close they are to the river. Where are the packages coming from?"

"Canada or possibly another drop-off?" I ask, remembering his comment about my expression. "Dollars to donuts is similar to the English expression 'pounds to a penny' and is believed to have originated in the late Victorian period."

He squints as if I've lost my mind, and I grin.

"What are you nattering on about? The cabins might be a drop site, but they are also nearly in the margin of the grizzly's habitat," he says. He stands and stretches. "I'm off to bed. We have a busy day tomorrow. We'll leave at eight a.m. sharp to go to Lodgepole Ferry and pick up your car."

"Michael, I can't. I'm singing in the choir tomorrow at both services. I can't miss that," I said, though I was thinking of what we would find at the cabin. "Can we go up after I finish at church?"

"I have a shift at Thayer starting at four in the afternoon," he says with a yawn.

I turn my head to shut down the computer, but Michael is gone. "Let me do research on these trappers and check with the other branches before I meet with Pam, Linda, and Dan. Can I do that?"

In response, I hear water running. Tssking under my breath, I stomp upstairs. I raise my hand to knock on the bathroom door, then stop.

****

I awaken to Michael pounding on my bedroom door. "I've called the police. Oh, my word. We have a situation. Joanne, wake up!"

Rolling out of bed, I glance at my phone, which shows the time as seven in the morning. I open my bedroom door to find Michael with beads of sweat on his forehead and his breath smelling of toothpaste and ginger tea. "What do you need?"

"I've called the police. We can't use the backyard, and they'll ask questions. Oh, my word," says Michael. "I didn't touch it, but…" He puts his hands on his knees as if he is getting lightheaded. He raises his head at me, his eyes filled with tears.

"Michael? What did you find in the backyard? Can you tell me?" I ask, still shaking off my slumber.

We both turn as red and blue lights flash against the wall. Seconds later, the doorbell rings.

"Joanne, you'll want to get dressed. The police are here. You'll give a statement." With that, Michael pads down the stairs. The front door squeaks, and then two voices ask if he's Michael Laysan, and then Michael asks them to come in.

I put on jeans and a shirt and walk downstairs to where Michael stands with two uniformed police officers.

"Good morning. I'm Joanne Corvus. Michael called you," I say, recognizing the woman as being a newer member of our church. The man is vaguely familiar, but I can't place him.

"Ma'am, you'll need to stay here with my associate while Mr. Laysan shows me what he found in the backyard," says the man. He and Michael walk through the kitchen and out the back door.

"Do you know what this is about? You look familiar. Don't you attend St. Olav's Lutheran Church?" I ask. "I'm sorry, I don't remember your name. Can I make you some coffee?" I offer, but the woman looks around the living room and back at me without a smile.

"I'm Detective Johnsrud. Yes, we recently joined the church. You're in the choir, aren't you?" she says in a noncommittal way. "Have you been outside this morning?"

"I woke up a few minutes ago. Michael, my roommate, knocked on my bedroom door. He's upset, but I don't know why." I search officer, oh, it's Holly, that's her name. "Holly, isn't it?"

"Detective Johnsrud. How long have you lived with Michael?" she asks.

"Michael moved from England several months ago. He and I were pen pals in high school, and he came here because he knew me," I say. "We're not romantically involved if that's what you are asking."

127

"I wasn't asking that. Pen pals? How long did you do that?" Officer Johnsrud takes out a pen and paper and writes down notes.

"Are you sure you wouldn't like coffee? I don't know what this is about. Michael called you and is upset. That's all I know."

"How long were you pen pals?" She looks up over her pad of paper.

"Two or three years in high school. Michael knew people who knew me. Six weeks after that, he showed up as I needed a roommate," I say, my mind spinning while she looks at me impassively.

"You haven't been out this morning at all?" she asks again.

I frown. "No, I haven't. I was asleep until a few moments before you and the other officer arrived. Can you tell me what this is about?" Again, Detective Johnsrud looks unblinkingly at me above her notepad. I look down at my watch. "I'm supposed to sing at the church in an hour. Will we have this wrapped up before then?"

Michael and the other police officer come back into the house.

"A set of tracks leads from the back door just past some bushes and then returns to the kitchen. I called our forensic team. They should be here in a few minutes. I took preliminary photographs so that the photographs reflect the footprints. I've also asked Mr. Laysan to give me his boots for evidence, and he has agreed to do so." The officer, A. Ropp, looks at me.

"Did you hear anything last night? What time did you go to bed?" he asks, sizing me up.

"I didn't hear a thing. I went to bed around ten last

night. What is this about?" I ask, looking at Michael. His eyes look out as if recollecting a memory or a place he'd rather be.

"I have to get to work. Can you release us so that she can go to choir and I can go to work at the lookout?" His mouth is in a straight line, and his brown eyes blink slowly.

"No, I'm afraid not," says Detective Ropp.

"I've been awake for fifteen minutes, and you have a person who is leaving for work who saw something. What I don't know," I say, my voice raising in volume, "and we're supposed to sit here while you look for what? Nothing? I'm confused."

Detective Johnsrud touches my elbow, and I jerk it away. "If you give us the names of people we can contact, we'll be happy to call them and let them know of your delay," she says.

"I don't know Pastor Jen or Shirley's phone number. Sorry," I say, my cheeks flaming in anger.

Michael rattles off a phone number, another for his supervisor, and one he identifies as the District Superintendent. It's a split second, but his mouth tightens before gesturing toward the couch. "May we sit down?"

Detective Ropp nods.

As I sit a foot away from him, Michael's hands splay over his kneecaps, his fingers pushing and stretching the taupe-gray twill of his pants.

Detective Ropp steps into the kitchen, and I lean back to catch his words. "Yes, Superintendent Tollerson? This is Detective Andrew Ropp. Michael Laysan will not be able to go to work—oh, he's not injured. There's been an incident in his backyard, and we have some questions. He will be delayed in getting to work, that's all. Yes, I'm glad you understand. No, I can't elaborate. Yes, thank you."

Detective Johnsrud excuses herself and goes into the bathroom.

Michael leans ever so slightly, his right elbow bumping my ribs. I look at him, and he shakes his head, and I return to looking at the still-life painting over the fireplace. He again nudges me with his elbow.

This time, my eyes go to where he rests his right hand over his left, massaging his left ring finger. With his right index finger, he draws it sharply across his left ring finger. Then he places his hands back on his knees.

The toilet flushes, and a moment later, Detective Johnsrud returns to the living room. "Andy? Detective Ropp? Have you contacted the people that are waiting for Joanne and—"

"Michael. Michael Laysan."

"Ms. Corvus. Can you give us the room? We have questions for Mr. Laysan. You aren't allowed to step outside. Is that understood?"

"Is it all right for me to sit in the kitchen? I'd like to make myself breakfast."

Detective Ropp nods, and I walk to the kitchen. Michael had made two omelets, and one lay in the pan on the stove. He's thoughtful that way. He's thoughtful in a great many ways. Taking a plate from the cupboard, I slide the egg, spinach, and ham concoction onto a plate and put it in the microwave above the stove. I crane to hear the conversation in the living room above the microwave's hum but fail. The microwave beeps, and I lean in, taking care not to jangle or jostle too much as I put the omelet on the table and remove utensils from the kitchen drawer.

"How long have you lived here?" asks Detective Ropp.

"Nearly two months," Michael replies, "I'm renting the house with my friend Joanne, but the property belongs to Bolton's Valor Security Forces."

"How long have you had pack rats in your woodpile?"

"Well, *Neotoma cinereai* or the bushy-tailed pack rat are quite common in this area. Unlike its cousins, the *Neotoma cinereai* prefers woodpiles, abandoned vehicles, and buildings and produces one litter each year. Their midden, which can extend to be larger than one meter in size, often has a latrine that can contain ectoparasites but is useful as an archeology tool to determine the history of the area. Packrat middens are a composite of the archeology of an area and have been used along with carbon dating to determine the time when an activity might have occurred. The packrat's urine and the salt it contains acts as a preservative of sorts."

Michael holds forth, and I have a vision of what a terror he must have been in school. "Legends in the area, though I have not confirmed it, and why I refer to it as a legend, state when pack rats appear prolific, it is going to be a hard winter. I observed a large specimen of the genus, probably a male. His fur was a lot thicker than usual. Coupled with the bounty of Oregon grapes and snowberries, my theory is that this year will have a lot of snow, and it will be cold."

I rub my mouth, trying and failing to suppress a smile. I should resist the temptation to walk back into the living room, but I have to see Michael's effect on others. It can't be only me reacting the way I do. Moving to the doorway, I delight in the two officers widened, uncomprehending expressions.

"Sorry. Though it would appear that I ramble, I forgot a salient point," says Michael, raising a finger in the air. "Pack rats, or wood rats, are attracted to shiny objects, so when I saw the ring, I thought that perhaps Joanne had dropped it. However, I didn't recognize the ring as the jewelry she would wear, and obviously, Joanne has all of her fingers. Sometimes I ramble on when I am nervous."

Michael turns to where two vans are parked in front of the cottage and shakes his head. "When I called the police, I didn't expect the number of people who are here, their hazmat suits, and the need for filtered respirators. Even the boots and gloves look high-tech. There are so many precautions brought to the scene."

He fixes a smile upon me as I stand in the doorway. "I have to be at the Thayer Lookout by four this afternoon. Am I free to go? And what of Joanne? She shouldn't be left here to tend with all of this business."

I walk to Michael and face the police. "Yes, I'm supposed to sing in the choir, but I've missed the first service, and I imagine that Pastor Jen isn't now expecting me to be there. Am I allowed to stay here?"

"Have you had breakfast?" asks Detective Ropp. "It might be easier if you leave because we will be working on this much of the day."

Michael's arm encircles my waist. I draw back for a second and then decide to play along with the coziness of our relationship. Actually, I didn't mind it. It feels good pressed close to him. His chest expands, and his fingers encircle my ribs a little tighter. "I'm expected up at the Thayer Lookout. Joanne can come with me for the day. That would allow you to work. You can use the house for bathroom breaks or to make yourself some coffee. Would that be all right?"

The detectives nod.

Michael drops his arm."All right then, we will gather our things and leave." He walks to the closet, takes out his coat, and places my Iris Blackrail satchel under his arm. I follow, pull on my shoes and coat, take my purse and my personal laptop from the closet, go down the steps, walk to Michael's Rover, and then climb inside.

He starts the car, the wipers clearing dew from the windshield. Ahead of us, the detectives walk out the kitchen door and down the back steps, where the hazmat team kneels in the grass. Two of them stand, turning their cocooned heads toward us, and then go back to their work.

"Look at that," I say in wonder. "I've never seen anything like it, except on television." A cocooned person photographs every inch of the woodpile, with the roped-off site extending about fifty feet in every direction from the midden.

"I wonder how much crime scene tape is used to secure the woodpile, the house, and the area surrounding the midden," says Michael, craning his neck at the scene before us. "The crime scene investigator moves as if in one of his daughter Katie's ballet productions. 'Step carefully over there, now don't trample that, watch your step.' I overheard him talking about her to one of his team members."

We must leave, but I want to watch, and from Michael's rapt gaze, so does he. In the four or five minutes after starting the Rover and warming up, we observe the workers. Bags resembling large trash bags sit outside the perimeter of the site. The team sprays a section. Then, using putty knives, they delicately pull and scrape the midden apart. All of this is put into the trash bags and labeled. Those bags are put into hard-sided plastic containers and again labeled.

"Detective Ropp repeatedly asked me if I had touched the midden, if I have had a hepatitis shot or picked up the finger," he said, putting the car into reverse.

"A finger? That was what your signal was about. I wasn't sure. I mean…" I shrink back at the thought, then shake my head in disgust. "How did you know it was a finger?"

"The diamond ring and the manicured nail. I didn't touch it, but there is no doubt a woman lost her finger. I don't know if the packrat found a body and carried off the ring or what, but that is not good."

Michael backs the Rover onto the street, and we drive west toward the center of town. As we pass by St. Olav's Church, I look at my watch, wondering if I can be in the second service. "Michael, I think I might hang out here. I can do the second service and have lunch somewhere. I'll be okay."

Michael slows and turns left, double parking in front of the church. "You sure?"

We are interrupted by a knock on my car window. Wally Harmon, his hands holding two donut boxes, smiles and gives a quick wave to Michael. I lower the passenger window, and Wally moves over to face me.

"I saw the police surrounding your house this morning," he says, placing a hand on top of the boxes to steady them.

"We called them a few moments ago. I didn't realize that you are on the police force, Mr. Harmon," Michael says, his tongue flicking something from the inside of his lip.

"Oh, I was getting donuts, and a clerk mentioned the hubbub at your house. We missed you at the earlier service, so I put things together." He puts the donuts on top of the Rover, and Michael glances upward, then turns back to Wally.

"You drive one of those foreign cars. I'm Wally Harmon, but everyone around here calls me Wally," he says. "I'd shake your hand, but the little missy is in my way." Wally smiles broadly.

It's odd that the clerk at the supermarket would know about the police. "I wanted to drop old clothes off at the church, but in all the excitement, I realize that I have forgotten them. I'm sorry, Michael. Can we drive back to the house so I can pick them up?" I say, shrugging my shoulders at what a dope I am. "Thanks for thinking of me, Wally. I'll see you soon."

Michael gives Wally a quick wave as I raise the window. As we leave, Michael floors the accelerator and then slams on the brakes. The two boxes fly off the roof and land just in front of the car. Michael then turns the car in the direction of the town, and I'm horrified as the two boxes collapse under the tires.

"Michael! Have you lost your mind? What is the matter with you? Wally Harmon has been a member of our church for decades. He's on the board of the bank, and he's on the board of the You Who Foundation," I say, my anger flaming my cheeks. "Now all of that is going by the wayside because he called me Little Missy? You need to get back there and apologize for your rudeness."

"It felt good to do that, and that's all I'm going to say." Michael turns right again and then stops at the traffic light. "He's met me before, and he should remember it since it was only about a month ago. I reported on my grizzly bear project, and he attended the meeting since his company is one of the regional logging companies involved. He was quiet during my presentation, but then he asked about my experience and why a foreigner is taking a job from an American."

"Wally said that? He's always been so nice to everyone," I say, recalling the times I've interacted with him and how positive he's been. "Are you sure—"

The light turns green. "I'm positive that I'm here with the proper permits. So I know he's all buddy-buddy with you and your biggest supporter, but I don't like him. The same stupid smile, the same bland words. I don't like him."

Chapter Ten

"We need to pick up your car in Lodgepole Ferry. I'll take the Willow Creek Meadows Road from Lodgepole Ferry and then go up to the lookout, and you can drive back down the road to Tamarack," says Michael, turning onto the highway leading toward the park.

"In all the excitement, I can't believe that I had forgotten about my car. I'm also wondering about Wally. I had no idea he was that much of a xenophobe," I say, thinking back to my limited interactions over the years and coming up empty. "I'm sorry that happened to you."

"Once you get back to Snowshoe, how do you plan to fill your time?" asks Michael as he turns the Rover east. "Will you call Belle? I suppose you could stay with her while the police get their evidence."

"I don't want to talk to Belle about the police. She'll have questions, which will be rocketed around town faster than anything. Sometimes, she doesn't have much of a filter." I purse my lips, unsettled by my cleansing assessment of my oldest friend "She's the first to reach out, but then, well, she takes over and dictates what I should do." I sigh as I contemplate my next move.

Michael slows as we approach Tamarack's outskirts. "I remember from our letters where you mentioned her when you went to band camp and choir festivals. But she wasn't as involved in sports as you were, am I right?"

"Good memory," I reply, still anxious to change the subject. "I think I will go to the bank and see if I can work on the Hinerman files. Maybe I should leave instructions for Abbie since she will be the one to take over once I get fired tomorrow."

"There's your dad's bar. I remember reading your letters and thinking about how great it must have been to live above a public house," he says, slowing to take a good look at the clapboard building that could stand a coat of paint.

"Now, it looks dreary—not even the least bit the public house of your village or your imagination, I'm afraid," I say with a rueful smile.

"Honestly, I don't believe you will be fired tomorrow, especially since Linda has asked you to look into some of her holdings. If she had been angry with you, she would have said so. This is coming from Pam. Maybe she caught wind of your dinner with Linda and is trying to sabotage you. But I don't think it will work. You have done nothing..." The Rover drives off the pavement and onto the graveled road, and its left front tire hits a small pothole. "...that's wrong. This road!" says Michael with a laugh. "Good thing our cars are able to navigate these roads."

"What is the road like up to the lookout? Do you have cell service?" I ask, turning over an idea in my mind.

"I have work at four this afternoon. I could show you the area, but parts of the road are narrow and may be iffy," Michael says, removing his foot from the gas pedal. "I can't let you stay up there while I'm working. It's against regulations."

"How far is the mountain where you found the drone

wreckage? We could hike there."

Michael puts his foot on the gas pedal and looks over at my sneakers. "No way are you going on that trail in that footwear. You asked about cell service. It's sporadic." He glances out the window at some gathering clouds. "I'm not sure we should take that chance. If you get caught in a bad rainstorm, it could spell trouble. And you don't have a satellite phone in your car."

We follow the river for ten miles, passing the remnants of recent forest fires. As we follow a bend in the road, I remember a story. "A forest fire jumped the river over there," I say, pointing at a large stand of blackened lodgepole pines. "The stand was so tinder dry, it exploded, and smokejumpers had to flee. Trees flew in the air, and branches blew off, becoming projectiles."

Michael slows the Rover down, seeing the arc of trees and branches lined like a blackened halo. "I read our log. We have been lucky this summer, with very few lightning strikes. I checked, and we recorded a small rain shower this morning, but the level of rain, or lack of rain, is worrisome." He slows the car down as a logging truck barrels toward us. "Isn't that like the truck we saw yesterday? Maybe we can see who it belongs to."

The truck thunders past us, creating a storm of dust in its wake. "Elizabeth Logging Company," says Michael.

I reach behind me and take out my laptop. "Let's hope for a signal," I say, forming an idea in my mind. I'm in luck, and I type in the name of the LLC I saw on the tax assessor's website. Four names pop up, and I open another screen and put the address into GPS. My heart skips a beat as I see we are five miles from the location of one of the trapper's cabins. "I'd like to check out an old cabin. It's about five miles from here, so we will turn off onto a Forest Service Road in three miles."

Michael nods, then flashes me a wide grin. "You have gumption. I've always admired that about you."

The GPS tracks the Rover's location, and in two long minutes, Michael slows the car down and turns left. Ahead of us are what look to be fresh truck tire marks.

"Michael, drive up about one hundred feet. I want to see if we can see tire marks turning onto the main road. With the misting that you mentioned, we should be able to see some mud splatters if it happened recently." I crane my head all the way back to see the direction of the truck's tires.

Michael stops the car, and we get out. He cocks his head, and I do the same, but all I hear are the sounds of magpies and the rustling of trees. He walks back toward the main road and then looks back toward the narrow logging path. "You can see where the driver applied the brakes here." He points to tracks that shimmy. "I don't hear anything, but we may have to pull over if another truck comes through here."

We walk back and get in the car. "It's another two miles from here. I don't know what I'm going to find, but, well, we will find out when we get there," I say, looking at the narrow road. I'm thankful that a truck has come down here because that means Michael's Rover should be able to drive to the cabin.

We pass stands of trees with orange markings on them, either painted or with ribbons, before crossing a small bridge that bears the still-fresh, muddy markings of the logging truck.

"How much longer, do you think?" asks Michael. His head turns back and forth, looking for a building.

"We will climb up a hill, and there is a meadow on the right. It should be close to that, I think." Though I am not sure of any such thing.

The road veers to the left and then takes a gentle, wide right-hand turn as it climbs the hill. Standing about thirty feet back from the road, nestled in a meadow adorned with fireweed and a stand of willows, stands a small, timbered cabin with a metal shed behind it.

"That's not what I expected. A trapper's cabin is supposed to be rough, like from a movie about a gold rush," I say, squaring what I see to what might be an explanation for the drones.

A chain-link fence marked with a "No Trespassing" sign prevents us from driving to the cabin, which appears to be painted and chinked. Michael stops the car and looks at me. "You're going to trespass. I should hide the car. There may be cameras, and you didn't bring your disguise."

"Well, let's pretend that we are lost and looking for help," I say as Michael puts the car into reverse and parks twenty feet from where I stand.

Scissor-legging over the chain, I walk toward the house, calling out, "Hello? Hello? Is anyone here?" not knowing what I will find. I walk up to the front door and knock, then peer inside the windows, but the cabin appears only to have a stone fireplace and old cookstove with a pipe leading to the chimney it shares with the fireplace.

Michael pulls on a ball cap and a non-Forest Service jacket to cover his identity, but he calls out in synch to my calls, taking a look into the windows opposite where I am peering.

We reconnoiter behind the cabin and walk toward

the metal outbuilding. "It could be a tanning shed or a place to do canning," I say.

"Doubtful," Michael replies. "Both require heat sources, and the only one would be in the cabin." He points to the remnants of a log structure with a pile of stone. "That would have been the shed. That's where the trapper would have tanned the hides. That's long gone. No, we are dealing with another matter entirely."

"Is there a padlock in the outbuilding?" I ask as we sidestep any tracks leading toward the building.

"I see ATV tracks, that's for sure." He pulls out his camera phone and takes a few pictures before walking around the building. He disappears from view and then calls, "No windows anywhere. We would need the police to get a warrant to search this, but I can say that an ATV is probably inside."

I look harder at the tracks and bend down as two different sets of tracks lead into the building. "Hey, Michael? I think we have two sets of tracks here. Can you come look?"

As he comes around the corner, he jerks his thumb back at a large pine tree behind him. "We're on camera. We have been since we arrived. More than likely, people are on the way here to see what we are doing. Let's leave while we can."

"Can you confirm what I see?" I ask, looking nervously toward the tree and seeing nothing.

Michael steps around the tracks leading into the shed and snaps some more pictures. "Let's go. Now. And let's not talk. I suspect there are voice recordings on those cameras."

We walk back to the car and get in. Michael turns the car around and speeds down the road. He turns left and begins to drive faster than usual. After a few miles, he says, "Look behind and see if you can see vehicles or dust."

I look and see nothing. But then, and it's a blink of an eye thing, I see a metal glint in the sky. "We're being followed. It's a drone, and it's following us. It's probably a quarter mile behind us, but I'm sure I saw a metal glint in the sky."

Michael speeds up, and I'm left to wonder how his driving skills seem a bit sharper than someone who was in the basic military forces. He rounds a corner and skids out a little, leaving a trace of dust in the air. The Rover rockets around the corner, and just as fast, he slams the car into reverse, weaving the Rover backward into a copse of trees. He backs in with only the nose of the Rover sticking out and then gets out. "Stay here! Don't move a muscle. Do you understand?"

Opening the car door, he props himself and a gun between it and its frame. Squatting, he waits for a few seconds as the drone flies above us, less than one hundred feet away. Michael pulls the trigger and fires.

The drone careens wildly before disappearing over the side of the road near the river.

Michael races toward the drone and then drops over the side of the road, returning seconds later, holding what, to the untrained eye, looks like a giant bird. He opens the back hatch of the car and throws it inside. Reaching underneath the drone's carriage, and pulling open a latch, he takes out a small camera and the battery. The drone's green, blinking tracking device goes dark. Michael's arm muscles flex as he twists the wires inside the body of the drone together. He jumps into the driver's seat and restarts the Rover. "We are going a different way. We are going to drive on the shady side of the road for as long as we can. They will be expecting us to drive where we can be seen, but that's no longer possible."

"Do you have another route?" I ask. "Can I look up something for you?"

"How far are we from Home Ranch Bottoms?" He ducks the Rover back into dark recesses as much as possible.

"That's across the river. You can't drive the Rover across the river, Michael, that's crazy," I say, though the last half hour makes me suspect he harbors the skills to take on an adventure such as what he's planned.

"We're about two miles away. Are you planning to float down the river and find our way to the other side? How are we going to do that?" I ask.

"We are getting out and guiding the car as best we can. If it's not too deep, we should be able to drive some and then guide it the rest of the way," he says, in a voice that tells me this has happened before.

"Won't it sink? It has to," I say, imagining rapids and swift-moving water.

"The Rover will tolerate water up to 900 millimeters deep," says Michael confidently.

"That's less than two feet. You have to figure out another plan," I say. "We can't do that. It will short out the electrical system and cause a host of problems. No, Michael. No."

"What do you suggest? That I keep driving?"

"Yes, we do this until we reach Camas Creek Road and then drive north through the park. Drones aren't allowed in the park and will be subject to intense scrutiny if they are caught. Stay hidden until we get to Camas," I suggest.

Michael says nothing for a few minutes. "That's a good plan. We need to stay hidden as long as we can and down the side of the road. Then we can shoot across the bridge and head north. It could work, but you can't come back on the road. You will need to go back through the park. That way, you'll be protected."

I peer out the left side of the car for drones and see nothing. Meanwhile, trucks and cars drive south, covering the Rover with dust. At last, the road widens, and we come to a clearing that announces that Camas Creek is one-quarter of a mile away. We cross the road and enter the park.

Forty minutes later, we arrive at the Lodgepole Ferry Ranger station and cross the river again. In a mile, we arrive at the Lodgepole Ferry Mercantile. I'm relieved to see that my car hasn't been disturbed.

I get out of the car, and Michael gets out as well. We meet by the hatch, and I pull out my satchel and turn to him. "Well, it's been fun," I say with a laugh, sticking out my hand, which he takes in his. "Oh, you have something in your eye," I say. "Come closer, and I'll brush it away for you."

He leans forward, and I do what I planned in all my decades of wondering. I take his chin in my hand and kiss him, slowly, gently, deeply. He doesn't pull away, and his lips warm against mine, pulling closer. I remove my hand, and he steps closer. The kiss continues.

He isn't inexperienced. He's unpracticed.

But we can work on that.

****

Rain splashes the windows of the Thayer Lookout. Ken, who Michael is replacing on shift, seemed grateful to be relieved of duty an hour and a half early. As we climb the ladder to the lookout's entrance, Michael makes easy conversation with Ken, stating that I am helping him work on the grizzly project and that I will be leaving for Snowshoe before he goes on shift at four p.m.

Ken walks down the hill toward the parking lot and gets into his truck. Turning the pickup down the mountain, he soon disappears from view.

Through the mist rising above the peaks surrounding us, trees appear and disappear, fleeting images. I walk to where Michael stands, a distance of maybe fifteen feet, but a lifetime of wondering away.

I take my jacket off, setting it on the cot. Michael puts his arm around my shoulders, but I turn to face him expectantly, wondering. I reach up and trace the small scar on his chin.

He presses closer to me, and I quiver. In truth, my experience isn't that much. But we press into each other, and as we meet, we explore. His hands are upon me, and my hands slip down his waist.

He pulls away, walking to the first aid kit. He opens it, removing a small square packet. I laugh that a condom is considered necessary field gear, but I doubt that either one of us has considered taking this next step until certain.

The act becomes a dance—a dance of exploration, curiosity, and decades-long pangs of desire. The rain creates condensation on the windows, and Michael probably should be outside, leaning out to view the landscape, but he and I are here, creating clarity of our own.

Getting up, I pad over to the first aid kit and then look back at him. He rolls over on the cot, watching me. "You'll need to replace that, you know. That is, if you want to," I say.

He sits up, and I walk over, straddling him as I arch my back. He grasps me in a fervor, but it's longer, and the experience is far more delicious this time. I hold onto his shoulders, and he grasps my waist. I lean forward, kissing him in a delight I'd only imagined was possible.

He shivers, but as I hug him, gladly giving him any warmth he needs, his thighs shift as if he wants to stand.

I stand, and so does he, pulling his pants from the floor and putting them on. I glance at the clock on the wall and see the reason. He has to be on duty in five minutes—which means I need to be leaving in five minutes—or no more than ten. My visit is logged, and the reason for my visit is listed as research. As I think back to the last hour, I agree. Decades-long thought and research have been done. Silently, I curse not having packets to spare.

He pulls on his Forest Service shirt, and I stand in front of him, still naked, still curious. But it can't be—at least not for now.

Michael opens the door to the deck and begins cleaning the windows, letting the foggy late afternoon light in. He'll be home on Tuesday morning after I meet with Dan, Pam, and Linda or when I'm at work.

I walk outside, the air nipping my skin, the gentle rain falling, then running in cool rivulets down my shoulders, waist, and thighs. I stretch out my arms, ready to embrace what comes next.

Michael puts down the squeegee and walks over to me, kissing the base of my throat, my chest, and my belly, and then stops. "I can't. I must work." And he glances inside to the area of the first aid kit. But then we move back inside, finding pleasures again, tasting and delving.

Thirty minutes later, I climb down the stairs, and Michael closes the trap door to the lookout station. With the thud of the door, I wonder if he will shut me out if I knock. But the evening light has fallen to such darkness that I need careful driving to return home. And return, I must. My home is in Snowshoe.

I take time to navigate the narrow, muddy road until I reach Willow Creek Meadows Road and pass Upper Snowshoe Road. Then, the lights of Snowshoe appear, and with it, the reality of my life comes on with the pinging of messages. Once back on the highway, I stop my car for a moment, passing a sedan parked by the side of the road, and look northward to where the lookout is.

I squint, imagining a lantern in a window, a beckoning call.

Ninety minutes after leaving the lookout, I am at the cottage. Putting my car back into the garage, I walk past the garden and woodpile. There are no stakes, no tape, no evidence of a terrible occurrence.

What I feel inside is unlike what I had felt with my ex-husband, nicknamed The Hole. I can't and don't want to turn this off.

****

I savor the last of the Portuguese Vino Verde as I scroll through the contents on my computer, nursing a lingering question about Paul Allegretti. The wine's crispness reminds me of the soft condensation that had rolled down my shoulders hours ago. I breathe deeply, luxuriating as the last of an initially frightening, then infuriating, then exhilarating day folds to a close.

Paul Allegretti of Hialeah, Florida, had been busy over the last five years. And, like most humans, he is a creature of habit. What worked once will work again. Rinse and repeat.

He has no social media presence, which, given the little that I know of him, isn't uncommon. But he found a pattern and has stuck to it. What I find curious is how he knew to buy trapper's cabins.

I set down my drink on the side table as I reflect on a cold, snowy evening nearly two decades before.

Thew, in a fit of anger, called me a whore. I pleaded, hot tears of recrimination pouring down my cheeks, saying it was a gift from Dr. Greene meant to help ease our family's pain after Mom's death, but Thew had none of it.

He walked over to my purse, dumping the contents on my quilted bedspread, snatched the keys of the car from the piles of notes and lip gloss, and then stomped down the stairs. I followed, my footsteps no doubt drowned out by the jukebox playing a loud singalong country song.

Stepping into the bitterly cold night, I chased after Thew. Neither of us had a coat on.

"Did you go to a clinic so that you can get protection? You know he's married, don't you?" Thew asked, his voice a hiss.

I blanched because I hadn't gone. "It only happened one time, and I didn't…"

"Are you? Oh, Joanne, what have you done? Did he force you?" His voice rocketing off the buildings around us.

My shoulders shook, as much from the cold as from the shame.

"Did you consent?" he asked, his eyes turning hard as the hatred boiled up within him.

I'd looked down and shook my head. "No," I said.

"I'm going make him pay. I'm going over to his house and let him and that wife and family of his know what he did to you."

"Thew? Dad? He gave me a car. Mom's car wouldn't start, and Dr. Greene thought I needed reliable transportation to get back and forth to school. I came back to return it, and that's when—" I looked down. "I'm late, but Belle says it's common."

"Oh, Belle knows about this? Of course, she does." Thew raised his face, and in the spotlight coming from the bar's back entrance, I saw tears streaming down his cheeks. "I'll follow you over to the office or his house. Knock on the door, tell him you are returning the car and that I am outside."

Thew waited while I started and warmed it up. He then walked over to his truck, and I watched as he hesitated, put his fingers on his face, and then swung his body inside the cab.

I drove carefully on the icy streets over to the Greene house, but the house was dark, and no tracks were in the snow in front of the garage. I then drove over to Dr. Greene's office, where two cars were parked. I pulled in front of his building and as I opened the car door, Thew stepped out of his truck, but I held up my hand. He nodded, and I walked to the back door, intending to open it, slip the keys inside, and then run toward the welcoming arms of my father, who would protect me.

As I approached, I heard voices, and I stopped, again raising my hand to Thew, who had sat inside his truck. I stepped closer, and as I put my foot on the back step, I could hear Dr. Greene. "I can get the money for you. The snowmobile hit a submerged tree, and the machine rolled over my delivery person." Then the office window rattled, and Dr. Greene shouted, "Please stop! I'll get you the money!"

I dropped the keys on the steps and ran back to Thew's pickup truck.

"You didn't go inside. Do you still have the keys?" Thew's tone told me how I didn't stand up for myself.

"He was with a customer, and there was an argument. I threw the keys in the snow on the back step. I'm sorry, Dad."

Dr. Greene didn't try to return the car to me. My period came a little late but came, and I shut that chapter of my life firmly away.

Months later, before my high school graduation, the body of a "Canyon Critter," our local term for a lowlife, was found north of town. He'd been considered trash, with the story being the talk of Tamarack, for maybe a week before dying away.

Opening another screen on my laptop, I type in the search words of snowmobile accidents, cocaine, and the year of my graduation. Up sprang newspaper articles about the rumored trafficking of marijuana and other illegal substances and how a local known to police authorities was found pinned below a snowmobile.

A nagging thought buzzes in my head. I pull up the Columbia County Recorder of Deeds page and then type in Alan Greene's name. I also put his name into the newspaper database.

The purchases began while I was in high school. The pattern was the same. An article popped up about how a trapper had found the title of his homestead had changed without his consent. I put the name of the buyer into the deed database, and Dr. Greene's office was shown as the address of the new owner. Three years later, the property was transferred back.

I sit deeply into the sofa's cushions, collecting my thoughts. Without any reports, there is no way that I can prove that Dr. Alan Greene and Paul Allegretti are drug traffickers.

****

"Hello, Michael?"

The voice coming from behind the front door is female and has a British accent. Closing my laptop, I get up from the sofa. "Coming!" I call out.

The woman in the stylishly cut black coat has high cheekbones, tawny skin, and a long black braid tied with a red ribbon, which drapes luxuriously around her neck. She removes a black leather driving glove and shakes my hand. "Hello," she says, "I'm Jessamine Nightjar, Michael's fiancée. Is he about?"

My eyes fly open, and I take a step back. "I'm sorry, no, Michael is at work," I manage, my head swimming. "Did you say you are his fiancée?"

She removes her other glove, revealing a diamond ring, and then steps inside the house. "You must be Joanne, Michael's pen pal from his school days. It's so nice of you to have allowed him to stay with you. He told me that his housing selection had come through, and with me being able to work remotely, we decided that it made sense for me to come here to live."

I gape as she walks over to the sofa and unbuttons her coat. "I am rather hoping to use Michael's room tonight and look at the new cottage first thing in the morning. I'll get my suitcases, and you can show me where Michael's room is. I don't want to disturb you." And she walks back out the door, through the porch door, and down the steps to where a car is parked.

An unknown emotion—maybe horror, maybe betrayal, maybe anger—washes over me, and I walk outside behind her. "Listen," I say, trying to keep my voice low, "Michael has never mentioned you, and I am not comfortable with you staying in his room. I'd prefer that I call him now and ask if he is okay with these arrangements. If he doesn't answer, I'm sure you can find a hotel in Snowshoe."

I don't wait for her to respond. Instead, I take the outside steps two at a time, fling the porch door open, and run inside the house, where I gag on the lingering scent of her expensive perfume. Opening the phone screen, I call his phone number, which goes to voicemail. "Jessamine is here, Michael. Jessamine, your fiancée," I continue in a clipped tone as I go back outside and down the stairs to where the manicured, coiffed, and everything I am not stands. "She wants to stay here in your room," I say, trying—and failing—not to hiss. "When I talked to you earlier, you hadn't mentioned that your housing change had come through." My mind goes to my straddling him. Was he thinking of Jessamine while I was doing that? "Could you call me back?" I ask.

Jessamine examines her manicured hand. Two designer suitcases sit at her feet. "I understand your need for caution," she says, revealing perfect teeth. She holds up her telephone. The name says "Shining Armor," and inwardly, I choke. "Sweetheart? Can you hear me? I'm putting you on speakerphone so that Joanne can hear you. Is that all right?"

"Hello, Joanne," says Michael, and my heart sinks. "I'm glad you have met Jessamine. We will make arrangements to have the furniture moved into our new cottage. Thanks for letting her stay."

"No problem," I say, glancing up at Jessamine's perfect face. She pats my arm and mouths, "Thank you."

"Joanne? I can't leave the lookout," says Michael in a quieter voice. "I've misplaced that square packet I showed you earlier today. As you know, per regulations, we need them up here at all times, and I'll get in trouble if I leave. It's an ask, but can you contact Ken tonight and remind him to bring the reinforced model?"

I knit my brows but nod at Jessamine like these requests happen all the time. "Of course, I will call him now," I say, walking back toward the cottage. "Good night, Michael," I call over my shoulder.

Once inside, I wrack my brain for Ken's last name but come up empty. Taking my phone from where it lay beside the laptop, I walk up the stairs to Michael's bedroom and open the door. It's orderly. I would expect nothing less. I scan likely places for an address book and spy a Forest Service manual below a Boy Guide book. Opening the manual, I thank Michael for writing his supervisor's name as well as the names of his co-workers. Ken Hammett. I breathe a sigh and call.

"Joanne? Are you upstairs?" Jessamine's voice has an edge of irritation to it.

"Yes, I'm calling Ken," I answer. "I'll help you with your bags in a minute. Help yourself to what's in the refrigerator. You must be hungry."

Ken picks up on the second ring. From his dull greeting, I can tell I've awakened him. "Ken, it's Joanne Corvus, Michael Laysan's roommate. He called and said that he needs a reinforced model."

"What?" Ken snaps to. "He specifically said he needs a reinforced model?"

"Yes," I repeat.

His voice is clipped. "A reinforced model? And he's at Thayer? Yes, of course, he is. I saw you this afternoon. Okay, thank you, Joanne. I'll take it from here."

Jessamine stands in the doorway. "I've decided to find a hotel after all, though I appreciate your hospitality. Perhaps you and I can meet for lunch or dinner this week. Good night." She turns and then walks down the stairs.

I follow her, but Jessamine walks through the house and puts the suitcases in the back of her car. She holds a telephone in her hand and then slams the car's hatch shut. She gets in the car and then drives off.

I go out to the porch, lock the screen door, and walk back into the house, locking the front door and the back door before returning to the living room, where my laptop has been moved from the couch to a chair. Prickles of fear course up my spine as I walk toward the hall closet. Opening the door, I'm pleased my Iris Blackrail satchel remains untouched.

Only then do I question my motives and what I truly know about Michael. Tears of foolishness course my cheeks, dropping hot and hurt upon my shirt—a shirt I had all too happily removed, thinking it was what Michael had wanted.

It appears now that I don't know anything.

Chapter Eleven

Twenty-one hours after my frightening wake-up call from Michael, I'm awakened by the pounding on the back door. *Pound, pound, pound!*

Forgetting my robe, I pad downstairs, through the living room, and turn on the porch light, which reveals a man that I couldn't wait to get rid of twelve hours before. Ken moves to the side, revealing Michael, who has cuts on his nose and a swollen lip.

Clasping my hand to my mouth to cover my scream, I unlock the door, and Ken, not so much allows as slides Michael past him. "Shut off the light, please. People may be watching," says Ken through gritted teeth.

"What happened? Did you fall?" I whisper as Michael shuffles past me.

"Can you cover up the windows with a cloth that can block the light?" Michael grasps his chest.

"Buddy, I don't think you can walk far. Not after the beating you had. We're in a pickle," says Ken. "Two people said they needed help, so Michael went down to see what they wanted. They looked like hikers, but then one of them kicked him, and Michael fell. They kicked him and probably broke one of his ribs."

"What were they after? Did they try to rob you?" My questions come in a stream, and Ken and Michael frown at me. "I mean, why would they hike all the way up to your lookout? I don't understand."

Ken and Michael heave simultaneous sighs that I

register as meaning I'm an idiot and need to shut up.

I back away from them and gesture to the sink and the refrigerator. "Make yourself at home. I'm asking what I think are basic questions." But as I speak, anger wells up in me. "I mean, you have a fiancée you don't bother to mention. This afternoon, you didn't seem to mind me making a fool…"

Ken gives me a stern look and then turns toward Michael. "Buddy…" he says. "Listen, Joanne, Michael might need to get some medical attention, and I need to relieve the guy I have up there. I'll file a report, but maybe Michael needs some rest. Do you think you can help me take him up to his bed?"

"Uh, no. I don't think I can do that. In fact, no, and hell no, I won't do that. He's not my responsibility. Michael, you have your fiancée. She's here in town. Call her. You are not my problem." I turn, go up the stairs, and slam my bedroom door. Of course, I listen for movement downstairs. A minute later, I hear a truck start and two truck doors close. Four minutes after their arrival, my cottage returns to quiet.

Then and only then do I scream as a sensation buried decades in the past rears up.

The metal cabinet door felt cool on my cheek. Alan hold my wrists in a viselike grip above my head, and he'd shimmied my sweatpants and panties below my hips. I'd wriggled and cried out, but he'd slammed into my back, the skin on my cheek dragging upward on the metal door.

The sting and burn of skin being pushed and hot tears streamed down my cheeks then and now. Then came the car and a story told by the daughter of the car salesman who had sold it to Dr. Greene. There'd been a wink and a nudge, no doubt. Bob Sethway's daughter,

Pam, always had the fanciest car and the best clothes. Like a telephone line, the rumors zipped along the lines of communication, painting me as a whore. Thew hadn't known, but the rest of the valley did.

Eventually, my stomach retches, and I run to the bathroom, my muscles stretching and heaving. I lay against the pink and white tiles of the bathroom, my head at first against, then enveloped by the soft towels behind me.

****

Two short hours later, I'm in my office reviewing Georgina's holdings against the records provided by the You Who Foundation. Abbie messages me. *Ken Hammett is here to see you.*

Oh, hell no. *Sorry, I'm knee-deep. Take a message and tell him that I will call later. Thanks.*

Outside the closed door of my office, I hear the low voice from a few hours ago and Abbie's higher-pitched voice delivering a message she doesn't believe. Seconds later, *He's gone. Can I help?*

No. Busy day. Dan and I are to have a meeting with Linda Taylor and Pam Clayton, but I don't see it on my calendar. Dan isn't on the messaging system right now. Can you find out when that meeting will be?

Sure thing. A few seconds later, I heard her chipper voice, "Winding Creek Bank Mineral Department, Abbie speaking. How can I direct your call?"

I stare at the box labeled Hinerman Legacy as an idea forms as to how I could get the information I want. I routed the pictures Linda had shared with me, which seemed like a lifetime ago, and sent them to the printer in my office. Then, I open the top bankers' box and pull out Georgie's files labeled "Forestry."

As I take the printed images from my printer and put them on top of the folder, there's a sharp rap on my office door. I fling open the door, ready to give Abbie a dressing down and come face-to-face with Detective Ropp.

"Your assistant Abbie said you're busy, but this will only take a few minutes," he says, stepping inside my office. "Would you prefer to talk here, or do you have a conference room?" he asks, but I'm not being given a choice.

"Here is fine, I guess," I say, gesturing to the chair across from my desk. Drawing in a breath, I smile. "How can I help you? Have you identified anything about what you found?" I place the pictures and file on my desk and take a seat.

"I'm sure by now you know about the item in your backyard," he says in a conversational tone. "People talk. Especially about things like this."

"Michael, my roommate, woke me up yesterday morning. He told me he had found a woman's finger with a ring on it."

Detective Ropp leans forward and then pulls out a notepad from his pocket. "Do you know who it belongs to?" He clicks the pen that he has taken from his shirt pocket and then frowns. "Can I use one of your pens, please?"

I shrug and tip the pen holder toward him. "Michael found it in the backyard, but as to who it is, I have no idea. Have you checked the missing person's database?"

Detective Ropp sits back in the office chair, pauses, and raises his eyebrows.

"Oh, sorry. Of course, you have," I say, blushing.

"The stone in the ring is large, and we've been able

Janet Yeager

to identify who bought it. Do you know where your boss is?"

"Dan?" I ask. Now, it's my turn to be confused. "I don't know." And I sit back in my chair, my mouth open as I recall how he had rushed to comfort Pam. I turn an idea over in my head. "Dan bought a ring? He took Pam home after she was here last Monday and mentioned her when he came over to our, er, my cottage on Thursday, but he said…" My voice trails off.

"Yes? What did he say on Thursday?"

"He was not himself. He hasn't been lately. Leaving the office during the day, wearing the same clothes two days in a row, and not washing his car," I answer, not coming up with an answer on how to say it. *And he's taken out a loan for diamonds that belonged to an old fur trapper. Which Michael and I thought was a horrible idea.*

"Not washing his car? Is that a crime?" asks Detective Ropp with a thin smile playing on his lips. "The whole valley is nothing but gravel and dust."

I blush. "Dan's particular about that Audi. It's bright red, and he makes sure it is in tip-top shape. Have you talked to him?"

"We haven't been able to find him. He's not at home, and we can't find Pam Clayton either. Do you know where they might have gone?"

I shake my head. "He mentioned trips to Missoula for a conference, but he never mentioned what kind. I wish I could be of more help."

"So you never saw the item that was lying in the garden?" Detective Ropp stands, putting his notebook and my pen in his shirt pocket.

"No, I didn't. I'm sorry that I don't know where Dan

is. He might have told Abbie, but he didn't mention anything regarding his plans to me." I pause as I realize he'd asked about Pam, but I hadn't answered. "You asked about Pam. I saw her last Monday. You might want to check with Linda Taylor. Pam works for Linda."

Detective Ropp fishes a business card out of his pants pocket and hands it to me. "If you think of anything, please let me know. Thanks for your help, Ms. Corvus."

The police station is across the street. I open the blinds of my office window as the detective jaywalks across the bank parking lot and then stops. He takes out his notebook and then turns back toward the bank. Glancing up at my window, he sees me, and I wave. I walk out of my office and down the stairs to the back door of the bank, where I meet him in the parking lot.

"I neglected to ask you about Pam, Detective. Is Pam involved with Dan? I am not aware of that. She had a nosebleed in my office last week, and Dan came over to assist, and he held her hand, but I—" I take a step back as the magnitude of what the detective is asking me hits me with full force. "Oh, no. No, no, no!"

Detective Ropp says nothing as I clasp my hand over my mouth. I bend over. "That's not possible," I say, through deep breaths. "I saw her last week. Dan would never hurt her. There must be a rational explanation."

"You are positive that you haven't seen Pam or followed Pam or Dan anywhere in the past week?" Detective Ropp's voice and eyes are steady, but he leans slightly toward me like he will snatch me if I flee.

I shake my head. "No, the last time I saw Pam was when she was in the bank last Monday," I say, straightening and squaring my shoulders. "Do you think

Pam is dead? I'm supposed to meet with Dan this morning, but I think you should be the one to tell him about Pam, not me. I'm sorry, I'm in shock. Is Pam dead? Can you tell me that?"

"I can't comment on an ongoing investigation," Detective Ropp says stiffly.

"Oh, of course. When Dan comes in, I will have him call you." I look up at him, tears pricking my eyes. "You think Pam is dead. You do. I know it. And you think Dan killed her. He wouldn't. That's impossible." A wave of nausea washes over me. "I'm going to be sick. I need to go right now."

I open the bank's back door and run inside, finding the bathroom in the nick of time.

****

Taking ten minutes to walk to Maple District Park and back won't be missed by the higher-ups, right? Wiping my mouth and checking my blouse and pants for telltale vomit and finding them clean, I walk out of the bathroom, go up the stairs, and step outside into a bright, warm morning. A thin dusting of snow sits at the uppermost reaches of Snowshoe's ski area. I close my eyes as a blanket of shame falls on me as I think about the lookout, Michael's betrayal of Jessamine, and my overeagerness.

Chatter to the right of me and behind the neighboring building makes me curious as a person riffs on a keyboard. I'd forgotten that Monday Musical Musings starts in a few hours. A lunch-hour favorite in Snowshoe, the hour-long concert features locals and even some celebrities who have moved to the Snowshoe area. You never know who is going to sit in or when you'll spot a future star.

I've been obsessed with a collection of musicians that take old and new songs and change the genre. Jazz becomes hip-hop, rock becomes country, the music is slowed down or up, and I think that's what I'm going to hear in a few hours.

For a split second, my conversation with Detective Ropp disappears, and I have something to look forward to.

"Good morning, Joanne," calls a pleasant voice behind me.

"Linda." I turn toward her and giving her a broad smile. "I'm sorry. We have an appointment."

"Pam was in one of her moods. I didn't tell her about our dinner last week. She's jealous of you. She hasn't turned up for work this morning, which is unusual for her. No, I have some errands to run, and then I'll be having lunch in town. Are you going to the concert?"

"I hadn't planned on it, but I like what I'm hearing, so I may change my mind."

I need one piece of normal, and I'm not sure how to ask. "Linda, I have a question. I heard, call it gossip if you like, but I heard that you are dissatisfied with my work."

"What? No, Joanne. Oh, that Pam. I can't believe she would take things this far. Apparently, she drove by my house last week and saw your car, and she called me all huffy-like. She didn't sound like herself, so I told her that I'd see her in the morning, but then I didn't hear back."

"When was this? When did you see Pam last?" I ask, working out the timeline.

Linda shrugs. "Wednesday, no, it was Thursday." She leans in. "You had excitement, I hear. My friend,

Paul, told me he'd heard a human object had been found in the backyard of your cottage. You're probably not allowed to talk about it."

"You're friends with Paul Allegretti?" I say, another layer of what I don't know added into the mix.

"He and I share some common interests," she says evenly. "We're friends, that's all."

"I'm not sure I have anything to share. Michael found a finger with a diamond ring on it in the backyard. We were hustled out of the house so the police could investigate. I talked to a detective this morning. We don't know who the finger belongs to. And that's what I told the detectives."

She clasps her mouth in surprise. "Oh, my word. A diamond ring?" She looks at me, her eyes shining like a curious bird's.

"I don't know. Dan hasn't been around, and I'm worried about him. I probably shouldn't have said anything. It's speculation. If you have information or concerns, you might want to talk to the police," I say as prickles of anger burble to the surface. "I probably should get back."

"Joanne, I didn't mean to upset you—"

"Linda, you caught me at a bad time. That's all. I received upsetting news, and it keeps piling on. I'm sorry, I'm being grumpy, but I can't tell you about the reasons why."

Her jaw drops at my directness. "Well, I hope things turn out okay," she says, her cheeks flushing. She squares her shoulders, fixes me with a stare bordering on contemptuous, and then walks toward the music.

"Linda, wait. I'm sorry. You deserve better," I say, running to catch her arm. As I touch her elbow, she whirls around, drawing her arm behind her back. "The police contacted me this morning about a finger found in my backyard. The finger had a diamond ring on it. My boss is behaving weirdly. And a person I thought I was beginning to care about romantically has a fiancée. I am told that you are unhappy with my work. I feel like I'm in a set of rapids, ready to capsize. And then, I snapped at you." I draw a breath. "There, I think that's all of it. I shouldn't have burdened you with this. I'm sorry."

"Were—no, are you involved with Dan? I'm surprised you would sleep with your boss to try to get ahead. Pam, well, Pam is jealous, and one time she said you had gotten a car from a gentlemen caller when you were in high school…"

My hand covers my mouth, and my eyes widen. "Pam told you I slept with Alan Greene to get a car? Oh, that's perfect. That's who Pam has been banging, by the way. She and her honey hook up outside in a huckleberry patch. Oh, and she snorts cocaine. But you take her version of events over mine. Great. That's just great." I walk a few steps away and then stop. "You know what? Here's a news bulletin. The police questioned me because they think Pam is dead. I should be unhappy, but I'm not."

****

Ten minutes have passed since I stepped outside to get a breath of fresh air, and I've upset everything and everyone. Opening the back door of the bank, I walk upstairs to the mineral management department and find Abbie engrossed in a project. Dan's office is dark. I slip back into my office, quietly shut the office door, and then turn on my laptop and put a Do Not Disturb message on my computer messaging system.

I can't stomach anything resembling Georgie or Linda's properties. I have a right to say what I did, I think, as beads of sweat form on my forehead. My phone buzzes in my purse, and I pull it out and then groan. "The hits just keep coming," I grouse as I pick up the phone. "Hi, Belle. Now's not a great time."

"I'm your friend, and I'm supposed to tell you the truth no matter how difficult things may be, right? Anyway, I should have done this face-to-face, but I didn't know how to say it. Michael has a girlfriend. He was hanging all over her at breakfast. I don't think that siblings hang on each other like this woman was on Michael."

"I have work to do, and I don't have time to listen to gossip," I say, angry with my humiliation, no longer able to hide under respectability but the horrible speed at which it has been exposed.

Belle laughed at my defense, and my cheeks burned at the tone I read as *First, you're an idiot, but we knew that, too. Now, I have dirt that you can't refute.*

"You can hide your head in the sand if you want, but I'm saying this for your own good. I sure hope you haven't gone all desperate and clinging because he is clearly not interested in you. Grow up, girlfriend. Your pen pal used you as an excuse to come here, but he was taken all along. He couldn't stop kissing her at breakfast. Finally, the waitress told them to get a room."

"Belle, I'm sure you think this is for my own good—"

"You're so naïve. And at your age, too. This isn't some romance novel that you have your nose in. It's real life. He's into her, not you. You're so trusting. You went to that dentist, passing it off as a rape when you didn't go to the police. Your hang-dogging over Michael—the invisible boyfriend. I've had to clean up your messes with our friends so many times—"

"That's enough, Belle," I say, closing off my future from the containment of the lies spreading further. "I'm done listening to your crap. You weren't slammed against a locker. You aren't forced to work with him…"

"Quit—"

"For the love of all things, will you please shut up!" I say, inwardly gleeful, as after thirty years, Belle sucks in a gasp. "I'm finished with your lies and your stupidity—all the years of listening to your half-witted, unsubstantiated lies. You're a bully. And I'm done with your idiocy. I'm blocking your number, and I will no longer speak to you."

"I'm not a bully."

"I no longer care, Belle. Don't call me or contact me again." I hang up the phone and then look at the number, doing what I should have done years ago, before the innuendo, the stories where she had protected me from others when there was no drama. I tap the circled 'I,' select 'block,' and then set the phone down, my shoulders wracking with tears. As I spend my tears, I realize I'm coming from a place of relief, like coming out of a tunnel and walking toward a clearing where I can stand, the sun on my shoulders enveloped only in possibilities. I dry my eyes, exhale, and then open the office door.

****

"Are you still talking to me?"

The cut lip, the swollen eye, the bruising on his cheekbone, all of Michael's traumas are visible. Mine aren't that easy. I sniff, glare at him, and wave him away as anger rolls over me. Abbie should have let me know Michael had come to my office. I exhale, probably louder than necessary.

"Please don't be mad at me. I need your help. Now it's my turn to have an 'I'm probably crazy' moment, and I can't talk to anyone but you."

To hell with being better than jealousy. "I can't. Why don't you talk to your honey, Jessamine?" I say, using his fiancée's name like the tip of a whip. "She should be able to help with whatever you need." I sniff away the tears and look straight down at the diamond paperwork as if it makes complete sense.

"Please listen to me. Please, Joanne." His Cotswold accent has wrapped my name into a stew of delicious desire. I squeeze my eyes shut and hunch forward. I inhale cool air through my mouth and exhale, mentally counting to four, and then repeat the calming method two more times.

Although any fool can see that I want to be left alone, I open my eyes just enough to confirm that he has not left. A big part of me doesn't want him to because maybe everything that happened in the last forty-eight hours was a weird dream. I recall his hands on me, and teardrops fall on the papers on the desk.

"It's about the packrat," he says in a voice not far from a recitation of a book report. "I have questions about its habits and the midden. You know, the nest is called a midden." I raise my head and glare at him as I nod, but Michael is looking to give me a stemwinder, and inwardly, I groan.

"What can the midden tell me? No training at the academy talked about the archaeology of pack rat middens, so I went online and did some research."

"Michael. I'm going to cut this short. I need to focus—"

"A pack rat's midden is a timeline. They can span decades, can tell of the climate, what people ate or wore," he says, and a heaping portion of my reading and rereading his informational letters draws me into what he's saying.

I hate myself.

"The packrat born in the midden comes from an area no more than a quarter of a mile away. If Pam Clayton is dead, her body is within a quarter mile of the midden."

Of course, Detectives Ropp and Johnsrud have talked to him. Why would they limit their questions to me?

"…that the finger with the ring had traces of cocaine in the tissue. The detectives confirmed that Dan bought a ring similar to the one found at the packrat's nest. That she more than likely was having an affair. Dan, or whomever she's been having an affair with, hit her. She had financial problems. Dan had business partnerships with Allegro, and he kept odd hours."

"Michael, I've had the worst day of my life, and you keep yammering on. Please go away," I say, cupping my forehead in my hand. I click on a file and look at the screen, scribbling notes that I already know will not make a shred of sense.

"…the finger was pecked on like it was carrion. Detective Ropp is an idiot and didn't want to hear about a large bird and changing the search area—"

Dammit. I'm in.

****

I shut my computer off. The strains of a great dance tune hit my ears. I'm insanely hungry and can't be inside

169

for another second. I want to go to the Monday Monthly Music gathering. I reach into my desk, take out my purse, and rise.

"Can I come along? I want to hear what you think about the large bird theory."

I sling my purse on my shoulder and walk past him. "Why don't you ask Jessamine? By the way, why isn't she here with you? You two should be like yoked oxen, don't you think?" I slide past him, turn off the office light, and walk out.

These kinds of exits only work in the movies. In the first place, I left Michael alone in my office, which wasn't secure, and secondly, I didn't get the response I wanted. You know. Pleading. Stammering. She's nothing.

"I closed up your office for you," says Michael. I'm barely outside the back entrance of the bank, and he's already caught up with me. "Jessamine told me I'm wrong about the bird theory and that I'm obsessive."

Score one for Jessamine.

I walk through the parking lot with Michael keeping his stride. "It'd have to be an eagle, of which there are only two types in this area, or an osprey. Perhaps a crow, but the picking marks are too large, so I think it's a raven, and we have a problem—"

I stop in front of a food truck selling sandwiches. I place my order while Michael rubs his eye and says, "Ow."

"You should probably have Jessamine take you to the doctor," I say, stepping aside to let the people behind me order. One hundred chairs ring the stage where The Modern Retellings are twisting popular songs into different genres. I spy a familiar face and sigh. Linda

Taylor sits shoulder to shoulder with Paul Allegretti. He reaches into his pocket, takes out a handkerchief, and then wipes Linda's cheek. I see Detective Johnsrud. She gives me a nod, and I nod back, unsure if any further exchange is needed.

The crowd cheers as the band breaks into their regionally known hit song. People stand and make their way to the cleared area before the stage, laughing and breaking into the two-step dance. Paul and Linda rub shoulders, and she cajoles him. He relents, and she guides him through the hand gestures associated with the dance. Paul looks sheepish, and both of them laugh with glee and embarrassment.

"I don't know the steps, but do you think you could teach me?" asks Michael, who has taken my elbow and led me to the side of the trailer so that others could walk to the stage.

"I haven't danced it in a long time. I don't think I would be any good," I say as the cook in the food truck calls my name. But he's here, right behind me, and seconds later, his name is called, so we stand, sandwiches in hand, and look at the crowd who is yelling the band's signature line of the song.

"The song is almost over. You might take Jessamine to the band's events. You can learn the dance moves there," I say, unpeeling my sandwich and taking a bite. Wiping my mouth with the back of my hand, I look up at the scar on his chin, thinking about how I had touched it, and then push that thought away as an elegant woman joins the throng. She's in an expertly cut, costly suede jacket, and she wears a flat-topped felt hat that suits her features perfectly. She waves at us, and I raise my hand, but I stop as Michael waves at her. I look at his face, searching his eyes, his mouth, his stance for what I still hope shouldn't be there.

But it is.

****

I cut in among the crowd who are returning to their seats and, once out of sight of the concertgoers, sprint into the office to check if Abbie or Dan are there. They are not, and despite my lack of running footwear and looking like an idiot, I sprint to the cottage, take out the Iris Blackrail computer from my closet, run to the garage, get my car, and drive north across the bridge, past the ski area turnoff, to the blockhouse and down the hill to the parking lot where a boat trailer and I share space.

I'm quite alone. A new addition to the sightline is a wooden picnic table positioned to give a view of the spectacular Kennedy Range and the rest of Snowshoe Lake. I get out of the car, tucking the computer under my arm, and walk across the clover-filled lawn. I sit so that I can stare at the lovely view. As I type in my password as Iris Blackrail and check my messages, I'm pleased to see that Jacy has approved my request for the additional surveillance equipment and that it will be arriving via courier tomorrow. Jacy asks in her e-mail if I will be available at the cottage or if I can arrange another location.

As I contemplate how I'm going to put the tracer into the Tamarack Springs Bar, the *putt-putt-putt* of a trolling motor comes across the water, and a lone fisherman, his hand on the tiller of the motor, his chin raised, surveys the lake for possible places to fish. A fishing pole, its line like a silvered strand of silk, bobs and weaves like the dancers dancing to the beat of the song I'd heard only an hour ago. What looks like a lone Canada goose flies steadily across the water, but as I expect it to flap its wings, it doesn't, and my brain and heart skip a beat.

The fisherman does not look at the drone as it passes but turns his head in the direction where it came. His body leans forward, and then he raises his hand. It's a slight movement, and if he'd been farther away, I might have missed it, but I realize that he is now moving his boat toward the shore, and I am about to become visible.

The computer pings that another VPN trace has started. This can no longer be a coincidence.

I also realize that I have no explanation for why I'm here. I must leave. Now.

As I do, the flash of a blue vehicle comes from the direction of the huckleberry patch. If I move, the driver or the car's occupants will see me, and with me is all the evidence to get rid of me like they did with Pam Clayton.

I freeze, holding my breath as my eyes follow the blue car as it passes the blockhouse and then disappears.

Slamming the lid of the computer screen down, I tuck it under my arm and run back to the car. Throwing it inside, I close the car door and turn over the engine. And it grinds. I plead, hoping and praying for a miracle. As the boat approaches, it slows and disappears.

The car's engine grinds again and stops.

The man's head appears above the hill, and he walks to me, his fingers not like the ones he uses in prayer every Sunday, framing his eyes to see who is in the car.

I put the computer under my seat as he taps the window.

Chapter Twelve

"What in the world are you doing out here, Joanne?" asks Wally. He smiles a toothy grin through the closed car window.

I open the car door and step out, thankful that I had thought to take my sandwich with me. "Oh, probably a dead battery, I'm afraid. I was having a bad day and thought that going out to where Thew and I had some happy times would cheer me up. When I was small, you took us fishing here, didn't you?" I ask, hoping that my speech isn't too rapid. "Did you catch anything?" I peer into the dinged and speckled bucket, which is half full of water and contains two nice-sized cutthroats.

"Got lucky. They weren't biting like they should. Pop the hood, and I'll go to my truck, and we'll give it a jump. Enjoy the sunshine. I'll be back in a jiff."

I watch his lanky frame take easy strides up the hill. I glance over the top of my car door to where the bottom edge of my computer peeks out. Had Wally seen it? What if he had? Can't a woman take her laptop out to a remote location? Do I even own a set of battery cables? Do I remember how to use them? I reach in and pop open the hood and then the trunk, take the laptop out, and put it in the trunk of the car, careful to cover it with a blanket. The batter cables sit in their original container, and I loop them over my arm.

The pickup appears, and Wally drives around the end of the parking lot so that it noses my car. He cuts the engine and smiles as I raise my arm, the battery cables looping my arm like climbing gear.

"Thew taught you well," he says, opening the truck door. He reaches to pop the hood of his truck and slides a well-used set of jumper cables from under the driver's seat. "He talked about the two of you doing craft projects. Having a bad day, huh?" Wally takes his jumper cables and leans over his truck's engine, attaching them to the block. He unspools the cables and moves toward my car, his long legs scissoring the parking lot log. "Let's see what we have here. Wanna talk about what you saw?" he asks, his fingers clamping the cable to the battery.

"What?" I say, startled at the question.

He turns his face toward me and studies me as he clamps the second cable. "Heard you saw a finger in your backyard. That's enough to spook anyone. No wonder you're out here having a bad day."

"I didn't see it, actually. That was my roommate, er, former roommate. We talked to the detectives. They might know more about it than I do. What have you heard?" I ask, breathing a sigh of relief about Wally's focus.

"You know, this and that. The choir was abuzz. Shirley counted a dozen people in and around your yard—" says Wally, sliding his slim frame back over the log and getting into the pickup. He starts the truck and then tilts his head out of the cab, and shouts above the diesel engine's roar. "Try it now."

I get back into my car, and the engine turns over. I wave at him, and he offers a broad smile in return.

We exit our vehicles, and I extend my hand in thanks, but he goes back over the log and removes the cables. Holding them in his hand, he cups his arm, and I lean in for a hug. "Thank you! What do I owe you?" I ask, thinking this is the closest I've been to him in my whole life.

"Nothing. Probably need to get that battery replaced. You don't want to get stranded. Heard you've been out with that roommate of yours in all sorts of places." He stiffens his arm.

"Showing him the area, though his fiancée has now arrived, so I doubt I'll be seeing much of him," I say, my stomach doing flip-flops.

Wally gives my shoulder a tighter squeeze and releases me. "Probably best. Well, I have to hitch my trailer and get my boat back into the blockhouse," he says, and I grimace at the smarmy misogyny packed into those sentences and the conversation in general.

"Again, thanks for your help. I look forward to furthering my work on the You Who Foundation and seeing the conveyances. Let me know if you need me to drop by your offices or if you have documents there." I say this as I slide back into the car, returning from Thew's little gap-toothed towhead daughter to mineral manager of hundreds of assets.

He slams the car's hood with more effort than necessary. I put the car in reverse and give a wave, a plastered smile on my face. As I climb up the hill and pass the blockhouse, I'm surprised to see the door open, revealing a vehicle I'd seen before. I tremble as I reach for my phone, roll down the window, and snap photos of Dan's Audi inside the blockhouse.

****

They huddle on the bottom of the cottage's front steps.

Jessamine looks up and tips her hat back. She stands, and Michael pushes off the step to gain balance.

I pull up and get out of my car, keeping the engine on. "I need to get the battery replaced on my car. Michael, did you lose your key?"

He raises his head and gives it a slight shake. "How about I follow you? I need to tell you the news, but it can't be here." He turns to Jessamine. "Can you follow us? I need to speak to Joanne. No, wait. Joanne, we'll follow you to the repair shop, and we'll wait outside."

I remember his admonition about my car being bugged. My eyes widen, and I nod. "We'll have to make a stop later."

"Okay," says Jessamine. Taking Michael's hand, she strolls over to the Rover with him.

I pull out ahead of Michael and drive to the repair shop, keeping the engine running while I go inside, explain the problem, and give them my information.

Michael and Jessamine watch me as I leave, and I get in the back seat of the Rover. As we go, a mechanic gets into my car and pulls it into a bay.

As Michael pulls out onto the street, I see Wally driving his pickup truck. I wave but then drop my hand. Wally continues past us.

"Wally jumped my car. I'm lucky he was there," I say, filling in the gaps of silence as I look at Michael's unsmiling face in the rearview mirror. Jessamine looks straight ahead.

I shiver at a horrible thought. "Where did Wally store his boat?" I ask. "Michael, we need to go to the blockhouse in a hurry. Dan's Audi is in there. I took pictures of it." Reaching for my purse and taking out my phone. "By the time the police get there, the car may be gone if someone took Dan's car somewhere else."

"Joanne, I'm sorry to say this, but Dan is dead," says Jessamine, reaching back and holding my forearm. "There was an accident in the park. He went for a hike yesterday afternoon and fell to his death. His car was found in a remote part of the park and was discovered by a ranger this morning. They went for a search along the trail and found him about four miles in. He had fallen from a height. Given the mental state that Michael described to me, it appears to be a suicide. I'm very sorry. You might have to break it to the bank's officers tomorrow, but the police have confirmed it."

I cry out as the details pour over me. "You said Dan was in the park, and they found the Audi parked there? That's not possible. I saw his car parked in the blockhouse not a half hour ago. I took pictures. I was working on a project and…" My mouth dries out. I'm silent for what was probably only seconds, but it seems much longer. "I can't believe that Dan is dead. It can't be. How can his car be in the blockhouse? Did he hitchhike to the park?" I'm babbling. I lower my head as my body wracks out sobs. *The repair shop. Oh no! The repair shop!*

"Michael, we have to get back to the garage," I say as a wave of paranoia takes over. "I left my Iris Blackrail computer in the car. I can't be without it. Please turn around right now!"

To their credit, neither Michael nor Jessamine contradict me. Instead, he slows down, makes a U-turn, and then speeds up. A few minutes later, he parks the Rover in front of the mechanic's garage, and I run inside. "I'm sorry. I left my computer inside my car, and I need to get it. Can I get it from the trunk?"

The mechanic shakes his head. "Your dad came in not three minutes ago and said you were worried you'd forgotten it but to check in the trunk. We let him look inside, and sure enough, that's where it was. He tried calling but couldn't reach you. Call your dad."

"He's not my dad! How could you hand it over to a stranger? What kind of idiot are you?" I scream.

"I didn't give it to him. He looked in the trunk and called you. The whole thing took less than five minutes. I was working on that blue crossover in a neighboring bay. Hey, he said he was your dad, and he described the location of the computer perfectly. I'm sorry, but if you don't apologize, I'll have you banned from this shop, and you can take your business elsewhere. He described you and where the computer might be, and sure enough, there it was. What was I supposed to do?"

Not-so-gentle arms pull me away from the clerk. Jessamine puts an arm around me and whispers in my ear. "I'm calling Bolton's Valor. They will deactivate the computer. Now, nod and apologize to the mechanic."

"I'm sorry for the outburst," I say, bursting into tears again. "I had a rude shock earlier today, and I took it out on you. Please let me know when the car will be ready. Again, I apologize."

Jessamine not so much walks as drags me out of the waiting room and pushes me into the Rover.

"Michael, do you know where the blockhouse is? There might still be time," says Jessamine. She pulls out her phone and switches to Farsi, and as I make out the words, she is telling an encryption officer to route the signals to another server. She says VPN, and I groan as I realize I was supposed to be available to have the tracker delivered to me. Jessamine then makes another call, and again, the British accent drops to one that sounds American.

"Ken is at the blockhouse," she says, pushing back her ball cap as she turns to look at me in the back seat. "Joanne, you are right. The Audi is gone and replaced by the boat, but your pictures and information should provide compelling evidence."

Drawing my shoulder blades together, I straighten. I look at the person in front of me, thinking back to earlier this summer in a darkened conference room in London's Financial District, where a person had mocked me. Just now, Jessamine had not said *infor-may-sion* but *infor-mush-on*. I study her hairline, looking for the adhesive tape strips used to secure a wig.

"Ken? Does Ken work for Bolton's Valor? Jessamine, do you work for them, too?" I stammer as everything that I know for sure has flown out the window. I blink several times, trying to take in the information, and then in a whisper, I ask as quietly as I can because if the information is taken in small doses, it will be less painful to swallow. "Dan is dead? He didn't commit suicide. He was killed. There has to be security footage of him driving the car into the park."

"Our officers got the information rather quickly from the federal officers. The person kept their head down and wore a wig. It was a woman. She wore a wig and was rather plump," says Jessamine.

I sit back hard. "What name was registered on the sign-in sheet at the park entrance?" I ask, already expecting the answer for which I have no excuses.

"Blackrail. Iris Blackrail. You have some questions to answer, I'm afraid," says Michael.

****

Nothing has prepared me for how to handle the worst day of my life.

Jessamine turns to me, undoes her seat belt, and then shimmies back out of the front seats to sit next to me, holding up her hand to Michael's howl about going to jail for these kinds of offenses. "Save it for someone who cares."

Tears of pain fall. The hand that rubs my back senses the appropriate spots and just how much pressure to apply. But right now, as the Rover jostles along, I can't form a thought that makes sense. Less than a minute ago, one word caused me to rethink the puzzle pieces.

I will be pinned for the murder of my boss. Iris Blackrail will. Dan and Pam are dead, and I realize I haven't asked precisely where the car was found. Rangers do not regularly patrol a remote part of the park. Odd.

Who had the strength to drag Dan or force Dan to walk miles when he couldn't manage…unless he was dropped? Not a stretch. A plane? Too noticeable.

"Who has Dan's body?" I say, stiffening. Jessamine removes her arm and pats my knee.

I close my eyes, imagining a remote trailhead, someone hitting Dan with a blunt object, either killing or subduing him, loading him onto the drone, and sending him off to a remote location. Who has the capability? Two names spring immediately to mind.

"The same people killed Pam and Dan. They talked or were going to," I say, straightening up and then shifting to the other back seat in the Rover so that I can face Jessamine and Michael can hear. "I need to go to the cottage, Michael."

"Why?" he asks, his eyes moving from the road to

the rearview mirror.

I shrug, looking for a tell from the front seat. "Please hurry."

****

Of course, the wig and clothing have disappeared from my closet. I run down the stairs to the powder room. Checking under the powder room sink reveals towels and cleaning products.

Jessamine could have stolen the wig I wore when I went to Lodgepole Ferry with Michael. But why would Michael betray me like that? Who would hire Jessamine to kill Dan? Was Michael really engaged to her? Why would she have been at the conference?

I flush the toilet, wash my hands, and take a hard look at myself.

What an awful mess. Bloodshot green eyes peer back at me. My cheeks are blotchy, and my nose, always prone to coloring, is nearly the color of the whites of my eyes. I open the bathroom door and walk over to the kitchen, where Michael and Jessamine sit at the table.

"I need to take a shower and change my clothes. I'll be down in an hour. I can walk back to work. I'll be fine," I say, turning and running up the stairs before they can respond.

Minutes later, with the hot water running down my body, I lather my hair, running my fingers through the thick, creamy lather, and reflect on what I know. Jessamine has to be the key. She knew who to call to deactivate my computer and appeared when I was knee-deep in the encryption project. Heck, she, or her alias, came to my talk at the conference in London. Again, is she working for Bolton's? She has to be. How did she meet Michael? Is he involved with Bolton's, too?

I lower my head, rinsing the lather from my hair. I flip back my hair, which lands with a resounding slap, and for the first time in days, I laugh. Turning off the shower, I reach for a towel and listen for movement below me. The bathroom window doesn't face the driveway, so I pad down the hallway from the bathroom to peek from my bedroom window.

The Rover is gone.

Taking clothes from my closet, I return to the bathroom, get dressed, apply makeup, and dry my hair. Reviewing the results, I've improved to passable but not great. Oh, well.

****

Five minutes later, I arrive at the bank. A sticky note is on my office door, and I recognize Abbie's large print. "Went home. Heard the news about Dan. I'll call you later – A."

Taking the sticky note from the door, I walk into the breakroom and peruse the stacks of mail that have arrived for Dan and I. As I riffle through the lease offers, division orders, and authorizations for expenditures on various wells, a hand-addressed square envelope flutters to the floor. I reach down and flip over the square envelope addressed to Dan. I slide my finger under the flap and rip the envelope open. Pulling out the card, I see a series of computer-printed numbers on one line and a similar, but not exact, set of numbers below it. I flip the envelope over, rubbing my finger over what appears to be a name and address written in felt-tip pen. I dab my finger to my tongue and run my finger over the address line. There are no pressure points on the paper, thus limiting the number of fingerprints.

I take the stack of offers, the envelope, and the card

back to my office. I look at the postmark on the square envelope. It was mailed several days ago.

A cough comes from the entrance to our department.

Bob Porter, wearing the Western version of formal business attire—a fleece vest, long-sleeved shirt, khakis, bolo tie, and cowboy boots—peers at Abbie's empty desk and Dan's office.

"Client meeting, Bob?" I call, forcing a smile. I can't be the one to tell him about Dan. That has to come from anywhere else. "Dan's out, and Abbie's out this afternoon. Can I help you?"

He strides toward me, hand outstretched, before coming right to the point. "Joanne, I am having a problem with a client of mine, and I need your help. The State Examining Board has flagged the amount of money going into my client's account, and I need an accounting of the assets. The client's name is Allegro Enterprises— oil, ranching, and airplane leases. It should have a Los Angeles or Spokane address. Here's the letter of authorization for your records."

"Oh, thanks," I say. "The Mineral Management Department files are on a universal computer drive, so Abbie, Dan, and I have access to them." I open Dan's computer files to the one named Allegro and then scroll to the Asset Listings while Bob talks in his folksy way about the weather and the baseball teams' scores from the past weekend. He pauses as I look at him expectantly.

"Bob, I don't see the problem. Allegro has partnership deals—listed individually. Let's see what they are doing." I open another tab, move it to my second monitor, and wave at Bob to stand next to me so that we can review these screens together. "Some leases are in Eastern Montana, North Dakota, and Wyoming. Most of the income is from minerals and hunting leases. Here's another partnership. Okay, some airplane leases, some mineral interests, pretty tame stuff in these parts. What is the bank saying?"

Bob shifts as if the balls of his feet ache. He lowers his voice. "One guy from the State Board of Examiners said the only time he had heard of something like this was in a small place in California near the Mexican border. Small banks were processing loans that were way too much money for the area. It appeared legit, but then they found that the assets were not what they appeared and the money was not coming from leases as they said."

I look at him blankly. "Well, we get mineral deeds and leasing documents from the client. Are you saying that Allegro money has a problem? Like laundering?"

Bob's cheeks flush at my directness. "I don't think that's it at all, but the bank wants to know what Allegro has on their books and start verifying that those assets actually exist. So, you have the authorization to release the information. Can you start sending those files today?"

My sigh is probably louder than necessary, and Bob's eyes widen in surprise.

"I will see what I can do. Does Dan have documentation on his computer? I feel like I'm coming in the middle of an investigation and expected to operate as if I know what led up to this point. Dan hasn't said a word about these variances, and I haven't received reports." I raise my finger to him as cognition of what should have occurred kicks in.

"I'm one of two money laundering officers at this branch. Dan is the other one. Either he didn't know, or, worse yet, he did, and he didn't bother to share this with me." I open another screen and type in a password. "Bob, this is the report we send the State and Federal Examiner's offices every month. Allegro isn't on this report. But now you want me to drop everything and jump into some rabbit hole because *now* you're getting heat?"

Bob steps away from my computer and walks around the desk to face me directly. He leans forward. "We bypassed the local and state levels since the people we are investigating are on the local board. The reports have been fixed to look normal for the past six to nine months."

A hard slap of recognition hits.

"Oh, hold the hell up," I say, no longer caring who hears me. "You represent Allegro and Paul Allegretti, the owner of Allegro, who wants to be on our bank's board. You got reports fixed." My eyes widen, and rising, I lean across my desk, the monitors brushing my rib cage. "State and local reports were fixed so as not to alarm them because the asset ratios are off. Just who in the hell do you work for? What kind of lawyer does that? If I'm hearing you correctly, I think you should be disbarred. What the hell?"

I've never counted out five seconds, but it's a long time. Bob squares his shoulders and, without a word, walks out of the bank's front entrance. In that stillness, with the droplets of my observations hanging in the air, I realize the magnitude of what I'm up against. If I don't leave now, like right this second, I've signed my death warrant.

Chapter Thirteen

I cry out as a pickup truck with a flatbed full of sound equipment and signage for The Modern Retellings startles me as it bounces onto the thoroughfare. The driver slows and gives me a friendly wave as he passes me.

I've never been to a police station. Snowshoe's smallness means it shares the building with the Justice of the Peace, the City Clerk, and the Library. A small glass door announces Snowshoe Police, with a second line reading "To Serve and To Protect."

I open the door and run down the stairs to a waiting room smaller than my office. On the right is a glassed-in partition where a young woman sits.

"Can I help you?" she asks.

"I need to see either Detective Johnsrud or Detective Ropp or both, please. It's urgent."

"Is there an accident?" the dispatcher asks, but I shake my head.

"Please. It's urgent," I say, nervously glancing up at the flight of stairs, half expecting Paul, Bob, or Alan to come down them.

The dispatcher presses a button on her console and then speaks in a low tone, glancing over to me. "What's your name?" she asks. I tell her, and she repeats it and says, "Okay."

"Miss Corvus. Joanne, hello," says Detective Johnsrud, opening a door and welcoming me inside.

"Is that door bulletproof? I, er, I mean, I need to talk to you and Detective Ropp."

The door clicks shut behind me, and I step onto a cushioned carpeted area. Six half-framed cubicles ring the room. Hunched people stare at computer screens with reports, maps, or spreadsheets. I see fingers clicking computer keys, but for all the activities, there is little sound.

Three photographs line the shelf above the detective's desk, and I peer at them as she motions for me to sit. The pictures are of a young, stern woman in uniform, a rafting photograph, and someone smiling on a ski slope.

"Can I get you some water or coffee?" Detective Johnsrud asks, and I shake my head, distracted by the lack of noise and the fact that she has a life outside of these four walls. I glance at her as she sits in her chair and then places her hands on her knees. "What is this all about?"

"I don't know where to begin. No, that's not true. I do," I say as Detective Johnsrud barely checks her eyeroll. "I'm Iris Blackrail, and I'm Joanne Corvus."

It's a sleight of hand how she manages to find a pen and a notepad in the seconds since I say that, but she is transcribing my words. "Hold on," she asks, "would you mind if we move into another room so that I can record this?"

I nod, and we rise. I follow her through another doorway to a hallway with three rooms. She opens the one directly ahead of us. Turning on the light reveals a metal table, four chairs, and a microphone. "Jimmy?" she calls to the wall. "Can you have Al join us in Room One? Are you sure you don't want coffee or water?"

I shake my head and begin.

She holds up her hand and says, "Detective Holly Johnsrud is in conversation with Iris Blackrail, aka Joanne Corvus." She says the date and time and then waits. There is a knock on the door, and Detective Ropp appears and shakes my hand.

"Detective Ropp, Iris Blackrail is also Joanne Corvus. She wants to talk to us and says that it is urgent," says Detective Johnsrud without a trace of sarcasm as Detective Ropp pulls out a chair, places a notepad and pen on the table, and folds his arms on the table.

"I'm only two people in one capacity. I'm an encryption officer for Bolton's Valor Security Forces and am investigating breaches of security at Winding Creek Bank. That work takes place on a laptop and telephone, which is different from my work and life as Joanne Corvus. Wally Harmon recently compromised the laptop registered to Iris Blackrail, but my password and all information on the computer are behind a firewall, and the password has been deactivated."

"You are reporting this because..." asks Detective Ropp, and I shake my head.

"I know that Dan, my boss at Winding Creek, was found dead in Alpine National Park, and a car was found near the trailhead. The person on the hike signed the trailhead register as Iris Blackrail. Dan was found four miles in, having fallen. That's impossible because he has a problem with one of his knees, and it pains him to walk across a parking lot, never mind walking four miles on a hiking trail. He never would have done that."

The detectives look at each other and return their gazes to me as I continue. "I saw his car, his real car, the red Audi, inside a blockhouse outside of town. The blockhouse is usually used for boat storage, but when I took the pictures a few hours ago on my telephone, it was definitely Dan's car."

"Can you send those pictures to us?" asks Detective Johnsrud. She tears off a sheet of paper and scribbles her e-mail and that of Detective Ropp and then slides it across the table to me.

I lean over and take my telephone out of my purse. I locate the photographs and send them to the addresses provided by the detectives. Two seconds later, pings come from their cell phones. "Shall I continue?" I ask, and they both nod.

"I've been asked to investigate breaches or potential breaches that are impacting Winding Creek Bank. We believe someone or a company is trying to create a hack into our bank's security firewall and that it is connected with drones flying parcels—drugs, and I believe, maybe even Dan. The drones may come from trapper cabins owned by Paul Allegretti and Alan Greene, who are directors in our bank. Alan is a director, and Paul will be nominated to the board after Bob Porter retires. Maybe I will take some water or coffee. My throat is drying out."

Detective Johnsrud looks at her watch, says, "Interview suspended at thirteen-forty-three," taps the microphone, and then rises from her chair and opens the door. "Do you need some water, Al?"

He shakes his head and looks at me impassively.

"I—" I begin, but the detective raises his hand. "We can't talk without the conversation being recorded," he says. "Detective Johnsrud will return in a second." He smiles as he says this, and I lower my shoulders, glad to unburden myself.

I pick at the cuticle of my right thumb and rub the

nail with my index finger.

"I have some lotion. Do you want some?" Detective Ropp slips his hand into his pants pocket and then slides a thin tube of moisturizer across the table. I unscrew the lid and squeeze a dab on the loose skin. I put the lid back on and slide it back. "Thanks."

"Got three bottles for us," Detective Johnsrud says as she opens the door, holding the water bottles as if they were bottles of beer. Under her arm is a manila folder.

Taking a bottle from her, I unscrew the lid and place the cap on the table. I take a sip of water and set the bottle beside the lid. I put my index finger on the lid, sliding it in front of me.

Detective Johnsrud taps the microphone. "This is Holly Johnsrud with Andy Ropp and Joanne Corvus, also known as Iris Blackrail. We are continuing our interview. Please continue."

I lower my head for a second, collecting my thoughts. "Forty-five minutes ago, I was in the bank working on a project, and Bob Porter, who you might know, came to see me." The detectives nod, and I continue. "He said he is representing Paul Allegretti's LLC, Allegro, LLC, and that the Local and State Bank Examiner's Board had contacted him because the accounts show too much cash flowing through it. And then he tells me that the reports the banks receive have been altered to appear as though the accounts are okay."

"Have you contacted the bank examiner's office?" asks Detective Ropp, rubbing an imagined spot from his face. "Why are you working today? Didn't the bank say to take the day off after your boss' death?"

I shake my head. "I don't feel safe in doing that. Dan and I are the money-laundering officers for the bank, and he has not, er, he did not tell me there was a problem with Allegro."

"Safe? Why don't you feel safe? Was Allegro your client?" asks Detective Johnsrud as both detectives lean forward.

"No, it was Dan's account," I reply, "but we are the officers who determine what is excessive and prepare reports on how we are handling it. There has to be transparency. Now Dan is dead, his girlfriend Pam has disappeared or is dead, but Pam was seeing Alan Greene. Alan Greene is on the bank's board."

I slide the bottle cap around in a circle, thinking about how I'm going to tell the next part. I let out a sigh. "As to why I don't feel safe, I need to tell you about what Dan did a few days before his death. He came to our, er, my cottage last week. Dan invested in a diamond loan, and the bank signed off on assets held by another bank. Michael, my former roommate, has seen Dan's car, the red Audi, on logging roads and in odd places. We have also seen drones fly across the Kennedy River next to Alpine National Park. Actually, one drone chased us when we went to see a trapper's cabin. I've seen drones three times on Snowshoe Lake and once at Willow Creek Meadows Lake. The VPN I was investigating, as Iris Blackrail says, is being controlled from the bar my father used to own in Tamarack. Paul Allegretti now owns the bar, using his company, Allegro. I had planned to put a tracking device in the bar below the living quarters. I might find out who is sending the drones out."

The detectives say nothing.

"Today, Dan received an envelope at the bank that appeared to have been handwritten. I opened it and found codes that appeared to be section, township, and range coordinates. If I had to hazard a guess, I think they are times of arrival and delivery of the drones and the coordinates of those places."

I slide the cap back and forth in front of me. "So, what happens now? I don't feel safe. How do I know that what happened to Dan and to Pam will not happen to me?"

Detective Johnsrud slides the manila folder over to Detective Robb. He pulls several pictures out and places them on the table in front of me. Of course, I recognize the photographs. I didn't realize Wally had put a camera on the blockhouse's garage entrance, nor did I know he had footage from the Tamarack Springs Bar. My squatting by the garage door entrance and looking for the key looks terrible. And the stupid, guilty expression that crosses my face as I exit the Tamarack Springs Bar's bathroom like I'm a common criminal. The two other photographs are taken at the boat ramp, and the last one shows me rolling down my car window and taking a photo of the opened blockhouse garage door.

"Why were you trying to break into the garage, Joanne? Or should I call you Iris?"

"I can't tell you that," I answer, wondering if Bolton's Valor Special Forces will cover my legal expenses. But in truth, I had been investigating those areas as both Joanne and Iris, so perhaps they would.

"The last time I checked, I didn't trespass at the boat ramp, and it isn't illegal for me to go into the bar my father once owned and take a look around, for old times' sake. I didn't enter the garage. I was looking for a toy I had placed there when I was a child and had gone with Wally, er, Mr. Harmon, to the boathouse garage. I was disappointed to see that the toy was gone. Am I being accused of illegal activity?"

Detective Ropp shrugs, and I give him a thin smile.

"Well then, I'm free to go. I hope you find the information I provided helpful." I stand and walk out the door, positive I am in danger.

****

Where do you go when you can't go back to work (too obvious), my cottage (under surveillance), restaurants (can't cause a scene)? Crossing the street, I walk two blocks and hope the choir door is open.

Padding softly down the stairs, I step inside the choir room, turn on the light, and then take a seat on a chair in front of the rack holding my choir robe and Belle's. My heart races at how things now look. The police didn't arrest me, but the evidence is damning. I close my eyes and bow my head, clasping my hands together. My thoughts aren't spiritual but tactical, and for a second, I wonder if I should go somewhere else to find a quiet place to think.

Curling my index finger under my nose, I continue to close my eyes. Tears form and roll down my cheeks as I search for a common point that will combine all of the jumble of data. I need help.

The knock on the door is gentle.

Startled, I rise to see Pastor Jen standing in the doorway.

"I'm sorry, Pastor Jen, I can leave," I say, wiping the tears from my eyes.

"Nonsense, Joanne. Did you forget something in your locker? I saw you on the camera and thought I would come by and say hello," she says, giving me a friendly smile.

"No, I'm fine. I'll leave. I need a place to think, and

I came here because…"

"I'm sorry to hear about your boss, Dan. I didn't know him well, but I would have liked to," she says. She steps closer as if offering an opportunity. "The activity at your cottage, too. It's a lot to process."

I pat the chair beside me, and she walks over and sits down, her knees and elbows nearly touching me but not quite. Again, I feel as though I'm being given an opportunity, but I don't know if it's to share or burden her.

"Do you want to come up to my office? Shirley is preparing a report, so it's just her and I," she says.

As she mentions Shirley's name, I square my shoulders and shake my head. "The acoustics in this church are perfect, aren't they?"

Her eyes widen as if she's not sure how to take the trajectory of my conversation.

"Do you have time to take a walk with me, Pastor Jen? I'd be more comfortable if we could walk over to Maple District Park if that's all right," I ask.

"Yes, I have time. It's a nice afternoon, and I could use some fresh air," she says.

We stand, and I follow her up the stairs. She holds the door for me, and we step outside into a noisier realm. Pastor Jen smiles at me. "I forget how noisy Snowshoe is becoming. Definitely more traffic."

"I'm not sure how to begin. Actually, this is the second time I've said that phrase today. I've provided information to the police, and now that information paints me in a way that isn't true and implicates me," I say. I blush as the words leave my mouth. "I'm sorry, that isn't helpful."

"Actually, it is." Pastor Jen plucks a leaf from a

silver maple tree, placing it flat on the palm of her hand.

I smile. "You're going to tell me there are two sides to truth, and though we expect the back to be green because the top is green, this is a silver maple, and in the fall, it turns a lovely silver color."

"Well, yes, there is that to be sure. I was going to say that our facts are only part of the story. You see a leaf, one with a number of unique qualities, but this leaf isn't the whole tree, and a number of these leaves will never be able to display their uniqueness."

"You've lost me," I say, flushing with embarrassment.

"Your truth is only one of the leaves. It isn't the only truth. It sounds like what you are working through has many layers or leaves. When you put the leaves and branches together, you will get a living, breathing entity, a tree, or the truth—the whole truth. You are welcome to stay in the church if you like. Shirley and I will be leaving in an hour. Maybe sitting in a peaceful place where all you can or have to do is to arrange the leaves on the tree might be the way to the truth, and what you must do to set things right will come to you." She hands me the leaf. "It sounds simplistic, but I think you have been exposed to a lot of noise. I think some quiet will do you some good."

I turn the leaf over, considering her words. "That you can come up with that on the fly is pretty impressive, Pastor Jen," I say with a laugh.

"Jen. Just call me Jen. My duty is to observe and listen. I suspect you carry many burdens and have convinced yourself that you are the only one who can take them and solve the issues that made you hold them in the first place."

That strikes a nerve. I nod, handing the leaf back to her, but she doesn't take it.

"Try this idea. Trace out the shape of the leaf in the center of a piece of paper. As you can see, the leaf has points. Put the name of each burden on the tip of each point and then trace another leaf above it. Name the person or thing that makes you uneasy about the burden. If it's a co-worker neglecting their duties, put the name of the job on your leaf and draw a line for that person on the other leaf. At some point, you will notice a pattern, and that pattern will lead you to the truth, and that truth will allow you to get some clarity."

"Thank you. I'm not sure it will work, but I'll try," I say.

"In my line of work, that's called faith. Not being sure of the outcome, but doing it anyway because it can give you an answer," she says, handing the leaf back to me. "If you need to talk about anything, I am always available."

I reach in to hug her, and she gives me a sisterly hug, one that I have always gotten from Belle and have now pushed away.

****

The cottage is quiet. I walk into the living room, kneel, and open the bottom shelf of the barrister's bookcase. Pulling out an artist's sketch pad and drawing pens, I walk to the kitchen table and turn on the light. Placing the leaf on a page of the pad, I trace it, reminding myself that each of the points on the leaf might represent a problem. After tracing the leaf, I laugh as I realize that I can't carry that many burdens.

I'm to label them and treat each point as a challenge. The late summer light fills the living room, and I have the urge to sit with the sun on my face. Carrying the sketch pad, I turn off the kitchen light and walk over to the sofa, finding delight in tucking my feet under me. I bend over the pad, and instead of listing the names, I list my questions. Maybe with a bit of faith, I'll find some of the answers I seek.

It takes me less than five minutes to list my questions, and I already feel better.

I take out my laptop and type in the Secretary of State for the State of Washington using Lake Chelan as the address. Then, I put Limited Liability Company into the search engine. Scrolling through them, I find the documentation and the registered agent who represents their interests.

Opening a newspaper database, I type in the name of the person murdered two years ago at Upper Snowshoe Lake. For a second, I believe in coincidences, but I shake that feeling away. Recalling my conversation with Michael only a week ago, I look at the names of the two people who died in the snowmobiling accident at Willow Creek Meadows Lake. '*One of them was related to a person who moved here from Florida, I think...*'

An internet search with the young man's name reveals several images. The young man had been on the tennis and sailing teams in Hialeah, Florida. A picture of a college graduation comes up, and there, behind the young man, stands Paul Allegretti. Another search of the newspaper database reveals a small article in the Hialeah, Florida newspaper stating that he would be starting with Elizabeth Logging Company as a sales manager. A photo is attached to the article, and there are the two young men who died and Wally Harmon shaking hands.

Allegro Enterprises, LLC owns the blockhouse on the tax rolls, but when I check the recorded deeds, I see that Elizabeth Logging Company transferred ownership to Allegro Enterprises. An addendum on the deed catches my eye and reveals that Wally Harmon can use the blockhouse garage as long as he lives, but the title remains in Allegro's name.

It's all circumstantial. I need to find proof, and for that, I have to eat a healthy dose of crow.

Chapter Fourteen

Belle's VW Bug is parked outside Hennessey's. A pang of guilt hits me, and I turn to walk in, tell her I'm sorry, and hope for a resurrection.

Then I catch sight of my, possibly former, best friend framed in the window with the Denver daisies and her head tilted back in a laugh. She raises a glass of wine, and Alan Greene does the same. He takes her hand in his, helping her set the glass down.

I slow my walk down, seething that my list of questions didn't include, "Is my best friend having sex with the man who raped me? She's not that much of an idiot, is she?"

Michael's Rover and Jessamine's rental car sit in front of a storybook-designed house on a small bluff above the Snowshoe River. The rounded front door, sloping roofline, and narrow brick and stone chimney are charming. The path, lined by flower boxes filled with petunias, is made of cobblestones. Climbing roses cling to trellises resting against the brickwork between the front door and the living room.

I knock on the front door, and a few seconds later, Michael opens it. He beams at me and calls out, "We have a guest."

The house is furnished in a style similar to mine. I'm disappointed that the rental department couldn't have decorated the house in the way it was intended to be furnished.

"It's late, and I should have called first. I'm sorry for barging in," I say, rubbing my hands together, though I'm not cold. Maybe I'm creating warmth to rekindle a friendship.

"Nonsense. Come into the living room. Would you like tea? I'd offer port, but that's still over at..." says Michael before breaking off at the awkwardness of the situation.

Jessamine comes in, her hair under a scarf, dressed in jeans and a sweatshirt. She gestures toward the sofa, identical to mine down to the lumpy feel. "Do you want something to drink?" She asks this in an English accent, straight out of boarding school. I'm left to wonder how close I'm getting to the actual Jessamine.

Michael gestures to Jessamine and back to me. "Do you want her to stay?"

So far, he hasn't said her name, only referring to her as "her."

I nod, and Jessamine and Michael take chairs opposite of me. "I was questioned by the police earlier today. The bank has been falsifying its liquidity reports, and Dan knew about it. For that, he could, er, would have gone to prison. The boys killed at Willow Creek Meadows and Upper Snowshoe Lake were related to Paul Allegretti. Paul owns the blockhouse, but Wally Harmon is allowed to use it as long as he lives. Oh, and the registered agent for the LLC in Washington has the same name as the guy murdered at the Upper Snowshoe Lake campground."

"There's been a development on the grizzly project," says Michael, beating me to my continuing my report. "I think this has a bearing on what you have discovered, Joanne. Come over to my office, and I'll show you." He rises from the chair, and I stand, but Jessamine scowls.

"I've heard nothing but this theory all day, so I'm stepping out." She rises, glares at Michael, and goes over to a table, taking a saucer with her. As she walks out through the kitchen, the back door slams.

"Michael, I should have called. I'm sorry if I came at a bad time…" I step forward, catching sight of Jessamine standing near the back door, a cigarette hanging from her lips. I shiver as she lowers it. I've seen that movement before. I suddenly didn't want to confess anything, least of all to her.

"Joanne? I'm in here." And I follow his voice past the staircase with its Douglas fir banister to a small room tucked between the kitchen and the dining room. The room has large topographical maps on its walls with red, blue, and black circles. Purple stars dot them. Michael walks to one that I recognize.

"That's Thayer Lookout, Upper Snowshoe Lake, and Lodgepole Ferry," I say. "That broad, black line follows the course of the river. What are the red, blue, and black circles?"

"Come over here. I have a theory, and I need to have you tell me that I'm not crazy." He glances up and swallows, his brows furrowing. A map of Snowshoe and Snowshoe Lake rests on Michael's desk. Green stars and yellow dots look like confetti.

He points at the map. "Do you remember the bears we saw up at Willow Creek Meadows Lake? I tracked them down. The sow has a technical name, but I call her Willow. The two cubs are yearlings, and I call them Bluebell and Forest. Although the bears have an extensive range, it's unusual for them to travel more than twenty miles in the Upper Kennedy Range Basin."

He taps his finger on where we traveled to the previous weekend. "We didn't see Willow when we were driving north of Lodgepole Ferry, but Bluebell and Forest were in the area. I've correlated the grizzly's activities with the drones and can, within an R-square of one confidence level, state that the drones are affecting the bear's habitat."

"That's a pretty high correlation," I say. "That will have a bearing on the man versus drone usage in the lookouts, right?" I look up at him with a new appreciation.

Michael peers at the alcove entrance and leans back over the maps. "The green stars are of the known raven nests, and the yellow dots are the known packrat middens. Raven aeries depend on food supplies. They prefer fresh food but will eat carrion if necessary. We know of one band of ravens that likes to go behind one of the local restaurants because the owner will often leave fishtails and fish heads out for them. That restaurant is here," he says, looking at me for confirmation.

"This yellow star is our, er, your cottage. I checked the prevailing winds around Snowshoe and the lake. I found that in the past week, the winds have been in a southeasterly direction, so the raven would have been able to pick up the finger along the lake, take flight, soar for five miles along the air currents coming off the Kennedy Range before dropping the finger in search of a better offer, the fish heads. I talked to the head chef at the restaurant, and he confirmed that he had left the fish heads out on Thursday afternoon."

"Which—" I break in, seeing the genius and tenacity

in Michael's peculiar mind, "means that Pam is probably at one of these places. This"—pointing to a large blue circle—"is by the ski area turnoff, and this area is isolated and only known for the lake trout that live in the deepest part of the lake. So, most likely, she's here," I say, pointing to the huckleberry-picking spot Thew and I had used all those years ago.

Michael leans over and places his left index finger over my right one. "Yes, I think you're right. I'm sure you are," he says.

I slide my finger out from under his, straighten it, and take a deep breath, dropping my voice to a whisper, coming as close as I can to him. "You're engaged. No. I can't be a part of this."

"Joanne, Jo-Jo, please," he says.

"I'm done with the lies and the secrets. I saw Belle a few moments ago on a date with Alan Greene, the man who raped me. Belle knows about it because she's the one I told. And do you know what she did? She apparently chose my rapist over me. Thirty-year friendship gone." I step back, widening my fingers like fireworks exploding. "And you. You're no different. I came here because I thought I could be the bigger person and let bygones be bygones, but no."

I turn, but Michael grabs my shoulder, and I turn around, knee him, and push him away. "No!" He drops to his knees with a thud, and I run back into the living room and race outside.

And that's when my feet fly out from under me, and I skid across the cobblestones, ending with my nose in a box of petunias.

****

"I don't think we finished our conversation,

Joanne," says Jessamine, rolling me over and grabbing both of my wrists. "Let's not make a scene."

"I'll scream—"

"And I'll say you tripped and are prone to hysterics. Let's do better than that." With that, she takes my wrists and half-slides, half-hauls me upward as if I'm on a meat hook.

I stand and eye her. "You're full of surprises. From a non-binary in London to an exotic, gorgeous creature now, I don't know what to think. Except maybe you're right. We need to talk."

She releases my wrists, and I pull away, but she takes my upper arm in a viselike grip. "Let's go into the kitchen."

"As if I have a choice," I say, nursing my right knee, which took the brunt in the fall.

Jessamine steps behind me as I climb the stairs and then closes the door behind her with a sharp *click*.

"What was it that gave me away?" asks Jessamine, pulling out a kitchen chair for me to sit on and pulling out a first aid kit from on top of the refrigerator. Turning, she pulls on her wound scarf, revealing a bald head. As she takes my wrist in her hands, I notice her up close for the first time. She is breathtakingly beautiful with tawny brown skin, her eyebrows shaped to accentuate her eyes. The anomaly is the beginning of a mustache.

"You said *information* the same way here as you did in London, though your appearance is different," I say, rubbing the reddened mound below my right thumb before nursing my aching knee. "I didn't put that together until a few days ago, but then I had a lot on my mind and hadn't had a chance to sort things out about why you might be here. I assume you met Michael on

205

one of your assignments?" I ask, keeping my voice neutral.

"You might have a small sprain, so I'm going to wrap it. You'll need to keep it elevated, and I can call in a prescription for you."

"You're a doctor? And you work in encryption. And you and Michael have been together for a long time?"

"I'll call in the pain medication. And you and I met twice in London. I was your driver. I work with the various Hinerman family members on their encryption and other needs." She takes a bandage and begins wrapping my wrist and lower arm.

"I don't remember you." But as I recall how I spent my afternoon explaining how I am Iris Blackrail and Joanne Corvus, I frown. "Why would you impersonate me and kill my boss? What had he done to you?"

Jessamine's eyes widen. "I didn't impersonate you, and I didn't kill your boss. My assignment is to protect the Hinerman family's assets."

"You're lying to me," I snap, pulling away from her. "You killed my boss. You and Michael are the only people outside of Bolton's Valor Security Forces higher-ups who know that I'm Iris Blackrail. You killed him and then sent a drone up to drop him in a remote location. He was scheduled to do a drop tonight. If I go now, I might see who is running the drugs."

"At least let me finish," she says, attaching a clip to hold the bandage in place. "No, I didn't kill Dan or Pam. You have to believe me. My only job is to protect the Hinerman interests against any encryption hacks."

"You have the location? Do you remember where it is? Will you let me help you, Joanne?" Michael stands in the doorway, his weight leaning against the doorframe.

"You winged me, but I think we might be able to put a stop to the drones. Can you show me on a map where it might be and when?"

I get up and walk past Michael into his office. He and Jessamine follow me, but Michael waves her off. "Let me handle this."

I look at the map with circles and groan. "I remember the section, townships, and ranges, but your maps have longitudes and latitudes." I close my eyes, recalling the card. Biting my lower lip at my foolishness, I look up at Michael. "I need to go into the bank because the card has the coordinates. I hope the card is still in my office."

"Let's go," says Michael, taking his coat and walking ahead of me, outside past the petunia boxes, down the steps, and opening the Rover.

I climb inside the car, and within a few minutes, we arrive at the emptied bank building. "I'll come in with you if you want," he says, but I shake my head. I pull out the keys to the bank, and the security lights light the staircase to the oil and gas mineral management offices. Unlocking my office door, I flip through the stack of mail and find the opened card. I stuff it in my hand, close the door behind me, and then run down the stairs and go outside. Climbing back into the Rover, I hand it to him, and he opens his phone to read the coordinates.

"You are right. This now makes sense." He puts the car into gear.

My phone buzzes, and I turn it over. "It's Detective Johnsrud," I say, answering the call and putting it on speaker.

"Hi, Joanne. It's Detective Johnsrud. I apologize for calling this late, but we have found some evidence that we need your help with. Would you be able to come to the station and help us review it? It shouldn't take long."

I look at Michael, and he slows the Rover, turning into a driveway to turn around.

"Yes, you would like me to come in right now?"

"Yes, your coming in now is appreciated."

"Okay, I will be at your offices in a few minutes," I say.

"Shall I stay with you?" Michael asks, but I shake my head.

"See what you can find out," I say as he stops the Rover in front of the police station. I open the car door and turn to look at him. I point my finger at him, and he leans over, putting his index finger on top of mine. I look up into his eyes and shiver.

I hate myself. I can't come between Michael and Jessamine. I can't. But here I am. Again.

****

After the dispatcher clears me, I take a seat in the waiting room, but almost immediately, Detective Johnsrud comes out and escorts me into the same interview room I'd been in this morning.

"We appreciate your coming in on such short notice," she says and then lowers the lights. "We need your help on a video that was taken a month ago and hope you can provide context. It might be disturbing, so if you need time to compose yourself, please let me know."

Detective Johnsrud taps the microphone and says, "Please run the interview," and Dan appears on the screen. He wears a white shirt and his grandfather's bolo tie, and I stifle a cry.

"He wears, er, would wear that outfit when he went

to an important meeting or a conference," I say, glancing over at Detective Johnsrud, who says nothing. The time stamp on the video indicates it was recorded six weeks ago. I go back to my mental calendar. Michael had been here for a few days, and I wanted to introduce him to Dan, but he'd been at a meeting. Missoula? No, he'd been to Spokane.

"He met with a prospective client around that time. He came in wearing that shirt and his good luck charm—his grandfather's bolo tie. 'It could be big,' that's what he said," I whisper. "You are right. This will be hard."

Detective Johnsrud hands me a tissue. There's a knock on the door, and she gets up. She opens the door and, after closing it, puts more tissues and bottles of water in front of me.

My eyes return to the screen.

Dan settled himself, and his expression changed. He frowned and then lowered his head, tapping his forehead on his fisted hands.

"My name is Dan Werner, and I have come to turn myself in."

I straighten and widen my eyes.

"I'm here to account for illegal activity perpetrated by myself and others. I'm here to tell you all that I know. I received a package—a cell phone—with directions to a remote delivery location nine months ago, but I think the activity has been going on a lot longer—probably years. It involves the smuggling of drugs, primarily cocaine."

Dan's eyes moved from the camera to points behind Detective Ropp. I'd seen that look when he had to deliver distressing news to a client and was framing how to say it.

"Paul Allegretti approached me at the Snowshoe

Plaster Bears charity event. I thought he was a rancher. He looked the part, wearing a corduroy jacket, dress jeans, and hand-tooled boots. The only giveaway was his hands. He has soft hands," Dan said with a sneer. "He'd asked if I was a benefactor. The Winding Creek Bank contributed twenty-five thousand dollars. The artist had proposed a First Nations outfit for the bear. The artist's rendering of the bear featured a headdress, beading, and buckskin. I told him I had contributed to one of the bears but not the total amount."

Dan shifted in his seat and shook his head. "Paul's tone was deliberately light and casual. 'Well, my company has just formed another partnership deal, and that partnership is going to put some money into the bear project,' he said. 'We are looking for investors, though. Are you interested?' I figured Paul was one of those ranchers who would make an offhand remark about doing some business in this and that—deliberately vague. I smiled and said, 'Why sure. Let me know where I can send my money. You got a business card on you?'

"Paul patted his breast pocket and pulled out a business card holder. It was silver with an inlaid 'A' in turquoise. 'Sure. The name's Allegretti. Paul Allegretti. Allegro Enterprises. Give us a call, and we will get you set up.'

"I offered my thanks and shook Paul's hand. I glanced down at the card: Paul Allegretti, President of Allegro Enterprises. The card had an embossment of an oil well, wheat waving in front of it, and a plane flying above it. The sky was blue, and the sun was shining. Offices in Spokane and Los Angeles. PO box. Local number and two with Washington and California prefixes. From what I saw, Paul Allegretti was just another rancher trying to figure out what to do with his money."

Dan rubbed his mouth and took a deep breath. "A couple of days later, I called Paul and mentioned how we'd met. Paul, whether it was true or not, remembered me and asked if I was still interested in the bear."

Detective Ropp leaned forward and tapped the microphone, stating he was pausing the interview with Dan Werner. He got up and walked out the door.

I sniffle and take a tissue. I inhale and then close my eyes. "This is awful. I haven't come to terms with Dan being dead. And to hear his voice?" I inhale again and shake my head.

"Take your time. I know this has to be difficult." At that, I open my eyes to see Detective Johnsrud looking intently at me. "Does anything click for you?"

"Coupled with what I told you this afternoon, I think Paul Allegretti killed my boss, Dan Werner. It also puts Bob Porter in a bad light if he knows he is working for a person who is trafficking drugs using drones. Paul is being considered for a position on our bank's board of directors. He and Alan Greene buy up trappers' cabins and use them as storage for the drones. And Alan is having an affair with Dan's fiancée, Pam Clayton."

I lower my head, biting my lip and wondering if I should say all of what I know.

"Joanne? What is it?"

I shake my head. "It's nothing you can do now. The statute of limitations—the he said, she said—passed long ago." I look up at the screen. "Run the rest of it, please."

Detective Johnsrud nods, and the video plays.

Detective Ropp returned with documents. He sat down and slid the folder over to Dan, though Dan didn't open it. Detective Ropp's voice softened. "Would the job have anything to do with paying the $250,000 loan? And why is Allegro Enterprises paying the interest on your loan? Aren't you in a partnership with them?"

Dan looked thunderstruck. "You guys are good. Yeah, I have a couple of deals going with Paul Alle…I mean Allegro Enterprises, and I do some odd jobs in payment. I don't have the money to invest in this deal, so Mr. Allegretti, I mean Paul, lets me work it as a sweat equity deal. I know that every month, the interest on my loan is paid, and I pay down the principal."

Dan grimaced. "Winter was starting to loom in the high country with the first dustings of snow at seven and eight thousand feet. The rains at the lower elevations made the roads almost impassable, and asking for a different route to transfer the packages was not an option. Worse, the packages were now in white or brown bags, making identifying them in the rocks or near trees more difficult."

Detective Ropp leaned toward Dan. "Are you sure the packages contain cocaine?" he asked, but Dan held up his hand. "I have to tell you in my way.

"I'd use the coordinates given on the card mailed to me, then wait and wonder. Over the past months, I've had doubts about my life. Pam is being weird. I gave her a ring and asked her to marry me. She flaunted the ring, going so far as to say it was from an admirer, but never told me yes or no. I have debts." Dan paused, and Detective Ropp cleared his throat. As he did, Dan again held up his hand. The detective fell silent.

"I've known what I ought to do. 'Come clean. You know it's the right thing to do,' " Dan says in a schoolmarm's voice. He then changes his voice like he's telling a child's nursery story. In a bigger, deeper voice, he says, "Do it, and you will be dead. You have allowed yourself to become part of this and have a code of silence to uphold. Death before dishonor. Dead. All because you were greedy."

Tears cascade down my cheeks. A week ago, he'd taken Abbie and me to lunch because it was "Par" Day at the golf course.

The fear on his face in the video is palpable—his absolute, abject terror. It was all held back—until it wasn't.

Dan's eyes are bright, and I realize he was losing his grip on reality. "Last night, I fell asleep and woke up cold and in the middle of nowhere." He closes his eyes and then opens them wide, boring the truth into what vessel would take it. "I found the packet and drove to the drop-off. I've been doing this to get out of debt, which I can't, and for what reason? I hate my life. But leaving will get me killed."

****

There's a knock on the door, and it opens, revealing Detective Ropp. "Joanne, Michael Laysan is here. Detective Johnsrud, should I let him know to wait?"

"Joanne, we couldn't match your fingerprints to those in the car left in Alpine National Park, and unless you gained thirty pounds and wore gloves, it appears you were never in that car. We may have other questions, but you are free to go."

I stand, shake the hands of both detectives and walk to where Michael waits. "Good to see you. Thanks for picking me up," I say as I follow him up the stairs and into the warm summer night. Michael walks over to the Rover and opens the passenger door. I slide in and watch him, still hobbling from my kick.

He starts the engine and then puts it into gear. Ahead of us, the stoplight pulses with a yellow light, and I glance at my watch. "It's late."

Two minutes later, we arrive at the cottage, and he opens his door. I open mine, curious as to what he could want. I stop, the streetlamp behind me elongating my shadow. "How did it go? Were you able to find the drop site from the card's coordinates?"

"Inside. I think this is best with some port, don't you?" Michael strides up the sidewalk and opens the porch door.

Pursing my lips, I scold myself for not asking for his house keys back when he moved in with Jessamine. I follow him inside.

He walks to the liquor cabinet and pulls out his grandmother's port glasses and the handblown bottle of port. He pours the ruddy liquid into the glasses and hands me one. "This evening's intended adventure was a bust, but it did provide clarity in other matters."

"Michael," I say, setting the glass down, "I'm exhausted. Can we meet for breakfast in the morning after we both have had some sleep?"

My reflexes are way off as he steps up to me, puts down his glass, and kisses me. There's been no invitation, but his lips find mine, and his hands hold me tight.

I attempt to pull back, and as he releases me, he says in a voice so soft, I'm sure I misheard him, "I love you, and I want you."

The second kiss is exploratory, starting on my cheek and moving to my lips.

"I can't. You and Jessamine—"

"Never were. Believe that. All those letters, all of my poems, I'm here. I love you, and I'm here. Believe me."

Chapter Fifteen

Planning was involved.

Forty-five minutes later, Michael rolls over on his side, not bothering to cover his torso. In my bedroom, with only the dim light offered by the streetlamp on the corner, his arm forms a shadow on the wall. "The grasses wave a greeting of surrender, the winds of longing stroke the blades in a labor of love. Rough-hewn granite, forged of dimmed heat..." he says before rolling onto his back.

"Oh, who is that? Please continue," I say, nestling into his chest.

"I made it up now. It's a work in progress."

I laugh and tickle his chest. "Best work on that."

"Oh, I have plans to work on a lot of things, but I do have to tell you about the coordinates you gave me," he says, his voice changing from tender to one more business-like.

"The coordinates are for a location forty miles from here. I parked behind a tear-down cabin. The front door has a work permit for the You Who Foundation posted on it. That's your new client, right?"

I nod. "The Conservation Authority is allowing a children's camp to be built on that land."

"Over the horizon, a light moved quickly toward me. As it neared the cabin, it pulsed, hovering over the trees. I got out of the car and heard a faint buzzing sound. The light came closer to the ground, and a drone's form took shape. A mechanism on the drone's legs opened—

it was a quick movement—and a package shrouded in white dropped near the front porch. The drone rose, and in a few seconds, all that was left to see were two blinking red lights."

"So, our theory about the trappers' cabins is correct. We have to tell the police!" I say, suddenly not sleepy.

Michael's hand reached out to mine to quiet me. "An ATV came out of the woods, heading for the cabin, but when the driver saw my car, it turned around and disappeared."

"Did you chase it? What kind of ATV? It's like what Linda Taylor talked about. She'd seen a clearing and ATV tracks in the dirt. You are on to who is behind this. It has to be Paul."

"I picked up the package and dropped it off at the coordinate. It was packaged well enough that whatever was inside wouldn't leak out. I think it's cocaine. I contacted people in that lookout to watch for vehicles in the area."

"Wait? You dropped it off? Why not go to the police? Wouldn't you be able to lure the people behind it that way by keeping the package? Jessamine—"

"Yes, Jess, they prefer Jess. I dropped the packet under a pine tree, walked back to my car, and then went to the police station to get you." Michael strokes my clavicle.

"I need sleep!" I say, but I want him to keep talking. And let's face it, other things as well.

"Are you sleepy? Do you need sleep?" His voice, throaty and full, suggests he is wide awake.

And I forget any need for sleep, too.

****

I awake to voices in the kitchen.

Pushing aside the rumpled bedding, I slide out and tiptoe to the bathroom to put on my robe. Foregoing the use of the railing, which will give a telltale squeak, I softly pad far enough down the stairs to eavesdrop on Jessamine, er, Jess, and Michael talking.

"The arrangements are designed for a certain appearance. You knew that is part of the assignment," says Michael.

I suck in my breath.

"We make a great team inside and outside of this assignment. I thought, after the lookout, we were moving forward," says Jessamine.

My head hitting the stairwell's wall ceases that conversation.

"You are such a jerk, Michael! All the pretty words and the poetry. All of it!" I say, stomping down the stairs and marching into the kitchen.

Jess wears a ball cap, jeans, and a running jacket. They hold a cup of to-go coffee in their hand.

I walk next to them, putting my hands on my hips, my chin raised. "You can't do that. Not to me and not to them," I say, pointing to Jess. "I'll make this simple for you, Michael. I'll have nothing more to do with you. Not now, not ever. We are not friends, we are not pen pals, we are not lovers, and you cannot take advantage of people when they are vulnerable."

Jess slides a look at Michael and, without a word, strides out of the cottage.

"Michael, you need to leave." I raise my hand. Biting my lip, I walk back upstairs to get dressed for work. The bathroom shower drowns out my tears and cries of frustration. Toweling off, I repair my red eyes and blotchy skin as best I can, all the while listening for movement downstairs.

Unlike in the movies, Michael is not waiting for me, and he has not left a note. Walking into the kitchen, I catch a whiff of coffee. I collect my purse and follow the scent. Jess, er, Jessamine, has left their cup of coffee on the laundry room counter.

When I open the back door—and in my mood, it seems to fit—there is a chill in the air. Walking along the side of the cottage, I catch sight of Wally Harmon. He carries a box of donuts as if he were turning in a science project that he's proud of. He stops and, balancing the box carefully, raises a hand in greeting.

I lope across the street and join him.

"We have a board meeting at the bank. You'll probably hear about it around the water cooler, but I thought you should hear it from me first. With Dan's passing, we are posting his position within the bank internally and will post it externally within a few days. You are, of course, welcome to apply. Bob Porter has unexpectedly resigned from his position on the board, even though he was scheduled to retire at the end of the year, so we are submitting Paul Allegretti's name as a bank board member."

"I see." Pretending, probably badly, that I know nothing about Bob or Paul. "I am glad you are letting me know." I glance at the box of donuts and breathe in the scent. "Wally, if I didn't know any better, I would say the bakery is nearly replicating the huckleberry bear claws baked at the Lodgepole Ferry Merc."

"They are from the Merc. I was up that way this morning. One of my logging truck drivers had a personal matter that came up and needed to leave. We are short-staffed, so I caught a ride with one of my drivers and stopped at the Merc just as they opened," he says with a toothy grin.

"It will be difficult to replace Dan," I say. "Please let me know how I can help. If the board has questions about Dan's portfolio, I'll be glad to let you know what I know."

Notably missing from our conversation is the easy camaraderie from a week ago when the You Who Foundation presentation occurred. Of course, in that week, my boss had died, my nemesis had disappeared, I'd found out that reports regarding the bank's liquidity were being forged, and I couldn't trust the people I considered to be the closest to me.

"Are you making headway with the You Who Foundation?" asks Wally.

Finally, a bright spot. "Yes, I am. I was able to work with the documentation you gave me and upload the information to our main server in Winding Creek, Colorado. Abbie has been a big help," I say, watching for and receiving the expected relaxed smile from Wally.

"We are so proud of her," he says. "She goes the extra mile. She can be counted on to show up."

We arrive at Winding Creek Bank. Despite my distinct feeling that Abbie has complained and I'm being reprimanded, I smile at Wally. "Yes, Abbie is a treasure. I'll be sure to tell her what you said."

Wally's phone rings, and he stops and waves me off.

The three-story windows of the bank reflect the Kennedy Mountain Range, the rooftop bar of the Snowshoe Hare, and Wally, who has put the box of bear claws on top of a car and is glaring at me.

In the one hundred feet from where Wally stands to the bank's front door, his conversation has been responsive. Only when I reach the front door and open it do I hear my name and the words "fired for cause."

****

"Good morning," says Abbie, juggling a paper coffee tray, two pastries, a banded packet of mail, and her purse. "Do you know what the board will do now that Dan is…" Her chin trembles as she looks around to place the drinks and sweets.

The tray looks like it will tip any second, drenching the picture of Thew and me, so I lunge, grabbing the drinks not a second too soon as the taller drink begins to tip. The hot coffee splashes my hand as I set the drinks on my desk.

"I walked with your uncle, Wally. He's bringing bear claws for the bank's board meeting. I'm sure he's already told you, but I think I should chime in, too. Your work is not going unnoticed. I appreciate your help."

Abbie drops her bag on the floor. "I'm sorry—" She puts the pastries on top of the tray of coffee and checks her coat pocket, pulling out a tissue. "I'm a mess. I can't believe that Dan is gone. They'll be giving you the job, right?" She blows, then wipes her nose and sets down the pile of mail on the edge of my desk. "Let me get some paper towels to clean the mess. The coffee nearly got your favorite photo."

"No worries," I say with a smile. "Thew and I are dry. Go ahead and put your bag and coat away, and we can go through the mail together." She turns to leave and then stops. "I do hope you are considering applying for the job."

"Thanks," I say. I stand with my back to the door over the mail, unbanding, then riffling through the leaflets, brochures, and catalogs, looking for a square

221

envelope. Two-thirds of the way down, I spot one addressed to Dan and slide it under one of my Current Project folders.

"Are you looking for something in particular?" asks Abbie, who has walked up behind me and is peering over my shoulder.

Good thing she can't see my face. "Nothing in particular. I looked through this stack"—my fingers grasp the mail—"and I think you can work on these," I say, as I place oil and gas envelopes into her arms. "You've been here long enough to do most of these. Let me know if you run into a problem." With that, I sit down, pulling the rest of the pile in front of me.

"Okay," she says, a seed of doubt in her voice. "Has anyone talked to Pam or Dan's family about the, uh, arrangements?"

"I suspect I know less than you, Abbie. I heard about Dan yesterday afternoon," I say, my lower teeth biting my upper lip. I shake my head. "I know the board of directors are meeting. I'm sure one of them, or more likely, the police, has contacted Pam and Dan's family. It's funny, I don't know anything about Dan except that he was kind and a good boss." My chin quivers as I recall the tormented man I'd seen in the video and the veiled threat he made in my living room. It is best to focus on the man I knew when I first started working for him. I give my head another shake. "Let's work through this pile of mail. It will probably help us cope."

Abbie leaves but a few minutes later knocks on my door. "Why would Iris Blackrail's mail be sent here?"

I should ask, "Who?" Or better yet, be so good at my disguise that I can look up without a trace of a tell and say, *"Oh, she was before my time, but we still get mail for her. I can forward it to her, or you can throw it out."*

Those thoughts come seconds after I raise my head a little too fast, suck in my breath a little too sharp, and break into a sweat. The best I can come up with is to give her a frown.

"Sorry, I thought you might know. I'll check with the others in the bank." She disappears.

Take a breath, Joanne. And another one. Breathe. Breathe. The only people who know about her don't work here.

Checking my watch, I see my heartbeat has slowed, though my stomach still churns. *Fake it 'til you make it! Take another breath.* I bring envelopes from oil and gas companies over to her desk. She looks up at me.

"You said Iris, right?" I ask, trying to pass for a person who has wracked her brain for an answer.

"Yes, Iris Blackrail. Do you know her?" Abbie's fingers stop dancing across the keyboard.

"Sorry, I should have asked if you are working on a project. I don't remember her, but I think there was a Blackrail in one of the other branches—"

"I checked the company directory, and no Blackrails are working for Winding Creek," she says, glancing at an envelope. The upper corner of the logo peeks out from under a Post-it note, and I relax. When I get my computer back, I will go to the Windsor Hotel's website and get Iris' address updated to my post office box.

"Okay, I must have been mistaken. Here are some projects that you can help with. If you have questions, let me know."

As I step into my office, a chill runs down my back. I'd paid cash for drinks at the conference in London.

Bolton's Valor paid for the registration, and the conference hosts covered the hotel and food. But that cover is gone, and I walked into a trap. Or maybe I missed walking into a trap. My response could make me look guilty and lead the police wrongly to the conclusion that I am Dan's killer.

****

"Joanne, can you join us in the conference room, please?"

I look up from the division order I'm calculating to see Alan Greene's hand poised in mid-knock.

"Alan," I say, my insides squirming as he scans my office. I don't have a metal cabinet to get my face slammed up against, but I don't think that would matter to him. He'd find a way to make me feel insignificant.

He tilts his head, catching sight of the picture of Thew and me. For a second, or maybe I only imagined its length, he looks away. I don't know if Thew talked to him after I returned the car, but Alan and I hadn't had an entire conversation in nearly two decades.

Wally Harmon appears behind Alan.

I rise. "Oh, of course. Do I need to bring anything?" I take a pen and a pad of paper from my desk's drawer. As I join Alan and Wally, I recall that I have never once seen Dan take a pen or paper with him to any meeting. I look like a receptionist. Or someone who can be manipulated.

Bob Porter and two women whom I recognize from corporate newsletters stand next to the conference table. Bob nods at me.

"I'm Constance Parrazzo. It's a pleasure to meet you, Joanne. This is Bonnie Sanchez, our human resources liaison," she says with a warm smile. "Please have a seat."

Alan, Wally, and Bob walk around the table and sit down. Constance and Bonnie flank me. Bonnie has placed a leather folder on the table and slides it to herself. She pushes her seat back so that she can talk to me and the others without having to swivel too much.

Constance sits to my left. She has placed her hands on the table, though her knuckles are risen and white. She clears her throat and begins. "We've been dealt a blow with Dan's passing. We have reached out to his family and will be creating a scholarship fund in his memory. You will see a notification soon. Of course, his death has consequences, as I understand that he considered his team as part of his family. Please consider counseling options. Bonnie will be able to assist you in that regard. Bonnie? Do you have anything to add?"

"Thank you, Constance. I understand that Dan's family has arranged for the funeral to be held in Snowshoe at the local Lutheran church the day after tomorrow. The mineral department will be closed that day out of respect for the family and his friends. We understand what a shock this might be, so we are letting you know that part of your health options is counseling. We urge you to consider using it should you feel overwhelmed by this tragedy."

This seems so canned. It's as if they memorized a speech and are now performing it.

I'm studying the dynamics and coming up blank. Bob is the chairman of the local bank's board, and after the conversation I had with him about Allegro and his retirement, I'm working out who will take over. Would it be Alan or Wally?

"I guess I do have questions," I say, looking at Bob

first, who licks his lips, and then to Alan, who is looking not so much at me as past me, and on to Wally, who isn't giving me a read. That he is neutral has me worried.

"Yes? What would you like to know, Joanne?" asks Bonnie.

Choose your words carefully. "Thank you for bringing me in on this meeting and for the information on Dan's funeral. I'm glad to be a part of the transition team. Abbie has been working with me to get acquainted with Dan's accounts, but I understand the need to bring a person in to handle the overload. I look forward to being a part of that hiring process." *Oh, to hell with it. It's time to shake out some things.*

I don't look at Constance or Bonnie but at Bob as I continue. "Since Dan was a member of the bank's board of directors, would my role be expanded to match his portfolio of business and to join the board in his capacity? I also understand that with Bob's retirement"—Bob blanches and Constance's knuckles turn white as I say this—"Paul Allegretti is being considered for a position on the board. Who will be the new board chairman?"

"My, you are such a take-charge person, Joanne," says Alan, his speech and eyes placid.

For a second, I'm back in his office, my face slammed against the metal cabinet, his hands on me.

And now, I'm not. As my eyes pass from Alan to Bob and on to Wally, I hear Michael's voice in my head. *You are better than you know. Use that. Use that.*

"Thank you, Alan. Constance and Bonnie, I have worked with or known these three men in some capacity, dealing with them inside and outside the bank. I've known Wally the longest—since I was a child. I briefly

worked for Alan when I was young and full of promise,"
I say with a mischievous smile, getting laughter from
everyone but Alan, who narrows his eyes. I turn to Bob.
"Bob and I have worked together on projects here at the
bank. In fact, Bob, I will be working on the report we
went over last week."

I laugh. "You could say, no, you should say, that
when you work or know people as long as I have, like
with these three men, you get to know things about them.
Oh, the stories I could tell!" I say this with the best
beguiling smile I can as I turn to Constance and Bonnie.
"What plans do you have for the department, and how
can I help you?"

*Oh, go ahead. Fire me. Go ahead. See what
happens.*

****

Constance smiles benignly at me—reaching for, but
not touching—my hand, and I realize that I've missed
my target.

The corners of Alan's mouth raise in the faintest hint
of a smile. He looks down for a second and then levels
his gaze to meet mine.

Wally's face remains placid, and then he smiles as
he looks past me.

"Joanne? You have visitors," says Abbie, who has
opened the conference room door. "They said it was
urgent."

I swivel and rise from my chair. "I apologize," I say
to the group, but Alan says, "Well, we certainly can't
fight urgent matters, now can we?"

My paranoia rises as the conference door closes with
a definite *click*, and I am sure I hear laughter. Abbie turns
her head toward me as we walk back to my office. "Linda

227

Taylor is here with Georgina Hinerman, and so is Detective Johnsrud. I'd put them in the conference room, but… We don't have an empty office."

Linda and Georgie rise from chairs next to Abbie's desk. "We can come back, if you like. Detective Johnsrud, please, you go ahead first."

I look at Detective Johnsrud, who nods at the cousins. "I need to ask Joanne a few questions. It shouldn't take more than twenty or thirty minutes, tops."

"Oh, we can be back in an hour. That's no problem," says Georgie. They wave at me and say, "See you soon."

"The conference room is busy right now, but we can use my office if that's convenient," I say, walking over to my office and opening the door. "Please have a seat."

She sits, glancing at my desk and the pile of mail, then around the room.

I close my office door and then walk over to my desk phone to mute my calls. I sit, looking for a clue as to what this conversation will be about. "How can I help you today?"

"A device and a note were sent to our offices, specifically to my attention. The note is anonymous but states that the monitoring device is from your car, insinuates clear proof of your part in the disappearance of Pam Clayton, and implicates you in the death of Dan Werner. The note goes on to implicate your boyfriend, Michael Laysan." Detective Johnsrud states this as if she is reporting what she had for breakfast.

"What? That's impossible!" I shout. "I don't know where or if Pam is dead. Has her body, or has she been found?" I ask, going over what to say next and wondering if I need a lawyer because I've done nothing wrong.

"The reason I'm here and we aren't meeting at the precinct is because we already talked to Michael. He told me about the bugging of your car, who placed it there, and why. I followed up with his information, and it checked out. Still, you could be called as a witness, so Detective Ropp and I are going over any threads we might have overlooked."

"So, I'm innocent. That's what you are saying? I don't know what to say." My mouth hangs open as the shock rolls over me. "You talked to Michael, who cleared me, but you barge in here and make me think I'm being arrested? I think I'm going to be sick. Have you found Pam?" I ask again. "Who put the tracking device on my car? Did Michael tell you that?"

"I can't comment on an ongoing investigation. I need to know how familiar you are with Heaven's Rest Road," she says as if my outburst means nothing.

"I went out to the boat launch parking lot on that road last week. My father and I used to go out there to fish, and it was near a huckleberry patch that my family used when I was little." I stop, considering why I had gone out there in the first place. "Heaven's Rest Road is also where Paul Allegretti owns a blockhouse garage that Wally Harmon uses to store his boat. I showed you the pictures I took of Dan's Audi in the garage. That was when Wally helped me with my car."

"Have you traveled by car or by foot any farther north on Heaven's Rest Road?" she asks.

I shake my head. "No." Thinking about any unusual places I did drive. I might as well set the record straight. "I did drive to Lodgepole Ferry to meet Michael and left my car overnight in the Mercantile's parking lot. When I retrieved the car, it didn't appear to have been disturbed. Michael told me my car was bugged while we were at MacFarland Lake, though I don't know why he would have known about that. I assumed Michael placed the bug on my car because maybe he didn't think he could trust me.

"When I was told about Dan's death, Michael, Jess, and I were taking my car to the garage to have the battery replaced. I remembered I had left my Bolton's Valor-issued computer in the trunk, so we went back to get it. I noticed it had been moved, so I contacted the company about the computer being compromised, and they remotely deactivated it. I didn't worry about it because there is no way Wally could break into the data," I say. "Wally is in the conference room. You could ask him why he took it out of my car, but more than likely, he will say that it was to protect it from being stolen by a person working at the garage when the car's battery is being replaced. He's an old friend of our family, so he was being his normal protective self."

"I see," says Detective Johnsrud, but from her tone, it's clear she has crowned me the Queen of the Idiots. "When was the last time you visited the huckleberry patch on Heaven's Rest Road?"

"I haven't been there in a long time, probably ten years or more. After my father's death, I didn't want to go back out there. It was 'our' spot, and the place made me sad. It's where I met Pam when I was a little girl. When my friend Belle recorded Pam's conversation with her hairdresser and how she was meeting Alan Greene by the huckleberry patch, I put two and two together."

Detective Johnsrud is an excellent poker player. She takes what I say without a reaction.

I continue. "Alan Greene is also in the conference

room. You might want to ask him if he drives a blue crossover car, if he can confirm that he and Pam were having an affair, and if they were meeting by the huckleberry patch."

"We've talked to Alan Greene," Detective Johnsrud says stiffly.

"And?" I ask. "Does he drive a blue crossover? Did he confirm that he was having an affair with Pam Clayton?"

Detective Johnsrud goes still. "Did you have an affair with him?" she asks, and in that question, I finally find the courage to lay down a decades-old burden.

I draw in a breath, picking off a piece of lint from my shirt, and then look up at her. "When I was seventeen, not long after my mother died, I worked for Alan Greene, cleaning his office. My mother's car was old, and Dr. Greene bought me a new car. And he raped me."

"Did you—?"

I hold up my hand. "I returned the car, never reported the attack, except to my best friend and eventually my dad, and this was way before testing kits, so no, it would be his word against mine." I drop my head, drawing slow breaths to calm myself. "The car salesman's daughter was Pam Sethway. Later, she became Pam Clayton. She heard about the sale from her dad and then spread rumors that I was Alan Greene's mistress." I run my tongue along my upper lip.

After a few seconds, I raise my eyes to hers. "I have done everything in my power to keep a distance between him and me. But now, he's using this story to get me fired."

"I can't comment on an ongoing investigation. You should have reported it and gotten help, but I can understand why you chose another path or did what you thought would bring you peace. Different times. Joanne, I am truly sorry."

She straightens in her chair, bringing her hands to her knees. "Your roommate is an out-of-the-box thinker."

"You can say he's weird," I say, a smile coming to my lips, and we both laugh.

"He has given us maps of birds—"

"The ravens and pack rats. One of the raven's nests is near the huckleberry patch. His theory is that the raven flew with the finger on the winds toward Snowshoe, dropping it near my cottage and going to get a fish head from the restaurant a block away from me. The packrat's range is small."

"He went over this with you?" she asks, and I nod.

"Once he gets a theory into his head, he's not one to give it up. But it actually makes sense," I say.

"How did you find out your car was bugged?"

"Michael told me when I went to Lodgepole Ferry. He's secretive about his work, though I don't understand why. It's a grizzly habitat study, but I didn't ask any other questions. I don't use the car very much, so, well, now that I think about it, I've been incredibly naïve. I should ask questions."

"Or you put your trust in a person who you have known for a very long time. Maybe that was it?"

As I think about Michael's arms around me and his kisses, I nod. "Yes, I believe that is it."

Detective Johnsrud pushes off of her knees and stands up. She extends her hand to me as she opens the door. "Thank you for talking to me. You've added a lot to the investigation. It looks like your next guests are here."

****

From my office door, the cousins could pass for twins. The brocade bag lays at Georgie's feet, and she leans toward Linda, motioning with her index finger. As I step closer, I hear her instructions to Linda. "Not too tight, that's right. Tip your needle down for a purl and up for a knit." She takes the needles from Linda's hands and then breaks out in a broad grin as she sees me. The knitting drops into the brocade bag, and Georgie stands, opening her arms. I walk with my hand outstretched, but she's having none of it. "Come here! It's wonderful to see you. I'm working with Linda on a knitting project."

Linda shakes her head. "I'll never get how yarn and two needles can befuddle a person so. We are sorry to hear of Dan's death," she says, and Georgie shakes her head too. "I've spoken to Paul and have put in a good word for you to be his replacement and to be placed on the board of directors."

Georgie motions to my office. "Can we talk in there? We need to address some issues that have arisen in the past few weeks."

"Of course," I say, "let's see how I can help you."

Georgie reaches down and picks up her brocade bag and purse. The three of us walk into my office, and I motion for Abbie to join us.

A few seconds later, Abbie squeezes into my office. "I want to introduce you to Abbie, who has been working with me on Dan's projects. We continue to work on his projects, and as soon as an additional person is hired, we will let you know about that, too."

Linda and Georgie turn to Abbie. "It's nice to meet you. We will be talking to you soon, but we need to talk to Joanne about another issue. I'm sure Joanne will bring you in on it, but we need her advice in private."

Abbie's smile loses wattage. She backs out of the office as if she has been spanked and told to sit in a corner.

"I'm bringing Abbie in on Dan's accounts, so making her acquaintance is important," I say, just loud enough for Abbie to hear as Georgie closes my door.

"You've met my assistant, Jess," says Georgie.

"I have," I say. "They introduced themselves to me several days ago. Do we need them to be looped in on what you need to speak to me about?"

"Jess urged Linda to get to know Paul Allegretti better," says Georgie. "We have always received offers to buy our assets. We ignore those but have always sent lease offers along with bids to purchase timber and ranch management issues to Winding Creek."

"I don't know how to wade into this except just to do it," says Linda. "Do you know about the diamond sale?"

"As I understand it, a trapper had an account with Winding Creek Bank. His wife, who I believe he was estranged from, died. The wife owned a large diamond that was in a vault in a bank in Washington State, not affiliated with Winding Creek. Our bank was trying to acquire the trapper's account and then buy the diamond from the bank in Washington."

"Yes," says Georgie, "that's the gist of it. But we are involved."

"Your family is involved? How?" I ask. "Did Paul ask you to invest?"

Both women nod.

"Paul mentioned the diamond to me and called

Georgie," says Linda. "But he made a major mistake. The estranged wife was our aunt—Josef and Edvard's sister, Janicke. For years, we had heard stories about her. She came to the United States and eloped with a man who was seeking his fortune in what we thought was Alaska. Being a trapper or miner's wife was not to her liking, but being a dutiful spouse, she agreed to go to Seattle and board a steamer to Skagway, Alaska. The last correspondence the family got was a postcard from Spokane, Washington. And then she disappeared."

"Go on," I say. "She was found somewhere else?"

Georgie picks up a strand of her knitting and knits, continuing the story. "When Paul mentioned the large diamond in the safe deposit box to both Linda and me, we realized this was no coincidence. The family story we heard was that it was a large diamond. It has to be the same one." She starts another row of knitting, her needles flying across the row as she speaks. "I had Jess contact the bank in Lake Chelan and had them check their records. The name had changed, but the birthdate on the initial documents of ownership of the safe deposit box was the same as was the handwriting."

"It belongs to the Hinerman family?" I ask.

"The diamond was a gift to Janicke from an admirer, a budding Western artist, who had courted her. The admirer had gotten paid for his art with what the buyer had, which was a diamond," said Georgie, giving me a sly smile.

"Frederick Remington was an admirer of your aunt? And then she ran off with a miner slash trapper instead," I say. "I suppose you have documentation that can support this? Old love letters? A letter of bequeathment?"

Georgie reached into the bottom of her knitting bag and pulled out a packet of letters tied with a bow. "These had been sent to the Historical Society in Lake Chelan. Jess went there to check if Janicke had a will and how the death and descendency laws in Washington work. I have set a meeting with the county's probate judge for next week to get a ruling on the matter."

"Linda, did you tell Paul about your aunt?" I ask, thinking of the conversations Dan had with Alan and what it cost him.

She swallows, then looks from Georgie to me. "I didn't connect the investment with Janicke until Georgie called me after Paul had contacted her. We thought the story about the Remington connection was just that—a story. But then Jess dug into it and retraced Janicke's steps."

Georgie digs into the knitting bag and pulls out a manila folder. "Janicke changed her name to Jane while she lived in Lake Chelan. Her marriage certificate was in the name of Janicke Hinerman, and she was married to Fritz Grebel. Janicke became Jane Smith in Lake Chelan. Plain vanilla Jane Smith."

Opening the folder, she lays it on the desk in front of me. "Here is a picture of Janicke Hinerman with her brothers Edvard and Josef."

I look at the young woman between the tall, thin man with the mustache I had seen in Georgie's paintings and sculptures and a larger young man. All three shared the same eye shape as Linda and Georgie.

"Here are the naturalization records filed by Jane Smith." The photograph on the second page of the record shows an unsmiling woman in a high-necked dress. Gone was the carefree girl in the other picture. But the shape of her eyes and the handwriting on the naturalization and the bound letters looked to be a spot-on match.

Linda and Georgie had not answered my question. "Does Paul know that the Hinerman family are the heirs? Does he know that he cannot have the diamond sold because the heirs have come forward?"

"I don't think it matters," says Linda. "It was a small part of Paul's portfolio."

"Dan died because of that diamond. He was a mule smuggling cocaine and all to be a part of Paul's diamond investment," I say, tears pricking my eyes. "Dan's dead because of this." Tears course down my cheeks, and I don't want to stop them. "You get the diamond, and you do what you will with it, but I think you should not have any more to do with Paul. I'm sure he had my friend, my boss, murdered."

I stand, placing my hands on the edge of the desk. "Go. Go get your diamond." I'm shaking as tears cascade down my cheeks. "Please leave. Please."

They leave without a word, and I shut my office door. I sit at my desk and find the two square envelopes. Pulling out the card that has the coordinates on it, I hatch my plan to be rid, once and for all, of the person or persons behind Dan and Pam's murders.

Chapter Sixteen

"You've had a lot of visitors today," says Abbie. "Can I take you to lunch? My treat." She holds a document in her hand. "I have a question about this Authorization for Expenditure. A letter was included, informing us this is a demand for signature. I'm confused as to why."

"Yes, I'd like that, though we can certainly split the bill. It's nice of you to offer. When do you want to go?" I hold out my hand, and Abbie gives me the AFE. Flipping the pages of the document to the expected expenditures reveals the reason for the demand.

"Working interest owners are the investors in the well or wells. A Joint Operating Agreement, called a JOA, is a document that outlines what actions the operator of the well should take to keep the wells operating. The JOA is sent to all of the investors. Typically, the operator only needs sixty-five percent of the owners to agree to the work that needs to be done. There are two exceptions."

I look up at Abbie to see if she is tuning out, but she leans over my desk as I point to the description of the work. "One exception is when the well is being drilled to a new formation, which is called a recompletion. The other exception is when the well is scheduled to be plugged and abandoned. In those cases, all owners must agree to the work."

"What happens if an investor doesn't agree to the

proposed work?" asks Abbie.

"The owner is deemed as going non-consent. The other investors take over the investment, and the owner gets a reduced amount until his portion of the investment is recouped. Or they can be barred from future investments until their debt is paid."

I stare past Abbie as an idea hits me. "Can we have lunch in an hour? I have an idea that I need to mull over."

"Oh, of course," says Abbie, turning back toward her desk. "I can work on the division orders that came in."

Paul Allegretti's drug cartel would certainly not have a JOA. There are no written codes of conduct or a list of investors, but what would happen if other investors had to pick up the slack in case one owner didn't pay their bills or died? Would payments from Paul to the investors change?

I suspect my personal telephone is being monitored. Phone calls from the bank should be tied to a client's activity. My Bolton's Valor-issued phone is deactivated, which leaves one person to contact to get a message to my contact in Cheyenne Mountain's encryption offices. Or I can do this face-to-face.

Five minutes later, I knock on the door of the Storybook-styled house. I listen for—and hear—a movement inside the home. Jess opens the front door and, after looking around me, ushers me inside.

"I need to get a message to Cheyenne Mountain. I don't know if you have clearance in that direction, but I need to know if Paul Allegretti's account, either personally or under Allegro, can be monitored. I'm looking for variances in their payments to its investors and who the recipients were. I also want to know about

Alan Greene's accounts and if he has accounts other than his account with Winding Creek."

"Hello to you, too," says Jess. "How's Michael?"

I bite my upper lip. "Complicated," I say, offering a slight shrug and smile. "I don't know what to make of him."

"I understand that," they say, giving me the once-over. "I can't make promises because my work is in a different sector, but I can let you know. Sooner rather than later? That's how soon you want it, right?"

"How will you let me know you have information?"

"You'll receive a phone call on your personal phone from a telemarketer in Boise, Idaho. I'll leave a voicemail about an extended warranty and mention a length of time. Meet me at Maple District Park at that time." Jess holds the door handle in their hand. "Don't say thank you. I haven't promised that I can do this, only that I will try."

Five minutes later, I return to the bank and go over to Abbie's desk. "Ready for lunch?"

****

"Hennessey's Steak House only recently began offering a lunch menu," says Abbie as we leave the bank. "I've wanted to try their sandwiches."

"Me, too," I say. Abbie's demeanor is more upbeat than an hour ago, and I take this as a good sign as we cross the street to the restaurant.

We join a half-dozen people in line.

"Oh, there's my Uncle Wally ahead of us," says Abbie.

At the mention of his name, he turns back and beams at us as Abbie moves in for a hug. "I'd planned a business lunch with these guys." Pointing to a man and woman I don't recognize. "I'd invite you to join us, but I'm afraid it'd be boring. Imagine an hour of my droning on about forestry permits and harvest totals to my favorite niece and favorite choir member. Sorry. But let's plan a rain check." Wally leans over, kisses Abbie on the head, and pats my arm. "I'll stop by on Sunday after church," he says as Abbie grins. "Tell your mother to make that famous huckleberry glazed pork roast of hers."

"Busy place," I say, craning my neck to see if I recognize anyone. "Do you know the people with your Uncle Wally?"

"He mentioned he was meeting investors in one of his companies," she says.

"Ah, I see," I say, chewing on how I want to ask more questions but without sounding nosy, which I am.

Wally and his investors are seated, and a few minutes later, we are seated at the table behind them. I take the seat directly behind Wally. The waitress hands us menus, and I scan mine, looking for the sandwich Abbie had mentioned and looking for an opportunity to eavesdrop on what Wally is talking about so I can speak to Michael about forestry in a more knowledgeable fashion.

"What are you ordering?" I ask as the waitress fills our water glasses.

"The Snowshoe Sidewinder," she says with a grin. "That's a silly name for a steak sandwich."

I laugh. "It does sound good. I think I'll have one of those."

The woman with Wally is talking about the Forest Service and its use of drones to determine a good harvesting area. The man chimes in, giving a laundry list of features that Elizabeth Logging could use to their advantage.

Wally says he has to use the washroom and stands. As he passes our table, he leans down to whisper in my ear. "I told you it would be boring. There's no need to eavesdrop." He then pats my shoulder and squeezes Abbie's as he passes by.

My cheeks flame in embarrassment. I didn't think I'd been obvious. Abbie looks at me and then at her uncle.

I shake my head as if it was a joke. "I couldn't help myself. Don't tell your uncle I said this, but I wouldn't mind learning more about the timber business. He's so smart."

Abbie looks over her shoulder as Wally disappears into the washrooms and then back at me. "He is. Most of the manufacturing is done overseas, but he keeps plugging away at it."

I nod, saved from a further comment, as the waitress comes to our table. As she takes Abbie's order, the woman at Wally's table says, "This is the third time I've tried to get a meeting with him, and frankly, I'm surprised. He's always using the excuse about declining timber sales in the US and how he's just straggling along. But this year, he has cash, and he wants to invest in our company. He wants some of the orders to be sent to Elizabeth Logging and some of the orders to go to a new LLC he's formed."

Wally comes from the washroom and glad-hands his way back to his table, avoiding any contact with our table. As he sits, the woman asks about the new LLC he has formed and where the drones will be used.

"I'll be changing my permitting with the Forest Service soon. I'll let you know when that is done. At any rate, our food is here, and I, for one, am hungry," says Wally in a hearty voice.

My phone vibrates in my purse. I reach down to answer and see that it is a call from Boise, Idaho.

****

"Do you come from a family of golfers, Abbie?" I ask, waiting for the message from Jess to go to voicemail. I lean forward, taking a sip of water. "When did you start playing?"

"Do you play golf, Joanne?" Abbie asks of me, and I shake my head.

"Actually, this is a great opportunity to talk outside of work, but I do need to say how much I appreciate all that you have done. I meant it when I said that higher-ups are noticing your work."

"Thanks," she says, but she doesn't smile.

I lean down as I hear the faint beep of a voicemail on my telephone. "Pardon me, I am expecting a voicemail about an upcoming personal appointment I have, and maybe this is it." I reach into my purse and flip over the phone, tapping in a code. I glance at the time and groan. I have to meet Jess in fifteen minutes.

As I raise my head, I purse my lips in apology, but Abbie is scowling at me. "I'm sorry, Abbie. I will have to cut this short. Let's reschedule, and I will take you to lunch when I have more time."

"It's fine," says Abbie, "just fine." She crosses her arms as the sandwiches arrive. "I'll see if I can sit in with my Uncle Wally, even if it is a boring logging meeting. I probably will learn from him."

"I promise to make it up to you," I say. "I have an appointment that I can't miss. I'll see you back at the office."

As I get out of my chair, I bump into Wally's chair as he's talking about pine beetle pesticides.

He turns and glares at me. "Another rendezvous with an admirer?"

"You're such a rascal, Wally. Abbie, I'll get the lunch, and we can reschedule lunch for another time," I say with a laugh.

****

They sit on a park bench, hands folded on their lap. This time, Jess is wearing a tee shirt and white jeans. Of course, they look fashionable.

"After we're through talking about Boise, I might need styling tips," I say, walking over to the bench.

Jess slides over, their gaze not departing from the Kennedy Range. Their hand pats the seat, and I sit. "Why would anyone want to leave this valley? You really do have it all. I hope you know that."

I slide my eyes over to their face and then drop them. "Can I ask how you met?" I ask, my voice trembling more than I expected.

They look straight ahead. "Michael has told you about the summers he spent with his grandparents in Bretagne, France, and the painting of their cottage?"

"When we were writing, he talked about his grandparents' whitewashed cottage and how he had to paint it every summer with a generations-old lime-wash recipe that went back to the French Revolution," I say, and Jess smiles and nods.

"*Oui*, ah, yes, that's correct. My father is a house painter and had given a bid to paint the house, but Michael's grandmother was a frugal, stubborn woman. It wasn't until Michael fell from a ladder and his grandfather complained of the heat that the old buzzard of a woman relented. I tagged along with my father to get spending money and ended up talking and, later, writing to Michael just like you."

My mouth drops open. I wonder how long Michael has strung us both along. "Let me guess," I say. "He wrote to you because he wanted to improve his French."

"Well, yes, and no. I was beginning to explore my duality, *n'est-ce pas*? My letters were about swimming and school and my time in the Boy Guide program. My duality came later after I left the military and joined Bolton's Valor."

Jess draws a breath. "I'm moving to a new post in Colorado. I interviewed several months ago and spent a long weekend with Michael in the mountains, hiking and reminiscing. Two years ago, when I began working for Georgie in London, I looked him up. I felt a connection and thought he felt the same way. That feeling continued in Colorado. And then he got the post in Snowshoe, and I met you. And I knew that while Michael enjoys my company, his heart lies elsewhere."

"Jess, I never intended—" I break in, but they lean over and pat my arm, still looking at the Kennedy Range. They shake their head.

"You want to know about the coordinates," they say, squaring their shoulders and putting their hand back on their knee. "Don't look at me. I'm going to point, and you're going to follow my finger as if I'm pointing out, oh, I don't know, a different kind of maple tree."

Jess' bicep flexes as they extend a long tapered finger and point at a maple tree thirty feet away. "Paul and Alan have been very busy. They have attempted to gain access to the diamond in Lake Chelan, going so far as to set off a smoke bomb near the bank to create a diversion. How about that for cops and robbers?"

They point their finger in a different direction. "Paul's connections are far wider than we realized. Keep looking straight ahead. He has access to drones and small planes. His connections are like a spiderweb, so we are bringing in a larger network as this trap has to be laid carefully. What this means, and please listen carefully, is for you not to go to Heaven's Rest Road. We have reason to believe that Pam's body is located there." With the tiniest shake of their chin, they silence my questions. "Please stay put. For now, your life as Iris Blackrail is on hold," they say.

I inhale. "I've done nothing wrong! Why would Bolton's do that?"

"It's temporary. We have back channels meant to create the illusion that Pam was Iris. That puts you in the clear. Once this is over, your encryption work will be reinstated."

Jess stands, brushing not only their bottom but reaching behind them to brush invisible dirt from the bench. "One last thing. Keep your head down at Winding Creek Bank. You are the leading candidate for Dan's position, so don't give them any reason to look elsewhere. Go back to work, now."

Chapter Seventeen

I know what Dan would have looked like in thirty years. David Werner, Dan's father, stands to the side of the crowd in St. Olav Church's narthex as the mourners pass by the family, offering their condolences. As each person murmurs a regret, David raises his head, his blue eyes and faded sandy hair nearly the same shade as Dan's. His restless hands pass between pants and coat pockets, a gesture I had forgotten about Dan, but one that makes my eyes sting with tears. Dan's father watches each mourner before reassuming a pose of disappointment.

Pastor Jen's sermon focuses on a life spent with good intentions. She holds up a maple leaf, and for a minute, I think she will ask the congregants to draw its shape and come to a conclusion.

Instead, she holds the leaf up and asks that we consider how maples can withstand harsh conditions and how some offer sweetness to people who draw from their trunks. Jen surveys us, and though I am probably wrong, I feel no grace settling on me as she gazes into the congregation.

"The oak tree is known for its strength, but the maple is known for its grace of movement. In my interactions with Dan, from when he was my raft guide on the river to his work behind the scenes on local arts and beautification projects to his stalwartness in the promotion of the best that Snowshoe and its citizens had to offer, he, like this maple, presented a beautiful grain, clean, supple, and full of potential."

Shirley, the church organist, played "Amazing Grace."

Afterward, as I step closer to where Dan's mother and older sister stand, it is Dan's father that I focus on. He needs. Maybe I will fall short.

David Werner's clasp is polite. He looks past me to the next person, doing his part, filling an unfillable void of grief.

"Mr. Werner, my name is Joanne Corvus. I worked for Dan. He was exceptional. Exceptional as a boss but greater as a friend on whom I could always rely. His void will be hard to fill, but his example will live on."

David Werner's response is wary. He draws back, taking a measure of me with his eyes, his nose drawing in against tears. He has been told of his son's erratic behavior, no doubt wondering if I truly knew him.

"In a way, he lived to a code," I say in a low tone. "He applauded others' successes, and when given a task, he stuck through to the end. In that way, he was and will remain exceptional. I'm sorry for your loss."

I move, my fingers releasing his, but he draws me in for a hug. His cologne is similar to Dan's, and I draw in its scent. His hands grasped my shoulders, and it was as though we drew strength from each other. I blink, and he does the same. Then, his eyes shift to the person behind me.

****

I stand in the narthex. Below me, tables creak in the basement as the last of the mourners and the church's Men's Guild fold up the banquet tables. A metallic slap of the folding chairs and the thump and swish of food, plates, and trash going into garbage cans, all signal the end of Dan's funeral service.

I walk down the steps of the narthex toward the front doors of the church. I could or probably should have asked if I could help. But I hear voices coming from the choir's practice room and draw back. I tread carefully up the stairs back into the narthex and walk over to my church mailbox, hoping for church bulletins to read as I listen to what is being said. My mailbox is empty, but I have picked up a schedule and am pretending to read about the upcoming summer camps at Columbia Lake Bible Camp.

The acoustics coming from the choir room are perfect.

"Have any other letters addressed to Iris Blackrail come to the bank? You're the one who sorts it. Think hard!" My skin crawls at Alan's oily tone. A locker door shuts with a thud. "You're a good girl."

If Abbie is in danger, I'll never forgive myself.

Abbie's laugh also makes my skin crawl. "She, er, Joanne, insists on helping me sort. Preparing me for bigger things, she says. I cover for her constantly. She's always off with that boyfriend of hers. Dan's job should be mine. I've earned it."

I don't dare to breathe, shocked by Abbie's seething anger.

"I'm afraid you'll have to cozy up to her for a while longer. But don't worry, we will set things right. Alan and I will talk to the higher-ups at the bank. We have pull, and they will listen to us. By the way," says Wally, his voice lowering, "if you see any squared-off envelopes that are addressed to Dan, can you be sure to collect them for us? We're in the process of getting the address list updated, but there might be a few stragglers."

"Joanne has taken those," says Abbie.

"Well, get them back. She's not involved in that partnership." Wally's growl is unmistakable. From the tone of his voice, he must have frightened Abbie because his voice changes to a soothing tone. "Dan was involved in an investment. We don't need to include her. Sorry if we scared you."

I tiptoe down the narthex steps, opening the front door of the church as quietly as I can, and run the two blocks from St. Olav's Church to Winding Creek Bank's offices. I fumble with my key to the back door for a few seconds, cursing my clumsiness. The door opens, and I take the steps two at a time before resuming a usual walk.

The mineral management offices are dark, and I unlock my office door. Rifling through my inbox, I put the two square envelopes into my purse. I then walk out of my office, close the door, and walk into the breakroom. Dan's stack of mail is in my bin, and I thumb through it, looking for another square envelope, but I can't find one. I eye Abbie's mailbox and pull out its contents. One square envelope is semi-tucked into the back of a large manila envelope, and I am left to wonder if that was deliberate. Based on the conversation I overheard a few minutes before, I bet that it is.

Slipping that envelope into my purse as well, I walk down the stairs and go into the bathroom. I sit in a stall, close the door, slide out the envelopes, and take out the papers. I photograph each one, then text them to the one person I hope I can trust.

As I leave the bathroom, I bump into a person I should trust.

****

"Can you come over to the station? I have information that might put your mind at ease," says Holly Johnsrud, who has dispensed with formalities. She is not in uniform. Instead, her blonde hair hangs in loose pigtails, and she wears shorts and a form-fitting jacket that a river guide might wear.

"Are you working on your day off?" I ask.

"Andy, er. Detective Ropp thinks he knows where Pam Clayton is. He's getting a search warrant for the premises as we speak, but we thought we would include you since you, in a way, cracked the case for us," she says. "Credit where credit is due."

We walk out of the bank building. An hour before, I'd been in the church comforting myself as much as Dan's family. Now, the detectives have information that is to set my mind at ease.

"I'm the only one holding down the fort in our department. I can't be gone very long, but if it has cracked the case…" I say as Detective Johnsrud gives me a quick shake of her head.

"It will be worth it, I promise," she says, walking to the entrance of the police station and holding the door for me. We descend the stairs, and she waves at the dispatcher, who nods at us. Passing through the cubicles, Detective Johnsrud opens the interview room I'd been to before. Detective Ropp sits at the table, reading from a file. He looks up and smiles at me.

"Andy? Do you want to tell Joanne what you found?" asks Detective Johnsrud, who has dispensed entirely with formalities.

"Joanne, please have a seat. You've had a busy day with Dan's funeral and all, but we caught a break, and we have located Pam's body. We are also arresting Alan

Greene."

"For Pam's murder," I say flatly. "That makes sense. She must have threatened to expose him—"

"No, Alan is being arrested on another matter," he says. "Can you run the surveillance video for us?" he calls, and the room darkens.

"You talked about a blue crossover, but there are a million of those in Columbia Valley. But when the surveillance cameras caught you at the blockhouse, and Paul Allegretti agreed to allow us to see that footage, he didn't realize that in the fine print, he was allowing us to have all the surveillance video. It was surprising since he used the blockhouse for the boat storage, but because that wasn't the only time it was being used. Watch this."

A blue crossover drives on Heaven's Rest Road, but the sun is shining in such a way as to obscure the features of the driver and passenger, who appear to be talking to each other. The time stamp stops and is replaced by photograph stills done in ten-minute intervals. Forty minutes later, the blue crossover goes by, but this time, the driver is unmistakable.

"Belle? What is she doing driving the crossover? She has a VW Bug!" I say, my mouth hanging open.

"Can you roll back the footage three seconds, please?" says Detective Ropp. The video rolls back, and I see Belle wiping her face with her right hand. "Look there! Do you see it?" Millisecond by millisecond, the blue car goes by until I see what is wrong.

I gasp. "There's a dent and a smear on the rear panel on the driver's side! But I don't understand. Belle couldn't stand Pam. Why would they…" I sit back in the chair. "Oh, no. Belle. Belle, no. Alan isn't worth it." I huff a breath and slump in my chair.

The dent and smear are on the screen. I stare hard at the image and then raise my eyebrows at the detectives. "This isn't making me feel better. Pam made fun of Belle for being friends with me after the, uh, you know, thing with Alan when I was in high school." I look down at my hands, noticing a thick sliver of dead skin. I flick at it with my fingers and bring my hand up to my mouth to tear at it.

Detective Ropp pulls a tube of lotion out of his pocket and slides it to me. I look up at the dent and the smear. "Thanks," I say, dabbing my skin and rubbing the lotion in. "But you don't know where the crossover is."

"Actually, we do. I brought my squad car in for an oil change and saw the crossover in the bay next to mine. I walked around it, and sure enough, there was the dent. The blood appeared to be gone, but the dent was still there. I asked the mechanic about it, and he said that Belle had used it when she had a repair done on her VW Bug. He said, 'Yeah, she's been coming in a lot lately for work on that car of hers, and we always let her use our crossover as a loaner. We do that a lot for our customers if they ask.' "

Detective Ropp continues, "I asked if she had admitted to the dent. The mechanic scowled. 'Didn't know a thing about it. It must have been someone else. Oh, and the snow shovel is missing from the trunk. We let that go, but we won't be loaning that car to her anytime soon.' "

"Was there blood in the dent? And does it match Pam?" I ask, and both detectives nod. "So you can pick her up. That's simple. Go to her shop, go to her house."

"She's disappeared. Left a message on her salon phone and catering line saying that she'd been called out of town and that she would be in touch when she can."

"Do you have video or photographs of Alan? He was meeting Pam at the huckleberry patch on Heaven's Rest Road, right?"

Detective Ropp smirked. "Oh yes, we were able to track Alan's comings and goings with not only Pam and Belle but others. Alan likes to think that he is a player, but a high school student from Tamarack has come forward. We have him on video with her on Heaven's Rest Road. The girl's statement says it was not consensual, but it doesn't matter. She is fifteen. Fortunately, she got a kit done. As we speak, his license to practice is being suspended, and charges are being brought against him by the parents of the young woman. That has to give you some satisfaction, I'm sure."

I bow my head as the tears fall.

****

"Can you give me a few minutes, please? This is a lot to take in," I say, my voice barely above a whisper.

The detectives rise, and one of them turns on the lights in the interview room.

"Can you turn them down, please?" I snap. Just as quickly, the lights dim, the door opens and closes with a click, and I'm left to think.

I should feel a sense of victory now that Alan has been arrested. But I recall the moments when I trusted Alan. I wasn't much older than the girl on the surveillance video. I recall the moment the trust was shattered and the disregard, no, the pleasure that Alan had taken toward me. I was powerless. I'm sure the girl was, too.

I think of Dan, who gamely went along with Alan's taunts and dismissed his physical and mental pain as being a challenge he could have overcome. He'd found a way. But he hadn't.

My thoughts turn to Pam. She was a shallow woman, a threatened woman for whom riches and adoration from a man who loved her wasn't enough.

The detective's words about my cracking the case were meant to bolster me. Yes, I did help the police find answers to a crime, but it all rings hollow. I'm left to wonder if I hadn't intruded if Dan and Pam would be alive or if the trajectory of their lives meant that their deaths were inevitable.

A few hours ago, I had sent coordinates to Michael. And now, more than anything in the world, I want to stop him, turn it over to the police, keep Michael safe, and keep us safe. If there was an us, keep us safe.

I open the interview room door and walk toward the police station entrance. Neither Holly nor Andy are around.

Walking outside, I shiver as a cold wind comes from the direction of Snowshoe Lake. From this angle, I believe I can see Thayer Lookout but then give myself a mental shake. Like everyone else, Michael is attending to other matters.

I cross the street, go back inside Winding Creek Bank, and enter my office. I have no new e-mails or new calls, and when I check the mail in the breakroom, my inbox is empty. I sit down at my desk and press on, working on my daily tasks because that's all I have now.

As the traffic hums, I realize that I have been in my office for hours, and no one has come to look for me.

Scanning my phone, I see the pictures I sent to Michael. As I scroll my messages, I find one from Belle that was sent ages ago. *Friends to the end.*

Taking my purse and turning off my office light, I pull the door shut and check the handle. Locked. I walk down the back stairs of the bank toward my cottage. I walk past St. Olav's Lutheran Church. Walking into the cottage, I set my purse on the table, open the refrigerator door, and take out some cheese and wine.

I have to try. I text Belle, take my purse off the table, and take out the car keys. Walking past the garden, I open the garage door, get into my car, and drive in the direction of the coordinates.

I have to try.

****

Fresh ATV tracks run across the road near the You Who Foundation Youth Camp's lone cabin. A metal hut, similar to what Michael and I saw on the way to Lodgepole Ferry, is open as a lanky man slides onto an ATV, gunning the vehicle down a narrow trail. Clods of mud fly up as I follow, but the trail leads into high grass and willows. I pound the steering wheel as I recall my words on the way to Willow Creek Meadows Lake. "Where there's willows, there's water!" I'd said, so confident in my abilities. But now, I dare not go farther.

The vehicle races into a barrow pit, zigzags down a hill, and then disappears. As the sun sets over the low hills of the Kennedy Range, a headlight appears on a trail in the distance.

I back up, finding comfort as the sounds coming from the car's undercarriage change from the slap of grass to gravel and then silence. To my right is the metal hut. An overhead light flickers off, and I hope that I'm the only one here. I drive slowly toward the entrance, and the light comes on. I watch for movement, and as I do, the light goes out.

The vinyl seat squeaks as I slide out of the car and approach the hut. Again, the hut's overhead light flickers on, revealing a dust-covered old boat, a dinged-up canoe with a broken oar lying against it, and two large drones.

Running back to my car, I rummage through my purse, retrieving my phone. I shut the car off. Again, the light goes out, and I walk ten feet toward the hut before the light stays on. As I walk to the opening, I spy a white object on the ground three feet from the entrance.

As I pick up the fresh, unlit cigarette, I realize how very wrong I've been about things.

****

After photographing the cigarette and the drones, I e-mail Holly Johnsrud and Andy Ropp the photographs and the coordinates I'd sent to Michael earlier today.

Retracing my drive to the camp, I cautiously drive farther up the road, looking for muddy ATV tracks. About one hundred yards from the metal hut, the tracks veer and go up a narrow dirt road. As I approach it, I see that it is labeled FSR 9, Cats Draw Trail Road. In the trees above me, I see a flash of headlights that seem to be coming toward me. Creeping forward, I look for a wide stop in the trail road, but it is very narrow, and if I meet whoever is coming down the trail, I will have to back down, and with the dimming light, I realize that will not be a good idea.

I pull over and nestle my car into the turnoff. Opening the door, I hear vehicles approaching me. The smaller-sounding engine, which must be the ATV, slows, and soft thuds follow a *pop, pop, pop*. The other, a car with a larger engine, grinds to a halt.

Gunfire? Pulling out my phone, I groan as I see that there is no cell phone service, even though I can see the town of Snowshoe's rosy glow over the moraine. I punch in the emergency code but can't get a signal, so I'm not sure if I should go up the trail to investigate or get in my car and drive down where the signal would be stronger.

"Stop! You have no right to be here!" The Cotswold accent, with its swallowed vowels, is unmistakable.

"Michael? I'm calling the police," I call.

"Joanne? Get away now! I'll handle this." A shot hits a metal object with a loud ding.

The trail is littered with rocks and mud puddles, but I can see the ATV tracks and the wider tire marks of a truck. Holding my phone in the air, I keep my eyes on the bars of cell service, willing them to rise above No Service to at least one bar. I stumble on a rock, catch myself, and curse out loud.

"Whoever you are, I'm coming for you next." The voice is male, and it is one that I've heard before. But why would he be here? He stands behind me every Sunday in church as he says the Lord's Prayer. Why would Wally Harmon be on an ATV up here? "I can see your cell phone. You have no business up here. Like I said, I will come for you next."

A light courses down the trail, followed by a thud probably fifty feet away from me up the steep hillside.

Michael's voice. "I'm putting you in my truck, and we will explain this to the police."

"You hit me with your flashlight. That's assault!" screams Wally. "I'll be so happy when your foreign ass is deported. You will never recover from this."

Keeping myself close to the uphill portion of the road, I climb up the trail, picking my way carefully around the rocks and mud puddles. The road widens and turns sharply to the left, and at this point, I see my phone getting one bar. Crouching down, I call 911 and try to whisper.

I'm interrupted by two woofs coming from nearby brush, which, as I inhale, isn't brush at all. I'm on a northwest-facing slope, somewhere between thirty-five hundred and forty-five hundred feet above sea level, and I'm next to a huckleberry patch. "Woo Bear! Woo Bear!" I call, and then I sing. *"My country 'tis of thee, sweet land of liberty, of thee I sing."* Wally Harmon half runs, half tumbles past me, followed by two collared bears that crash through the huckleberry patch brambles, followed by Michael, bellowing, *"Long live our noble King, God save the King!"* Michael lunges from the top of an outcrop toward Wally, and I hear *"Send him victorious…"*

Wally looks at me and fires his gun.

The bullet whizzes past me as I run toward Michael. Wally twists and squirms, but as he rolls over, I see he still has the gun in his hand. "Michael! Look out!"

Michael raises his arm to subdue Wally, and as he does so, I see a flash of light and hear the pop as he falls on top of Wally. As Wally drops his head, he hits it on a small rock.

Rising, then crouching again, I check for a cell phone signal and am rewarded with one bar as I stand above Michael. "You can't leave me. You can't."

Turning him over, I see the blood pooling on top of Wally. As the moon rises over the sky above Kennedy Creek, I sing through my sobs, *"My country 'tis of thee, sweet land of liberty, of thee I sing"* over and over until the police and paramedics arrive.

Chapter Eighteen

"It's early for lunch, but I can't not talk to you. I'm glad you texted me."

I look up from my computer screen to see Belle. "Does the other guy look worse?"

"You're one to talk. I don't have enough makeup in my shop to make you look better. Your runny mascara makes you look like a horror show extra."

The first one to laugh loses. That's the thing about fights with best friends. It's written somewhere. Insult until the other person laughs.

I'm about to lose. Again.

"What if I start going to the other shop? Offer to buy all the mascara and makeup they have since you are running dry," I say.

"Could work, but you probably shouldn't go outside until your vampire friends know it's safe to be seen with you."

And with that, it's game, set, and match for Team Belle. Again.

"Dammit, you really are good at this."

"Natural talent and lots of practice with you."

"Shut up."

"No, you."

"Cut that out!" Now, I have tears again, and I wave my hand at her. "You lose. Since we're playing verbal tennis, that would make it 40-all. Service!"

"I nearly lost a lot. That's why I'm here."

I eye her. Her chin's wobbling, and she's gulping. This has happened maybe three times in a multi-decade friendship.

"It's all right. You had it coming, full stop."

"So, I win again."

I get up from my desk, walk over, and hug her. Nestling my nose near her ear, I whisper into her rat's nest hair. "Not this time." I release her and my former best friend of decades steps back into the waiting handcuffs held by Detective Ropp.

****

The Range Rover chugs to life. The picnic basket I'd set in the back contains Japanese bento boxes and a Portuguese Vino Verde. Sitting beside it is my rucksack, which includes a satellite phone, a battery charger for my cell phone, bear spray, and a packet in case, well, just in case. Inwardly, I sigh as Michael limps down the stairs, giving me a half-hearted wave.

Under his jacket, his arm is in a sling, and a small bandage covers the scar received from his fight two weeks ago with Wally Harmon.

Despite the limp, he hustles over to me and points to the passenger seat. "I'll drive. I got a report of yearling bear cubs separating from their mother. I hope to see them from a distance. Since it's a grand day for a trod, we should get a good start."

"You're crazy and in no shape. Can we track Bluebell and Forest now?"

"We owe Bluebell and Forest a debt of thanks, so I do hope that I can see them, or rather, we can see them. Their scattering when the drones came in with their packages helped crack the case. When Wally requested the grizzly activity near the trapper cabin at the You Who

Foundation's summer camp, my antenna went up."

Michael has made an error in his calculations. I close the driver-side door and point to the passenger seat. "Your injury is on your left side. How are you going to drive a stick shift if your left side is in a sling?" I ask, happy to win an argument in logic at long last.

He says nothing for a few seconds, and rather than admit any defeat, he walks to the passenger door, opens it, and slides in, closing the door with a small sigh.

"You'll be able to do this soon. The doctors say you are making progress," I say with a light laugh.

His jawline moves a fraction of an inch, and I see a person who is coming to terms with something he has no control over.

Fortunately, I am also coming to terms with things I have no control over either.

****

Although Constance and Bonnie promoted me to Dan's position as vice president of the bank, the last two weeks had been more tumultuous than I'd ever thought possible. Abbie had resigned, taking an accounting position at Elizabeth Logging Company. Wally's death was ruled accidental due to the grizzly's claw marks on his body, and he was buried last week. Pam Clayton had been cremated, and her family scheduled a celebration of life service in a few months.

I chose not to attend Wally's funeral, deciding to take the afternoon that had been granted me by the bank to go to the Maple District Park and then go huckleberry picking on Snowshoe Ski Area's hills. As I sat on a log, picking the plump, blue-black berries, I could hear tourists in the distance laughing as they rode to the top of the jackrabbit gondola.

I returned to the cottage where I'd attempted, and failed, to make huckleberry bear claws. I laughed at that, knowing I could use my bad baking as an excuse to drive to the Lodgepole Ferry Merc. Later that evening, I'd stopped by the Snowshoe Hare, picked up two of my favorite burgers, and after clearing it with Michael's doctor, brought them to the hospital.

Michael wore sweats and sat in a chair. "I smell burgers," he says, patting a small side table. I set the bag of food down, perching on the hospital bed. Opening the bag, he took a hungry bite of the brioche bun, meat patty, tomato, and avocado before speaking.

"Jess convinced Linda to have Paul show her his airplane as she said she might want to purchase it. While in the hangar, she recognized two octocopter drones. Their size convinced her that one of them could have been used to transport Dan to the Alpine National Park location. She said nothing about the drones but spent time inside the airplane, where she sat in one of the chairs, slipping a tracker behind a chair leg. She was terrified, but later, Georgie and Jess calmed her down."

"That was brave of her," I say. "She has gumption."

"Jess is remarkable and a good friend to both of us," he says, taking another bite and not raising his eyes to meet mine. "These burgers are so good. They are returning to London. Their life is there, not in Colorado, but I will keep in contact with them as they have put in an offer on my grandparents' house in Bretagne," he says, pushing the bag of food away from him.

My lips fold in as I frown. I'm looking for a tell. I know what he said when he was shot, but...

"What do you think? Do you want to drive there?"

I scramble. "I was thinking about Linda. I'm sorry.

What did you ask me?"

"When I'm released from the hospital, can we have lunch at MacFarland Lake and dinner at the Aurora Borealis Saloon? I'd like to take you on a trod."

****

Ten days later, and despite his orders not to stress out about the drones and trafficking, it seems that nothing is slowing Michael down as we drive toward the Lodgepole Ferry Merc.

That's not true. My driving is causing consternation as I swerve to avoid a rock. Micheal utters what could only be a curse in a language I don't know.

He draws a long breath. "Jess hears that Paul Allegretti has disappeared. Anyway, Paul told the Conservation District that he had business and couldn't attend a meeting with the You Who Foundation tonight. Jess' sources told them after receiving initial clearance, his plane went below radar levels once he was over the Continental Divide. He is nowhere to be found," says Michael.

"What does that mean?" I ask as the Rover hits a pothole directly. Michael groans, and I reach to touch his belly in a comforting gesture.

"It means that I need to drive since you cannot keep your eyes on the road. I feel fine," he says, but his hand moves to the exact spot I had touched seconds earlier, and he grimaces.

"We're having a picnic at MacFarland Lake to celebrate my promotion and that you are a—" As we hit another pothole head-on. "—live." I flash my winningest smile and am rewarded with a less serious scowl.

"Yes, that's true. Local airstrips have been notified along the projected flight path, so the authorities might nab him when the plane refuels. Plus, Jess says the VPN tracking device they put in the Tamarack Springs Bar, along with the tracking device Linda placed in his plane, can monitor him. We shouldn't have to worry about Paul for much longer."

A brown and yellow lettered sign appears on the road and shows that Lodgepole Ferry is one mile away. "I'm looking forward to having dinner tonight at the Aurora Borealis Saloon and that you pulled strings to get a Forest Service cabin for the night."

I recall an afternoon in Michael's hospital room. I'd held the ring finger of his left hand, watching the monitor, gazing at the man who, at long last, had been pronounced by his doctors as being out of the woods. I'd cried and had called his parents in Birmingham, England, to tell them that their son had stabilized at last.

After I end the call with Angus and Brenda Laysan, a song lyric floats into my brain about not being afraid. There'd been anxious moments between my phone call to the police, pushing on Wally to check if he was dead, cradling Michael in my arms, and singing as loudly as I could until the police arrived.

I'd been terrified. In many ways, I still am.

As I hummed the tune in the hospital, Michael's mouth began to move.

I leaned in to hear what he was saying, but he only said, "King," before sinking into a deep slumber.

But now, ten days later, as I slow the Rover to make the right-hand turn into the town, I'm no longer afraid.

I gasp. *Welcome to The Modern Retellings! One Night Only. Lodgepole Ferry Square.* "They're here! I wonder if we can get tickets for the concert? Wouldn't that be great?" I exclaim, keeping an eye on the road but stealing a glance at Michael, who is no poker player.

"We have tickets? Oh, you got tickets?" I say, squarely hitting another pothole and bouncing into a parking space in front of the saloon. Opening the car door, I take in the scent of baked goods coming from the Merc's bakery next door and the smell of pine. A sign on the front door of the saloon flutters in the breeze, and I climb onto the porch to read it.

I groan. "Michael, the saloon is closed for a private event. Are you sure we have reservations here tonight? Did you get the date wrong?"

A bearded man opens the saloon door and steps onto the wooden porch. "Mr. Laysan. Ms. Corvus, I presume," he says with a laugh. "Actually, Mr. Laysan, your Rover is every bit as distinctive as you said. Your timing is perfect. We have closed the saloon to tourists while you dine. We will open it for the concert-goers after that. Do you need directions to your accommodations?"

Michael shakes his head, but I'm confused.

"I thought we were having lunch at MacFarland Lake," I say. "I brought bento boxes and wine."

"Another opportunity to celebrate has presented itself. I think you will like it," says the man. "I can refrigerate your bento boxes and wine for you, but I think you will find the menu that Michael planned with us will be pleasing."

"What do you say, Joanne? I've promised you dinner here on more than one occasion. Now's my chance to make it up to you," says Michael. He opens the back seat of the car, retrieves the bento boxes and wine, and walks over to the chef.

A phone buzzes in my purse, and reflexively, I reach in to check what it says.

I look up to see Michael scowl at me, but I smile at the message. *Let us know when you want another encryption mission. Bolton's Valor Security Forces salutes you. —Jacy and Vince.*

"Well, what is it? Are you being whisked away?" asks Michael.

"Not a chance. It's good news, but I'm here," I say, gasping as the chef opens the door to reveal a dazzling scene.

A table, set with linens, has roses and willows in a vase. A bottle of champagne sits in an ice bucket. A waiter pulls out our chairs, and Michael and I sit down. A bowl filled with lemons and kiwis sits next to two lit candles.

"I should introduce myself," says the chef. "My name is Stefan, and this is my assistant, James. We'll be cooking for you. The menu Michael suggested to us is a melding of your backgrounds but will be presented with a twist."

I cringe at my flowery handwriting but laugh as I read words from long ago.

Dear Michael, or do you go by Mike?

My name is Joanne Strong, and I am a sophomore at Tamarack Public High School. For our history project, I was given your name and asked to write to you to learn about England and the history of your area.

I live near Alpine National Park and like to fish and hike. I also read English history and want to study animals.

I look forward to corresponding with you.

Your friend,

Joanne

"Each course begins with a letter that Michael saved

from your correspondence over the years. The starters will be crispy phyllo shrimp, followed by Catalan gazpacho and angel-hair pasta with trout bisque. Bon appétit!" says Stefan, pouring champagne into the glass flutes placed on the table.

"Congratulations on your promotion at the bank, and thank you for everything you have done for me. This, this," says Michael, pointing to the mountains outside the window, the candlelight flickering, and the exquisite food, "all of this should be yours. All the time."

James presents another letter from me along with Japanese spiced shaved ice as a granita.

Dear Michael,

Your letters about your trods are interesting. How did you get interested in the legends of King Arthur? We are studying MacBeth in our English class.

I live above a bar, what you might call a public house. My dad owns it. I help him take care of my mother as she has gotten sick. I think I might like to be a doctor, but I will see how my grades are.

I will write more when I have time.

Your friend,

Joanne, but you can call me Jo-Jo.

Stefan and James bring a beef tenderloin with a wine glaze, asparagus, and a garden salad.

The clouds above the mountains take on a pink and orange tinge as we eat.

"This is one of the best days of my life. So much work went into this. I'm overwhelmed," I say, reaching over and kissing Michael's cheek. He quickly turns his head, and the next kiss is softer and full of possibilities.

Outside, a band tunes, and I want to celebrate.

As if by magic, Stefan and James appear. "Would

you like your dessert to be served later? I understand that part two of the surprise is about to start," says Stefan with a grin.

Michael stands and extends his hand toward me. "Do you want to dance with me?"

James opens the saloon's door, and Michael and I stroll outside, hand in hand.

Twenty feet away, The Modern Retellings are tuning up. As we walk toward them, the bandleader cheers and whistles. The crowd joins in, but the bandleader holds up his hand.

"Our opening song is a song dedicated to a special couple. Please give it up for Michael and Joanne. Michael composed a poem in Joanne's honor—" This is met with hoots of awe. "—and Michael suggested an English style of play. We hope you will enjoy this." The bandleader turns to the musicians and gives them a beat.

Michael removes his sling, taking me into his embrace. "I am ready to fly. I have found you, Joanne. My love soars above and around you. I love you."

As we kiss and swirl to the jazzy beat of the song, two ravens fly above the saloon before perching on top of the Merc.

"Corvus is the genus name for ravens, and Laysans are birds that mate for life. We are perfectly suited. In fact, the genus of both species—"

I twirl away and back to him and reach up to kiss him. As we do, the ravens rise, eager to spend a life together in a nearby nest.

A word about the author...

Janet Yeager is the author of Brothers by Honor and Two Birds, One Stone. Her award-winning short stories have appeared in E-Merge magazine, the Montana History Portal, and the anthology Echoes of Tradition. She is a proud member of Sisters in Crime, the Tulsa NightWriters, the Red Sneakers Writers Group, and the Oklahoma Writers' Federation. A Montana native, she lives in Tulsa, Oklahoma. janetryeager.com

Thank you for purchasing
this publication of The Wild Rose Press, Inc.

For questions or more information
contact us at
info@thewildrosepress.com.

The Wild Rose Press, Inc.
www.thewildrosepress.com